John S. Abbott

The Life of General Ulysses S. Grant

Containing a brief but faithful narrative of those military and diplomatic

achievements which have entitled him to the confidence and gratitude of his

countrymen

John S. Abbott

The Life of General Ulysses S. Grant
Containing a brief but faithful narrative of those military and diplomatic achievements which have entitled him to the confidence and gratitude of his countrymen

ISBN/EAN: 9783337110444

Printed in Europe, USA, Canada, Australia, Japan

Cover: Foto ©Raphael Reischuk / pixelio.de

More available books at **www.hansebooks.com**

UNIVERSITY OF CALIFORNIA
LOS ANGELES
SIGILLVM·VNIVERSITATIS·CALIFORNIENSIS
FIAT
LVX
MDCCCLXVIII
EX LIBRIS
GIFT OF
U. C. Library

U. S. Grant

THE LIFE

OF

GENERAL ULYSSES S. GRANT.

CONTAINING

A BRIEF BUT FAITHFUL NARRATIVE

OF THOSE

MILITARY AND DIPLOMATIC ACHIEVEMENTS

WHICH HAVE ENTITLED HIM TO THE

CONFIDENCE AND GRATITUDE OF HIS COUNTRYMEN.

BY

JOHN S. C. ABBOTT,

AUTHOR OF "LIFE OF NAPOLEON," "HISTORY OF THE FRENCH REVOLUTION," "HISTORY OF
THE CIVIL WAR IN AMERICA," "LIVES OF THE PRESIDENTS," ETC.

ILLUSTRATED.

BOSTON:

B. B. RUSSELL, PUBLISHER, 55 CORNHILL.

CINCINNATI: WHITE, CORBIN, BOUVÉ, & CO.

SAN FRANCISCO: H. H. BANCROFT & CO.

868.

GEO. C. RAND & AVERY,
STEREOTYPERS AND PRINTERS,
3 CORNHILL, BOSTON.

PREFACE.

 ENERAL GRANT is emphatically a man, not of words, but of deeds. His eloquence is the eloquence of action. He will be renowned, through all future time, for the achievements which he has performed, — achievements which, every impartial student of history will declare, give him position among the ablest men the world has known.

We are, in our day, apt to give undue importance to fluency of speech. There is a charm in popular eloquence which captivates the mind. And one is led to suppose that the man who can give utterance to noble thoughts in glowing sentences, who can soar in dazzling flight upon the wings of imagination, who, with fluency which never fails him, can on all occasions make an apt and taking speech, must surely be a man of wide reach of intellect, of sound judgment, of executive ability.

But no student of the past, no careful observer of the present, need be informed that such a conclusion may be very erroneous. The voluble talker is often the very inefficient actor. The man who can elicit shouts of applause upon the platform may be the very last man to plan and execute an important enterprise. In fact, speech-making has become the pest of the present day in legislative halls, consuming the time, and clogging the wheels of action. Moses, whom God chose as the ruler of Israel, was " slow of speech."

In these few pages we present the character of a thoughtful, reserved, taciturn man, — a man of tireless energies, of great breadth of comprehension, of the highest order of administrative genius. No man can read these pages without being convinced that General Grant is, in mental capacity, one of the foremost men of the present age.

To lead a charge on the field of battle requires but little save the heroism of courage. But to conduct a campaign like that of Vicksburg, or Chattanooga, or Richmond demands the highest order of intellect. All the resources of which the mind is capable are called into exercise. The man who has thus been tested proves himself qualified for any administrative duty which may be assigned to him.

We speak of General Grant as not being a man of *words*. And yet there is great power in the few words which he does use. His despatches are models : brief, comprehensive, clear, no man can misunderstand them. The energy with which General Grant grappled with the Rebellion, the self-denying patriotism with which he consecrated himself to the service of the country, and the achievements to which he led the glorious armies of the Republic, giving our nation new renown throughout the world, surely entitle him to the confidence and affection of every American citizen.

JOHN S. C. ABBOTT.

New Haven, April, 1868.

CONTENTS.

CHAPTER V.

THE BATTLE OF SHILOH.

CHAPTER VI.

THE VICTORY AT PITTSBURG LANDING.

CHAPTER VII.

THE SIEGE OF CORINTH, AND THE ADVANCE TO VICKSBURG.

CHAPTER VIII.

RUNNING THE BATTERIES.

CHAPTER IX.

THE MARCH TO THE REAR.

CHAPTER X.

THE ADVANCE TOWARDS VICKSBURG.

CHAPTER XI.

THE CAPTURE OF VICKSBURG.

CHAPTER XII.

THE PERIL AT CHATTANOOGA.

CHAPTER XIII.

PREPARATIONS FOR BATTLE.

CHAPTER XIV.

THE BATTLE OF MISSIONARY RIDGE.

CHAPTER XV.

THE PURSUIT.

CHAPTER XVI.

THE RELIEF OF KNOXVILLE.

CHAPTER XVII.

NATIONAL HONORS CONFERRED UPON GENERAL GRANT.

CHAPTER XVIII.

THE BATTLES OF THE WILDERNESS.

CHAPTER XIX.

THE MARCH FROM SPOTTSYLVANIA TO THE PAMUNKEY.

CHAPTER XX.

THE MARCH FROM THE CHICKAHOMINY TO PETERSBURG.

CHAPTER XXI.

THE SIEGE OF PETERSBURG.

CHAPTER XXII.

PROGRESS OF THE SIEGE.

CHAPTER XXIII.

GRANT'S BATTLES AND SHERMAN'S MARCH.

CHAPTER XXIV.

THE FINAL VICTORY.

LIFE OF GENERAL GRANT.

CHAPTER I.

COMMENCEMENT OF HIS CAREER.

Parentage. — Anecdotes of his Childhood. — Enters West Point. — Development. of Character. — Studies and Rank. — Stationed on the Frontiers. — Ordered to Mexico. — Battle of Palo Alto ; of Resaca de la Palma. — Capture of Monterey. — Joins the Army of Gen. Scott. — Promotions. — Battle of Molino del Rey ; of Chapultepec. — Conquest of Mexico. — Withdrawal of the Troops.

PON the banks of the Ohio River, about twenty-five miles above the city of Cincinnati, there is the little village of Point Pleasant, containing three or four hundred inhabitants. It is a pleasant point of. the beautiful stream (*la belle rivière*, as the French call the Ohio), and lies on the northern or Ohio side, in what is now known as Clermont County. Not quite half a century ago, a very worthy young man of Scotch descent drifted to that remote region on the tide of migration which was then, as now, sweeping, with ever-increasing flood, towards the setting sun. He had brought with him from his Pennsylvania home the Bible in his chest, and its principles in his heart, and became a respected member of the Methodist persuasion. He found him a bride in an excellent maiden who had accompanied her parents to this frontier settlement from Pennsylvania.

On the 27th of April, 1822, a son was born to them, who received the baptismal name of Ulysses S. Grant. The babe was scarcely a year old, when the parents removed about twenty miles up the river, to Georgetown, Brown County, Ohio, about seven miles back from the stream. Here the little family found themselves in a more progressive region, and in the midst of a more energetic, intelligent, and thriving community. Ulysses was sent to the village school, where he obtained the rudiments of his education. He developed at that early period no qualities which indicated that he was destined to distinction. He was a good boy, — faithful in his duties, peaceably disposed, of sober character, and solid endowments. A few incidents have been gleaned from parents and friends, so few and so trivial as only to prove, that, in those early years, there was nothing particularly to distinguish him from the other farmers' boys who were his companions and friends.

We are told, that, when the child was but two years old, his father was one morning holding him in his arms, in a public part of the village, when a boy came along with a loaded pistol. Curious to see how the babe would stand the fire, the boy asked the father of the child to let Ulysses pull the trigger. They curled the tiny finger around it. The child pulled, and the charge was exploded. Delighted with the loud report, the little fellow shouted, "Fick it again!" One standing by said, "That boy will make a general." None will question but that the prediction has been verified.

The father of General Grant, in an account of his

childhood published in "The Ledger," gives the following interesting narrative: —

"The leading passion of Ulysses, almost from the time he could go alone, was for horses. The first time he ever drove a horse alone, he was about seven and a half years old. I had gone away from home, to Ripley, twelve miles off.. I went in the morning, and did not get back until night. I owned, at the time, a three-year old colt, which had been ridden under the saddle to carry the mail, but had never had a collar on. While I was gone, Ulysses got the colt, and put a collar and the harness on him, and hitched him up to a sled. Then he put a single line on to him, and drove off, and loaded up the sled with brush, and came back again. He kept at it, hauling successive loads, all day; and, when I came home at night, he had a pile of brush as big as a cabin.

"At about ten years of age he used to drive a pair of horses alone, from Georgetown, where we lived, forty miles, to Cincinnati, and bring back a load of passengers.

"When Ulysses was a boy, if a circus or any show came along, in which there was a call for somebody to come forward and ride a pony, he was always the one to present himself, and whatever he undertook to ride he rode. This practice he kept up until he got to be so large that he was ashamed to ride a pony.

"Once, when he was a boy, a show came along in which there was a mischievous pony, trained to go round the ring like lightning, and he was expected to throw any boy that attempted to ride him.

"'Will any boy come forward and ride this pony?' shouted the ring-master.

"Ulysses stepped forward, and mounted the pony. The performance began. Round and round and round the ring went the pony, faster and faster, making the greatest effort to dismount the rider. But Ulysses sat as steady as if he had grown to the pony's back. Presently out came a large monkey, and sprang up behind Ulysses. The people set up a great shout of laughter, and on the pony ran ; but it all produced no effect on the rider. Then the ring-master made the monkey jump up on to Ulysses's shoulders, standing with his feet on his shoulders, and with his hands holding on to his hair. At this there was another and a still louder shout, but not a muscle of Ulysses's face moved. There was not a tremor of his nerves. A few more rounds, and the ring-master gave it up: he had come across a boy that the pony and the monkey both could not dismount."

We are told, that, when he was twelve years of age, his father sent him to a neighboring farmer to close the bargain for a horse which he was wishing to purchase. Before Ulysses started, his father said to him, —

"You can tell Mr. Ralston that I have sent you to buy the horse, and that I will give him fifty dollars for it. If he will not take that, you may offer him fifty-five ; and I should be willing to go as high as sixty, rather than not get the horse."

This is essentially an old story, probably having a mere foundation in fact ; but the peculiarity in this case was, that when Ralston asked Ulysses directly, "How much did your father say you might give for the horse ? " he did not know how to prevaricate, but replied, honestly and emphatically, —

"Father told me to offer you fifty dollars at first ; if that would not do, to give you fifty-five dollars ; and that he would be willing to give sixty, rather than not get the horse."

"Well, I cannot sell the horse for less than sixty dollars," Mr. Ralston replied.

"I am sorry for that," was the rejoinder of young Grant, in a tone of decision which satisfied the farmer that he meant what he said; "for, since I have seen the horse, I have determined not to give more than fifty dollars. If you cannot take that, we must look elsewhere for a horse."

Mr. Ralston took the fifty dollars; and Ulysses rode the horse home.

A brother of Ulysses' father had settled in Canada. As there was no school in his settlement, he sent his son John, who was about the age of Ulysses, to Georgetown, to board with his uncle, and to go to school with his cousin. We are told, that, on one occasion, John, who was imbued with British prejudices, said, —

"Your boasted Washington was a rebel and a traitor. He fought against his king."

"Repeat that," said Ulysses, "and I will whip you."

The pluck of both boys was roused. There was a fierce battle between the American Eagle and the British Lion. Though the eagle suffered severe handling, and had its pinions ruffled, and showed some crimson spots, the lion was compelled to retire from the field smothered with bewildering blows. It is said, that, many years afterwards, the two cousins met in Canada, when stalwart young men. As they were pleasantly talking, John suddenly exclaimed, —

"I say, U. S., do you remember the thrashing you gave me at school for calling Washington a rebel?"

"Yes," Ulysses replied with a quiet smile; "and I should do the same thing again under a similar provocation."

In the year 1839, Ulysses, then seventeen years of age, entered the Military Academy at West Point as a cadet. His progress here, as at school, was steady, not rapid; his qualities solid, not brilliant. Whatever he gained in advancement he kept, never falling back. He was faithful in every duty; securing the approbation of his teachers, and the affection of his associates. The four years passed at West Point were four years of intense application, devoted to the attainment of all those sciences, and all that knowledge, which can be rendered available in the art of war. He was led through the various branches of a thorough English education; studied the French and Spanish languages, chemistry, experimental philosophy; was taught the essential art of drawing; received instruction in ethics, and in constitutional, military, and international law; in mineralogy and geology; and was thoroughly drilled in infantry and artillery tactics; in the use of rifled, mortar, siege, and seacoast guns; in small-sword and bayonet exercise; in the construction of field-works and fortifications, and in the fabrication of munition and *matériel* of war. Thus he became, by long and severe training, a highly-accomplished man, well prepared to meet the emergencies and great struggles which lie across every one's path through life.

Such are the *legends* which have floated to us from Grant's early years. We do not vouch for their accuracy. They merely show the general character which Ulysses S. Grant had established as a boy, for patriotism, firmness, and unboastful bravery. He graduated in June, 1843, standing in rank about the middle in his class, and immediately entered the United-States army as brevet second lieutenant of infantry. He was despatched as a super-

numerary lieutenant to join a company of infantry stationed far away on the frontiers of the Missouri Territory,
to watch the Indians. The region was then a wilderness,
which civilization was just beginning to penetrate. The
Indians, exasperated by the treatment which they were
continually receiving from vagabond white men, had become very menacing and dangerous. Ignorant, degraded,
and brutal, they knew not how to discriminate between
the innocent and the guilty. In retaliation of their
wrongs, they often inflicted vengeance upon the families
of the peaceful settlers, — vengeance the recital even of
which causes the blood to curdle in one's veins.

Nearly two years Lieutenant Grant passed in these distant and dreary solitudes, far removed from the intellectual and refining influences of civilized life. But
there was a cloud gathering in our southern horizon. A
war with Mexico was manifestly approaching. Quite a
little army of United-States troops was gradually being
concentrated in Texas. The boundary-line between
Texas and Mexico was disputed. .

The American troops took possession of Corpus Christi,
an important Texan post upon the Gulf of Mexico. In
the year 1845, Lieutenant Grant was sent, with his regiment, to this place, commissioned as full second lieutenant
of infantry. The anticipated struggle soon commenced
in Texas, without any declaration of war. The hostile
troops were facing each other upon the opposite banks
of the Rio Grande. There was a small garrison of American troops at Fort Brown, opposite Matamoras. After
a severe bombardment, the Mexicans crossed the river,
six thousand in number, to attack the fort in front and
rear. General Taylor was at Point Isabel, twelve miles
distant. Major Brown, in command of the fort, signalled

his peril by firiug, during the night, eighteen-pounders at stated intervals. Lieutenant Grant was then with General Taylor. Early on the morning of the 8th of May, 1846, they commenced their march, with about twenty-two hundred men, for the rescue of their comrades. As they pressed eagerly and anxiously along, the thunders of the Mexican bombardment rolled heavily over the prairie, proclaiming that their comrades must be sorely beleaguered.

It was nearly noon when the American troops encountered the Mexicans, drawn up to meet them, in line of battle, on the field of Palo Alto. General Taylor promptly formed his line at the distance of half a mile from the foe. Thus the two hostile forces, nearly equal in number, faced each other on a vast plain, where the prairie-grass waved densely around them, and where not a hillock, a tree, or a shrub obstructed the view. The battle soon commenced; and, as the forces were too far distant for musketry to be effective, it was mainly conducted by artillery on each side. The Americans had the best gunners, and the heavest weight of metal. With this advantage, our round-shot, grape, and shell tore through the Mexican ranks with great slaughter. The American infantry threw themselves upon the ground. Some of the Mexican shot passed over their heads, though most of it fell short in its range. It was a very foolish affair on the part of the Mexicans. They stood stubbornly at their post, to be slaughtered by our guns; while the Americans were almost entirely out of the range of theirs. Probably they were not aware of the inefficiency of their fire; for the prairie-grass was soon in flames, rolling along in fiery billows ten feet high, and enveloping the contending hosts in dense and suffocating smoke.

Night closed the scene. Neither party knew what had

been the effect of its cannonade upon the other. But the Mexican loss had been two hundred and sixty-two. The Americans had lost but four killed and thirty-two wounded. This was Lieutenant Grant's first battle. There could be but little opportunity for any display of gallantry upon such a field.

At night, the Mexicans retired, and stationed themselves in a new and more formidable position, a few miles in the rear, called Resaca de la Palma. They had left behind them their dead and many of their wounded. General Taylor pressed cautiously on, and soon found them posted in a ravine surrounded by dense and almost impenetrable thickets of dwarf-oaks. Again the battle was opened with artillery ; but it was soon followed up with charges of infantry and cavalry. The Mexicans fought with great pertinacity. But the Americans, more intelligent and better disciplined, fired more rapidly and with surer aim, and gained a far more signal victory than that of the day before. The Mexicans were soon seen on the rapid retreat, having lost, in killed and wounded, a thousand ; while the American loss did not exceed a hundred and fifty. This was Lieutenant Grant's second battle.

The army marched up the left bank of the Rio Grande a distance of one hundred and forty miles, and then crossed the river, and marched upon Monterey. The city was garrisoned by ten thousand Mexican troops. General Taylor led an army of six thousand two hundred and twenty men. On Sunday morning, Sept. 20, our army arrived before the city. A careful reconnoissance showed that it was strongly fortified, and that its ramparts and bastions were armed with heavy guns. After a terrible and bloody conflict, which lasted, with few intermissions, until the 24th, the city capitulated.

While at West Point, young Grant, who, from his vigorous constitution and frame, excelled in all athletic exercises, acquired the reputation of being one of the boldest riders in the school. He lost none of this faculty in his experience with the Indians on the boundless plains of the West.

At the battle of Monterey, the brigade, with which Lieutenant Grant served, had exhausted nearly all of its ammunition. They were in the heart of the city, from which there was no egress but through a narrow street, the houses on one side of which were held by the Mexicans, who fired from the windows and the roofs. Some one must be sent through this street to Walnut Springs, a distance of four miles, for ammunition. It was so perilous an adventure, that the general in command hesitated to *order* any soldier to go upon it. He therefore called for some one to volunteer. Lieutenant Grant stepped forward with the offer of his services. Throwing himself upon a fleet horse, and adopting an expedient which he had learned of the Indians, he caught his foot in the crooper of his saddle, and, grasping the flowing mane with his hands, he hung upon the side of his horse, so as to be shielded by his body from the shots of the Mexicans, and then, spurring the animal to its utmost speed, safely ran the gantlet. In an hour he returned with a wagon-load of ammunition and an escort.

The loss of the enemy at Monterey is not known: it must have been dreadful. Our balls and shells swept their thronged streets with awful carnage. The American army also lost heavily. Twelve officers, and one hundred and eighty men, were killed; and thirty-one officers, and three hundred and thirty-seven men, were wounded. This was Lieutenant Grant's third battle.

Thus was Providence preparing him for the great events in which he was subsequently to attract the attention of the world.

During all these movements, Lieutenant Grant had retained his connection with the Fourth Infantry, the regiment with which he had commenced his career in the wilds of the Missouri Territory.

General Scott had landed at Vera Cruz. A portion of General Taylor's force on the upper Rio Grande was sent down the river to co-operate with him.' Lieutenant Grant accompanied the Fourth Regiment, which was a part of this detached force. Vera Cruz was besieged and captured. Lieutenant Grant was very efficient in this great military achievement. His rank was, however, too humble, thus far, for him to take any part so conspicuous as to attract the eyes of the nation. Still, it is evident that he was gaining constantly in the confidence and esteem of his fellow-soldiers.

As the army was preparing for its march into the interior, to the halls of the Montezumas, Lieutenant Grant received the honorable and important appointment of quartermaster of his regiment. This office brought him more prominently into the view of his commanding officers. Though not necessarily called into the field, he was ever eager for active service whenever he found that he could be useful. At the battle of Molino del Rey, fought on the 8th of September, 1847, his gallantry in the field caused his promotion to a first lieutenancy. In the fierce strife at Chapultepec, on the 13th, he won the high approval of his superior officers by his bravery and the sagacity of his tactics while under fire. He was consequently promoted to the brevet of captain.

Upon the fall of the city of Mexico, and the peace which

ensued, the United-States troops were recalled; and Captain Grant returned with his regiment, the Fourth Infantry, and disembarked at New York. The regiment was soon after distributed in companies along different points of the frontiers of the States of New York and Michigan. Captain Grant went with his company to one of these points of defence.

The father of General Grant writes, in 1863, of the son of whom he may justly be so proud: "When a child, and all the way up to the present time, he has been extremely modest and unassuming. Some called it bashfulness; but that was not the proper name. For those who knew him best said, that if he were required to meet a company of crowned heads from Europe, male or female, he would approach them with as much ease, and confer with them as free from embarrassment, as he would meet his playmates in the streets."

And here let it be remarked, as one of the crowning glories of his character, that, when Ulysses S. Grant had been in the army seventeen years, he had never been known to utter a profane or an immodest word. This is the instinct of a noble nature. In this he resembled Washington and Napoleon, both of whom he has rivalled in his military achievements.

CHAPTER II.

THE BATTLE OF BELMONT.

General Grant stationed in Oregon. — Life on the Frontier. — Resigns his
Commission. — A Farmer. — A Merchant. — Commencement of the Rebellion. — Raises a Company. — Promoted to a Colonelcy. — A Brigadier-General. — Seizes Paducah. — In Command at Cairo. — Expedition to Belmont. — The Battle. — Its Results.

HE discovery of gold in California was now
pouring a flood-tide of emigration into that
far-distant land. Of course, many of the
desperate, the vile, and the reckless followed in the crowd. There were such
scenes of lawlessness enacted on the part of the whites,
provoking the Indians to the most cruel reprisals, that it
was deemed necessary to send a United-States force there,
to preserve the semblance, at least, of order. A detachment of troops, which included the Fourth Infantry, was
accordingly despatched to the department of the Pacific.
Captain Grant went with his company. The battalion to
which the company was attached was sent into Oregon,
and took up its quarters at Fort Dallas, in that wild and
distant territory.

Life in garrison there must have been almost insup-
portably wearisome. The days came and went in the
same dreary monotony, with no exciting adventures, no
sense of usefulness, no opportunities for progress, no

prospect of promotion. The earnest spirit of Captain Grant soon revolted from such a career; and resigning his commission, in July, 1854, he turned his attention to the more attractive and remunerative employments of civil life. Returning to the States, he resided for a short time in the vicinity of Saint Louis, Mo.

Having previously married Miss Dent, of that city, he took a small farm, at a short distance from its crowded streets, and engaged in the labors of a practical farmer. He worked hard, sparing himself no toil, and indulging in no luxuries: but he was not a trained farmer; his military education had not given him those habits of close calculation, and of attention to the minutest details of economy, so essential to one who, from the culture of the soil, would gain his bread. He soon became satisfied that farming was not his vocation, and entered into mercantile life under very favorable auspices.

He formed a partnership with a younger brother in the leather-business, commencing operations in 1860, in the city of Galena, Ill. His brother was practically acquainted with the business; and aided by the energy, the sobriety, and the unwearied industry of Ulysses, the firm soon became widely known and very prosperous. The integrity of both the partners was such, that, to an unusual degree, they enjoyed public confidence.

Captain Grant never forgot that he was a United-States soldier, that he had been educated under the patronage of the stars and the stripes; and he ever recognized his duty to abandon all the tranquillity of civil and domestic life, should his country claim his services. When infamous Rebellion fired upon our national flag, and smote the walls of Sumter with insulting blows, the spirit of Captain Grant was roused to its utmost intensity. He said to a friend, in those calm tones of deliberation which ever marked the man, —

"Uncle Sam has educated me for the army. Though I have served him through one war, I do not feel that I have yet repaid the debt. I am still ready to discharge my obligations. I shall therefore buckle on my sword, and see Uncle Sam through this war too."

Going into the streets of Galena, he speedily raised a company of volunteers. Ambitious only of being their captain, he led them in person to Springfield, and tendered his and their services to the governor of the State. His plain, straight-forward demeanor and unaffected zeal so impressed Governor Yates that he wished to secure his co-operation in the volunteer organization then forming for government service. He was accordingly assigned a desk in the executive office. His familiarity with military regulations and all the routine of military life enabled him to render invaluable service in the department of the adjutant-general.

But it was very evident that his qualities as a military commander were of so high an order that he could not be spared from active service in the field. It was also his own wish that he might be engaged in those duties for which his military experience and education so eminently fitted him. He was first assigned the command of several camps of organization, which were being formed at different points. The Twenty-first Regiment of Illinois Volunteers, through peculiar circumstances, had become very much demoralized. Governor Yates was anxious to find an efficient officer to assume the command. He offered the colonelcy to Captain Grant. The offer was promptly accepted; and his commission was dated from the 15th of June, 1861.

Under his efficient action the regiment, which had become greatly weakened in numbers, was in ten days brought up to its maximum of a thousand men, and was raised to a state of discipline rarely attained in the volunteer service. The regiment was soon taken across the Mississippi to guard the Hannibal and Hudson Railroad, which crossed the northern part of the State of Missouri to the border of Kansas. General John Pope was then in command of the district of North Missouri. There were various movements made by Colonel Grant's regiment, of local importance, but which did not attract public attention; but, in all these, Colonel Grant distinguished himself as a regimental commander in the field. His success in organizing and disciplining his regiment was signal. He was already an experienced officer; for he had served for fifteen years in the regular army, as lieutenant and captain, and had seen much hard fighting.

In August, 1861, he was detached from his regiment, and promoted to the rank of brigadier-general; and was placed in command of the very important post at Cairo, at the confluence of the Ohio and Mississippi Rivers. This post commanded the mouths of the two rivers, and controlled wide reaches of the Missouri and the Illinois shores. Kentucky had assumed a nominal neutrality; and the rebels found much sympathy on the soil of that State, and rendezvoused there in large numbers for their attacks upon the national flag.

Treason's foul banner was unfurled at Paducah, an important point at the mouth of the Tennessee River. General Grant promptly seized upon the post, trampling the traitorous banner in the dust, and unfurling the stars and the stripes. He then advanced and occupied Smithland, at the mouth of the Cumberland River; and thus blockaded the entrance to, or the emergence from, the rebel States by those important streams. His military eye had selected these points as bases of future military operations.

The rebels had assembled in great force on the bluff at Columbus, a few miles down the Mississippi River, on the Kentucky shore. They thus, with their heavy batteries, commanded the stream, and were preparing to send a force across the river to Belmont. The point upon which this insignificant hamlet was situated, on the Missouri shore, was low, and was commanded by the bluffs on the Kentucky shore, where the rebel General Polk had planted very formidable batteries, and had gathered a force which was rapidly increasing, and which already numbered twenty thousand men.

The rebel General Price was fronting a small army under General Fremont in south-west Missouri, and was eagerly awaiting re-enforcements, that he might attack the small band of national troops with certainty of success. Colonel Oglesby had been despatched to attack Jeff. Thompson, who was on the St. Francis River, hastening with re-enforcements to General Price. General Polk was rapidly sending troops across the river, and establishing them in camp at Belmont, that he might soon be able to push forward a force into south-western Missouri, sufficient to crush the little band under Colonel Oglesby; and then, effecting a junction with General Price, to overwhelm the troops under General Fremont, — or rather, at that time, under General Hunter.

Such, in brief, was the object of the rendezvous at Belmont. It was a sagacious scheme, and promised efficient results. General Grant resolved, if possible, to break up the encampment, scatter its forces, and capture its guns.

Even though another encampment should immediately be formed, the delay of a few days would be very important.

It was a perilous adventure. The rebels were in great force, and with heavy batteries on the bluff which commanded Belmont. They had twice as many men in the camp at Belmont as General Grant could take to attack the fort. They had gunboats and transports with which they could rapidly send re-enforcements across the river. But General Grant trusted to take them by surprise, bewilder them by a sudden and very impetuous assault, and then, having destroyed their camp, to retreat to his boats and return to Cairo. In order to bewilder the enemy still more, and to prevent him from sending large re-enforcements from Columbus, he ordered feints to be made upon the garrison there. General C. F. Smith marched out from Paducah, which was about twenty miles east of Columbus, to attack the garrison in the rear. At the same time, a small force was sent across the river from Cairo to the Kentucky shore, to co-operate in the movement. Thus, perilous as the adventure was, every precautionary measure was adopted to secure success.

On the evening of Nov. 6, General Grant in person, with three thousand one hundred and fourteen men, embarked on transports, and, convoyed by two gunboats, commenced the descent of the river. The night was intensely dark. Heavy clouds obscured the sky, and a dense fog rested upon the forest-fringed and solitary stream. Very cautiously and slowly the little fleet moved in the gloom, and it was eight o'clock in the morning before the designated point of debarkation was reached. This was about three miles above Columbus, just beyond the range of its heavy guns.

The troops were speedily landed; and the gunboats

gallantly steamed down the river a couple of miles farther, and opened fire upon the rebel batteries. The troops were immediately formed in line of march, and advanced as fast as possible towards the fort at Belmont. They had a distance of three miles to traverse, through the woods and clearings of a very rough country. On the road, they encountered at several points serious opposition, but they fought their way through.

The rebels at Columbus had witnessed the landing; and General Grant soon beheld transports, crowded with troops, crossing the stream to the Missouri shore. Four regiments were speedily sent across. Fortunately for the national troops, the rebels at Belmont had felt so secure under the guns of Columbus that they had not fortified their position with earth-works of any great strength. They had, however, constructed a rude sort of abatis, by felling about twenty acres of the forest directly in front of their camp. This proved a very serious impediment to the advance of our troops.

The rebels, thus protected, and with re-enforcements every moment coming to their aid, fought desperately. As our troops struggled through the prostrate forest, impeded by the trunks and interlacing branches of the trees, a storm of grape-shot and bullets was hurled into their bosoms. A rebel battery, upon an eminence, caused great carnage by its rapid and accurate discharge of grape-shot and shell. The heavy guns of Columbus also took part in the deadly strife. Now and then was heard, above the roar of the battle, the deep boom of a distant gun of heaviest calibre; and an enormous shell came shrieking through the air, and, dropping in the midst of the struggling patriot troops, exploded with terribly destructive power.

All — officers and men — were alike exposed. General

Grant had his horse shot under him. General McClernand lost three horses, and a bullet was flattened against the pistol in his holster. But, heroically, the patriots forced their way from stump to stump, until after a struggle of two hours, in which many perished, they had crossed the abatis. The order was then given to charge.

It is estimated that there were from six to eight thousand in the camp. There were three thousand in a semicircle rushing upon them, frenzied by the excitement of battle, and uttering shouts which rent the skies. The contending hosts were soon mingled in apparently inextricable confusion, grappling hand to hand in the deadly struggle. The rebels broke and fled; and the cry of onset gave place to the shout of victory which burst from three thousand lips as the stars and stripes were proudly unfurled over the conquered fort. Perhaps the rebels were the more ready to abandon the field from the consciousness that the batteries at Columbus would immediately disperse their assailants.

It was a glorious victory, but a victory which required an immediate retreat. It was manifest that the guns of Columbus would be turned upon the fort as soon as it was evident that the rebels had abandoned it. From the garrison at Columbus re-enforcements were being rapidly pushed across the river, to cut off the retreat of the victors. General Grant had no baggage-wagons with which to remove the camp equipage he had captured. The torch was consequently immediately applied to every thing that would burn. The fort, as we have mentioned, was on a gentle eminence; and the flames soon enveloped the whole hill-top.

The guns of Columbus were now brought to bear upon the audacious assailants. But the victors did not remain to encounter the fire. Their end had been attained, and, thus far, their expedition had been an entire success. The fort had been utterly destroyed, and the rebels had been routed and scattered with great loss. But the peril of the little band of patriots was now greater than ever. Numerous re-enforcements had crossed the river, under whose protection the discomfited rebels had rallied; and they now prepared to cut off the retreat of the patriots to their gunboats. But no one thought of surrender. The spirit of the leader animated the whole band. As an officer rode up to General Grant, and announced with no little excitement, "We are surrounded!" the general calmly replied, "Very well: we must cut our way out as we cut our way in. We have whipped them once, and I think we can do it again."

The patriot troops, made bold by their victory, cut their way through their foes, consisting of thirteen regiments of infantry and two squadrons of cavalry. The patriots had four six-pounder field-guns and two twelve-pound howitzers. These were admirably handled by experienced gunners, causing great carnage in the concentrated ranks of the foe.

According to the rebel account given in "The Memphis Appeal" of Nov. 12, General Pillow in person, at the head of his troops, charged the patriots three times with the utmost determination. Three times the rebels were repulsed, leaving the ground strewn with their dead. With slow but resistless steps, the national troops pressed on, until, just before sundown, they reached their transports. The gunboats opened fire upon the pursuing rebels, keeping them at a distance. They threw terrible missiles with great rapidity and accuracy; and, under the protection of this fire, the troops were safely re-embarked.

General Grant, when the main body was on the boats, rode back with a single staff-officer to withdraw a battalion which he had left as a rear-guard. But, in the confusion of the hour, these men, inexperienced in military discipline, had withdrawn without orders. General Grant was thus entirely outside of his own lines; and, as he ascended a knoll, he saw the whole rebel force directly before him. Many of these troops were in a corn-field, not fifty yards from where the general stood. They were all pressing forward eagerly, taking advantage of such protection as the forest or the inequalities of the ground afforded them, seeking a chance to fire upon the troops who crowded the decks of the transports. The general wore the overcoat of a private, and was not recognized as an officer. General Polk, however, saw him as he sat upon his horse, and, pointing him out to his men, said, "There's a Yankee: try your aim at him." But the men were so eager to get within gunshot of the transports that no one fired at him. The general then turned his horse, and rode rapidly back to the boats. It was near sundown. The rebels, with rapidly-increasing re-enforcements, were now pressing on as skirmishers, and were firing upon the boats from every protecting rock and tree. A plank was put out for the general; and, under a heavy musketry fire, he trotted his horse across it.

But, in the retreat through the pathless forest, amidst the tumult of battle, one regiment — the 27th Illinois — had been lost. The foe, swarming along the river banks, had become so numerous that it was not safe any longer to await the arrival of the regiment. There was every reason to fear that it had been cut off and captured. The boats now commenced the return. The current of the river was rapid, the boats heavily laden; and their progress was necessarily slow. Twilight was fading away on the dark river. Many thousand men were running along through the forest on the shore, firing incessantly upon the boats as they could get opportunity. The gunboats were dropping continually their heavy shells into the forest, while the sharp-shooters on board the transports allowed no rebel upon the banks to expose himself with impunity. The scene presented at this hour was picturesque in the extreme, with the continued flash and roar of musketry and artillery from the river and the forest.

But soon the increasing speed of the boats, and the increasing darkness, rendered all further pursuit impossible. The storm of war ceased; but its terrible ravages were left behind in the mutilated, the dying, and the dead, who strewed the ground. General Grant lost four hundred and eighty-five of his gallant band in killed, wounded, and missing. One hundred and twenty-five of his wounded fell into the hands of the rebels. Such was the price of the victory, — a sad price when we reflect that every one, probably, of these nearly five hundred men had friends who loved him, and that in five hundred homes bitter tears were shed and hearts were wrung with anguish. But such is war, such its necessary sacrifices. In a military point of view, the victory was worth far more than it cost. General Grant took also one hundred and fifty prisoners and two guns. Four guns that he had captured, but could not remove, were spiked. The rebels lost six hundred and forty-two in killed and wounded, and were so alarmed by the boldness and impetuosity of the assault that, apprehensive of an attack upon Columbus, they kept their troops concentrated there.

As our heroic little band slowly ascended the river, their spirits were saddened by the loss of the Illinois regiment, which was commanded by Colonel Buford, who had greatly distinguished himself by his bravery during the battle. They had, however, ascended but a few miles when they were signalled from the Missouri shore. There they found the lost regiment. A shout of joy burst from their lips, which echoed far and wide along the dark banks of the river. Colonel Buford, having lost his way in the intricacies of the forest, and being separated from his associates, had very sagaciously evaded the enemy, and reached a point of the Mississippi where his troops could be taken on board. The expedition now returned rejoicing to Cairo.

General Grant is emphatically a man of action, not of words. There was no very full explanation, at the time, of the object of the enterprise, and of the reasons which controlled its tactical movements. Consequently there was not then ascribed to the achievement the merit which it deserved. And, though there is not in the narrative now given any special difference from former accounts, subsequent revelations have explained some things which were previously obscure. The victory of Belmont was one of the very important events at the commencement of the war. It inspired our troops with confidence in themselves; and General Grant on that occasion displayed that coolness and indomitable persistence which so characterized him throughout the whole of our eventful struggle. It was then that public attention began to be directed to him.

CHAPTER III.

THE CAPTURE OF FORT HENRY, AND THE MARCH TO DONELSON.

The Military Line of the Rebels. — The Strategic Importance of the Posts. — General Grant's Views. — The Co-operation of Commodore Foote. — The Naval and Land Force. — Plan of Attack. — The Battle and Capture of Fort Henry. — Preparation for the Attack upon Donelson. — Strength of the Works. — Peril of the Attack.

HE rebels were well aware of the importance of Columbus, which gave them entire command of the river from that point to its mouth. They soon collected one hundred and forty guns upon its bluff, and surrounded them with such intrenchments as rendered the post, in their view, impregnable. They had also established themselves in very considerable force at Fort Henry, on the Tennessee River; at Fort Donelson, on the Cumberland; and at Bowling Green, on the Big Barren, in Central Kentucky. This military line — running from east to west, a distance of nearly two hundred miles — was intended to prevent the national army from advancing into the south either by land or by water. The Cumberland River, whose headwaters are formed on the Cumberland Mountains, and the Tennessee River, which takes its rise far south, among the highlands of Mississippi and Alabama, approach within twelve miles of each other at

the points selected for Fort Donelson on the one, and for Fort Henry on the other.

General Grant clearly discerned the importance, in a strategic point of view, of these posts on the Tennessee and the Cumberland, which the enemy had so skilfully chosen, and had so strongly fortified.

God does not confer upon any man all gifts. He had given General Grant a remarkably clear head; but he had not conferred upon him a voluble tongue. In the eloquence of action he excelled. In the eloquence of words he failed. Almost instinctively, he discerned the elements of military success; but he had not the power of forcibly conveying his ideas to other minds. Deeply impressed with the importance of the capture of the Forts Henry and Donelson, he visited General Halleck at St. Louis, — then in command of the department of Missouri, — and laconically asked permission to undertake the enterprise. General Halleck abruptly refused. General Grant was not prepared to support his plans with arguments; and, somewhat wounded in feeling by the brusque reception he had met, returned to Cairo.

Still impressed with the importance of the measure, a few days after his return to his post, notwithstanding the repulse he had encountered, he wrote to General Halleck as follows: —

" In view of the large force now concentrating in this district, and the present feasibility of the plan, I would respectfully suggest the propriety of subduing Fort Henry, near the Kentucky and Tennessee line, and holding the position. If this is not done soon, there is little doubt that the defences upon the Tennessee and Cumberland Rivers will be materially strengthened. From Fort Henry it will be easy to operate, either on the Cumberland (only twelve miles distant), Memphis, or Columbus. It will, besides, have a moral effect upon our troops, to advance thence towards the rebel States. The advantages of this movement are as perceptible to the general commanding as to myself: therefore further statements are unnecessary."

Commodore Foote was then in command of the gunboat fleet, which had been gathered with great vigor at Cairo. Some of these boats were iron-clad, and carrying heavy guns, yet requiring but a light draft of water, were capable of very efficient service. Commodore Foote was in entire accord with General Grant upon the policy of attacking the forts. He wrote to General Halleck, on the 28th of January, as follows: —

" Commanding-General Grant and myself are of opinion that Fort Henry, on the Tennessee River, can be carried with four iron-clad gunboats, and troops permanently to occupy."

Two days after, they received the desired permission. This was on the 30th of January. The energies of both of these extraordinary men, who co-operated like brothers in the herculean enterprise, were so roused that in three days the combined naval and land expedition started from Cairo. The land force was under the command of General Grant; the naval armament was conducted by Commodore — subsequently Rear-Admiral — A. H. Foote.

The fleet consisted of seven gunboats, four only of which were iron-clad. The land force embraced seventeen thousand men, who were conveyed by transports.

The little squadron steamed rapidly up the Ohio River about forty miles, to the mouth of the Tennessee; and thence up that river nearly ninety miles, till it approached the fort. Three gunboats then slowly ascended the stream, shelling the forest on each side to ascertain if there were any concealed batteries, and advanced near enough to the fort to throw into it a few shells. This drew the fire of the foe, and enabled Commodore Foote to judge of the calibre of the rebel guns and of their range. In performing this interesting experiment, a thirty-two pound shot passed through "The Essex," though without doing any essential damage.

Fort Henry was on the eastern bank of the river, and, garrisoned by twenty-eight hundred men, was under the command of General Tilghman. It was a strong field-work, with bastioned front, and mounted seventeen guns. Traverses were formed of sand-bags between the guns. Outside of the fort there was an entrenched camp, and beyond this an extended line of rifle-pits. Great care had been taken to protect the fort from assault, both on the side of the river and on that of the land. A communication, called the Dover Road, connected Fort Henry with Fort Donelson, at the distance of twelve miles, on the left bank of the Cumberland.

The troops were landed about four miles below the fort. They could not all be conveyed in the transport at once, and the boats were sent back to Cairo for those which were left behind. It was not until near midnight on the 5th, the rain then falling in torrents, that all the troops were put on shore. On the west bank of the stream, upon some heights which commanded Fort Henry, the rebels were in possession of another stronghold, called Fort Heiman.

The plan of operation was as follows: Commodore Foote, with the gunboats, was to attack the fort from the river. It was confidently hoped that, with his powerful ordnance, throwing both solid shot and shell, he would be able to drive the foe from the fort. Two brigades were to be sent, under General C. F. Smith, to seize the heights occupied by Fort Heiman. General McClernand, in command of the remainder of the national forces, was to take a circuitous march through the woods, so as to get into the rear of the foe, and to cut off their retreat through the Dover Road. If necessary, after the works had been bombarded for a sufficient length of time, General McClernand's force was to take them by storm. Commodore Foote, having great confidence in the power of his gunboats, urged that the land-force should start an hour before the boats. But as the troops had, as they supposed, but a two-hours' march before them, it seemed impossible but that they could reach their position in ample time. Still Commodore Foote, as he informed the writer, said to General Grant pleasantly, as his gunboats pushed from the shore, " I shall take the fort before your forces get there."

It was half-past ten o'clock in the morning of Feb. 6, 1862, when the little fleet got under way, and steamed gallantly up the river to encounter the guns of the fort. Commodore Foote led, in the flag-ship " Cincinnati," the three remaining iron-clads keeping in a line abreast of him. The three wooden boats followed, a short distance in the rear, also abreast. Their mailed companions thus served as a rampart for them, and they were to throw their shells over the boats in advance. The Commodore gave the following very judicious order : —

" Do not attempt rapid firing, but take deliberate aim. Rapid firing wastes ammunition, heats the guns, throws away shot in their wild range, and encourages the enemy with a fire which proves to be ineffectual."

When the gallant little fleet had approached to within a

mile and a quarter of the fort, while still keeping steadily underway, the boats opened a vigorous, accurate, deadly fire. Every shot accomplished its mission, ploughing through the earthworks, knocking about the sand-bags and gabions, dismounting the guns, and scattering the gunners. One eighty-pound shell killed or wounded every person at one of the rebel guns. One of the rifled cannon of the rebels burst, creating fearful carnage and dismay. While the Commodore kept up this tremendous and unceasing fire, his boats were continually approaching nearer to the forts, until it seemed as though it were his intention to grapple the foe and to take him by storm. The fire of the enemy was much less effectual: The targets at which he aimed were small, and were continually changing their position. The shots which struck the heavily-armed bows of the iron-clads glanced off harmlessly. Thus, for an hour, the battle raged with unequal results, but with equal desperation on either side.

At length a twenty-four pound shot struck the plated "Essex" upon a weak spot, and pierced one of the boilers. The scalding steam instantly filled the boat, dreadfully scalding the crew. As the rebels saw the crippled steamer drift helplessly down the stream, their waning courage was for a moment revived, and they raised a feeble shout of triumph. But, unfalteringly, the remaining ships still pressed on, until they were within six hundred feet of the muzzles of the foe. Every shot was so destructive that soon but four of the rebel guns could be brought to bear upon the fleet.

The garrison now raised the white flag of surrender; but, buried in the blended smoke of the combatants, it was for some time not seen, and shot and shell from the fleet mercilessly swept the fortress. The rebels could endure this no longer, and in wild confusion they fled. As soon as the Commodore perceived that his fire was not returned, he signalled to cease firing ; and a perfect calm succeeded the roar of battle.

Then came that most exciting shout which can burst from human lips, — the shout of victory. A boat was sent on shore ; and the stars and stripes waved proudly in the breeze over the ramparts which treason's banner had degraded. Most of the garrison escaped. Sixty-three, with their commanding officer, General Tilghman, were captured.

It was eight miles from the place of landing, by the circuitous route through the woods, to the point on the Dover Road where General Grant's troops were to cut off the retreat of the garrison. There had been very heavy rains. The country, low and marshy, was now very extensively flooded. Several streams had to be bridged. It was not until an hour after the surrender of the fort that General Grant arrived with his advance guard. The garrison had escaped by the Dover Road, across to Fort Donelson, leaving behind them only the heavy guns. It appears, from General Tilghman's report, that he had no hope to defend the fort against the gunboats; and that he fought only with the endeavor to retard the capture until he could send off the main body of his troops, with as much of the *materiel* as they could take with them. Commodore Foote lost five men killed, and about fifty wounded. The gunboat " Cincinnati " was struck by thirty-one shots. " The Essex " was struck fifteen times. The other two armored vessels received, one six, and the other seven shots. The rebels reported five killed and sixteen wounded. All but enough to work the guns had been sent out of the fort to a station about two miles off, from which they were ordered to retreat upon Fort Donelson.

The captured fort and prisoners were turned over to the army. The cavalry pursued the retreating foe a short distance towards Fort Donelson, when it was found that the enemy had got too far in advance, and the pursuit was relinquished. General Grant telegraphed to General Halleck, —

" Fort Henry is ours. Gunboats silenced the batteries before the investment was completed. I shall take and destroy Fort Donelson on the 8th, and return to Fort Henry."

The capture of Fort Henry gave great animation to the national troops. The three great avenues to the rebel States by water were through the Mississippi, the Tennessee, and the Cumberland Rivers. The rebels had barricaded the Mississippi, at Columbus, with fortifications deemed impregnable. The Tennessee was barricaded at Fort Henry, and the Cumberland at Fort Donelson. But the rebel line was now pierced. Fort Henry had fallen. The Tennessee was open to our gunboats; and, wherever they could go, our army could follow.

General Grant now prepared for a vigorous movement on Donelson. The rebels, alarmed by their defeat on the Tennessee, gathered all their strength for the defence of the Cumberland. The troops which had garrisoned the works at Fort Henry, variously estimated at from three to seven thousand, joined the garrison on the Cumberland. The position there was very strong, and the works elaborate. The fortress, including many acres of land, was placed upon a ragged, rocky eminence, on a bend of the river, a little below the town of Dover. This elevated plateau commanded the stream, both north and south, as far as shot could be thrown.

The engineers who had constructed these works, and had raised over them the banners of treason, had been well taught in their art at the military school of West Point. Two water-batteries at the river's edge, of twelve guns, throwing thirty-two and sixty-four pound shot, swept the stream, protected by earthworks which no ball could penetrate. Back of these batteries, the bluff rose quite precipitately to an elevation of nearly a hundred feet, when it spread off into a broad plateau of more than a hundred acres, densely wooded, and cut up by ravines and gullies. A better position for defence Nature could scarcely have created. Here an army of twenty thousand determined men was stationed. Skilful engineers had erected ramparts and bastions and rifle-pits, and had so surrounded them with impervious abatis of felled trees as to render approach, even unopposed, extremely difficult. The precipitous nature of the hill itself, at many points, rendered the ascent almost impossible. Upon every commanding position batteries frowned. Thus Donelson was a cluster of forts surrounding a vast central fortress. General Buckner was in command of the post; but, in view of the impending danger, General Pillow was sent with heavy re-enforcements from Columbus, and, as the senior officer, superseded Buckner in command. Immediately after the fall of Fort Henry, General Floyd was despatched with still additional re-enforcements; and this man, of unenviable notoriety, assumed the command.

The fall of Donelson would leave the path open to Nashville; and therefore the Confederate Government roused all its energies for its defence. Guns, ammunition, and all other *matériel* of war, were sent in great abundance down the river to Nashville; and the garrison worked day and night, in preparation for a desperate resistance.

General Grant was deeply impressed with the necessity of an immediate attack. He was aware that large re-enforcements would be continually poured into the fortress, and that the defensive works would rapidly increase in strength. The day after the capture of Fort Henry, orders were issued for the whole military force there, infantry and cavalry, to be ready to move with the dawn of the next morning to take Fort Donelson. They were to advance in the lightest marching order, with but two days' rations in their haversacks.

But the rain had for some time been falling in torrents. All the streams were swollen into turbid floods. The low grounds were inundated. The only road of advance was speedily trampled into deep mire, through which it was impossible to drag the baggage or the artillery. General Grant wrote, —

"At present we are perfectly locked in. The banks are higher at the water's edge than further back, leaving a wide margin of lower land to bridge over, before any thing can be done inland. I contemplated taking Fort Donelson to-day, with infantry and cavalry alone; but all my troops may be kept busily engaged in saving what we now have from the rapidly-rising water."

This delay was not all a loss. It is doubtful whether the force then at the command of General Grant could have taken the fort under circumstances so adverse. The most vigorous measures were adopted to secure re-enforcements. The gunboats, which had gallantly run up the Tennessee River as far as Florence, Ala., steamed down the Tennessee and up the Cumberland, to co-operate in the assault. The gunboats needed some repairs before they would be prepared for another battle. Commodore Foote repaired to Cairo, and rapidly made ready to ascend the Cumberland, convoying six regiments of troops in transports. These were all to be landed on the western banks of the Cumberland, just beyond reach of the guns of the fort. On the 11th, General McClernand, who by his gallantry at Belmont had won from General Grant the highest commendation, as " proving, by his coolness and courage, that he was a soldier as well as a states- man," moved out three or four miles with his division, from Fort Henry towards Fort Donelson.

Early on the morning of the 12th, General Grant, with the main column, fifteen thousand strong, marched from Fort Henry. Eight light batteries accompanied the expe- dition. They took neither tents nor baggage, and but few wagons followed in their train. The soldiers were supplied with such rations only as they could carry in their haversacks. Each man was furnished with forty rounds of ammunition. The necessary supplies for the great conflict were to be sent from Cairo up the Cumber- land, and, with the six regiments in the transports, were to be landed, under protection of the gunboats, within two or three miles of the fort.

The distance, as we have mentioned, between Henry and Donelson, was but twelve miles. About mid-day, Grant's little army came within sight of the rebel lines. His whole force for the attack did not exceed the force he was to assail, in the strongest position, and protected by works which the most skilful engineers had reared. Twenty thousand stood behind those ramparts, while sixty-five pieces of artillery frowned from the command- ing heights. No ordinary courage could have ventured upon the attack. No ordinary sagacity and energy could have led to a successful result.   But the genius of Grant and the heroism of his soldiers, as will be seen in the next chapter, triumphed over all these obstacles.

Much has been said respecting the origin of the proposition to take possession of the Cumberland and Tennessee Rivers.   Probably the idea occurred to many persons of military intelligence about the same time. General Frémont urged it unavailingly upon the department at Washington, when the rivers could have been taken without sacrifice of life.   As soon as General Grant was placed in power, he appreciated the importance of the movement, and suggested the plan to General Halleck ; but his suggestions were not listened to.   It is probable that General Grant then proposed the plan to Admiral Foote ; for the Admiral, *after* General Grant had spoken to General Halleck upon the subject, telegraphed to this latter officer, " General Grant and myself are of opinion that Fort Henry and Tennessee River can be carried," &c.   General Halleck, perhaps recognizing General Grant as the originator of the plan, sent the orders to him to make the movement under convoy of the flotilla, and directed him to show to Admiral Foote his orders.

CHAPTER IV.

THE CAPTURE OF FORT DONELSON.

The March to Donelson. — Investment of the Fort. — The Bivouac. — Commencement of the Conflict. — The Wintry Storm. — Action of the Gunboats. — The Repulse. — Interview between Foote and Grant. — Desperation of the Foe. — The Attempt to Escape. — Energy and Sagacity of Grant. — The Final Conflict. — The Capture and its Results.

HE two divisions of General Grant's army were under General John A. McClernand and General C. F. Smith. General Lewis Wallace was left with a small force in command at Fort Henry. It was a serene and sunny morning as they commenced their march ; and, as the roads were now dry and solid, it was a pleasant excursion of four hours which brought them to the outworks of the foe. Here General Grant brought his force into position, enclosing the fort with an almost unbroken semi-circular line, extending from Hickman's Creek on the north to a point near Dover on the south.

The enemy's defences were so concealed by the forest and the thick underbrush, and the ground was so broken by gullies and ravines, that it was necessary to proceed with the utmost caution. All the afternoon was spent in this operation, during which there were many very spirited engagements with the foe. Whenever any suspicious spot was reached, a few shells were thrown into it, frequently awakening a very emphatic response. Before nightfall the fort was pretty effectually invested. General Grant's left rested upon Hickman's Creek, by which he could communicate with his transports and gunboats. The only possible escape for the foe was by boats from Dover, up the river; and but few could escape in that way.

General Smith's division occupied the extreme left. General McClernand was placed upon the right, near the town of Dover. General Grant established his head-quarters near Smith's division, where he could be in easy communication with his transports and gunboats, which were hourly expected, but which had not yet arrived. A careful reconnoissance had shown that the enemy was in such force, and his position was so strong, that the utmost caution would be necessary in conducting the assault.

The night had been beautiful, with a brilliant moon and a cloudless sky; and the air was as serene and bland as in a summer eve. Neither party ventured to kindle camp-fires, as the light would surely serve as a target for the batteries of the other side. The combatants slept in peace, while no sound disturbed the chirping of the cricket or the pensive song of the night-bird. As in nature an unusual calm often precedes the earthquake, so did this night of quietude and repose prove to be the precursor of one of the most terrific tempests of war.

The morning of the 13th dawned, warm and beautiful. Still no boom of cannon announced the arrival of the fleet. The centre of the line of investment was weak. It was to be filled by the troops which accompanied the gunboats. Until their arrival, and the land force could be aided by the efficient co-operation of the gunboats, it would be the height of imprudence to venture upon an

MAP
OF
FORT DONELSON.
SCALE.
FORT
DOVER
CUMBERLAND RIVER

attack. Still, all day long the forest echoed with explosions of artillery, as the opposing batteries exchanged shot and shell. Riflemen crept from tree to tree, and with unerring aim harassed the rebels at their guns. During the day there were several very severe and sanguinary battles, in which the national troops gradually drove in the outposts of the enemy, and gained important positions. Birge's celebrated riflemen did effectual service. With a weapon which threw a heavy, conical ball, they would strike with almost certain death any one who appeared within the distance of half-a-mile.

In the afternoon, one of the rebel breastworks was stormed with great gallantry. Three Illinois regiments, under Colonel Morrison, rushed, at the double-quick, down one declivity and up another two hundred feet high, upon the summit of which the redoubt was placed. They seemed to pay no more heed to the bullets which swept their ranks than if they had been so many raindrops. The sun shone down brightly upon them, as if animating them to their heroic deed. Over stumps and felled trees, and the sharpened, intertwining branches of the abatis, they pressed on until within a few feet of the battery they wished to seize. Here their colonel fell, struck from his horse by a ball. The redoubt was crowded with rebel troops, who, in large numbers, had gathered for its defence; and the heroic assailants were compelled to file off to the left, leaving their object unaccomplished. Many valuable lives were lost in this endeavor, which, though unavailing, was one of the most gallant of the exploits of those days filled with acts of heroism.

Thus passed Thursday the 13th. As night came on, the wind veered to the north, blowing with wintry chill, while clouds darkened the sky, and the cold rain began to fall.   The soldiers, shelterless, were soon soaked to the skin.   The previous day had been so warm that many of these heroic but improvident men had thrown aside their overcoats and blankets, and in the darkness and the rain they could not be found.   Soon the rain changed to sleet, and then to snow.   No fire could be kindled, as they were in the midst of the batteries and sharpshooters of the enemy.   The sufferings of that night were dreadful.   Through all its dismal hours the enemy kept up a deliberate fire, dropping shells here and there into the forest, at whatever points they thought their foes might be gathered.

The national troops were cut off from the view of the river, by the bluff and the forest occupied by the rebels ; but, in the afternoon, the booming of heavy artillery announced the arrival of at least a portion of the fleet.   For a moment the desultory battling ceased, as a shout of joy burst from the lips of all the beleaguering host.   It proved to be only one of the gunboats, the " Carondelet," which had arrived in advance of the transports.   Heroically Lieutenant Walker, in command, ran his little iron-clad up the river, and engaged the hostile batteries.   Most of the balls thrown from the rebel guns glanced harmless from the iron bows of the steamer.   But one enormous missile, weighing a hundred and twenty-eight pounds, entered an open port-hole, and, wounding eight men, buried itself in the coal-bags which protected the boiler.   During the short conflict " The Carondelet " threw over a hundred of her enormous shells, which, exploding within the water-batteries of the rebels, caused great devastation.

At midnight the remaining gunboats, with the transports, arrived.   With the earliest dawn the disembarkation was commenced; and by noon, these troops, ten thousand in number, were on the march through the forest to occupy their position in the centre of the line of investment. The ground was covered with two or three inches of snow, which was swept by a freezing, wintry wind from the north. It was nearly nightfall before the newly-arrived troops were established in their positions. The whole day was passed in this movement, and in vigorous endeavors to promote the comfort of the shelterless troops upon whom wintry cold had thus suddenly fallen. Still, during the day, a rambling fire of sharpshooters was kept up, with frequent discharges of artillery.

In the afternoon, at three o'clock, six of the gunboats — four of which were iron-clad — opened fire upon the fort at a distance of but four hundred yards. The guns of the rebel water-batteries were well manned and admirably placed, so that almost every shot struck its target. The crash of these heavy balls hurled against the iron mail of the boats, where they were often crumbled to powder, produced a ringing sound, which was distinctly heard above the thunders of the cannonade. One vessel alone received fifty-nine shots. Fifty-four men were killed or wounded. Commodore Foote, when standing with his hand upon the shoulder of the man at the wheel, was severely wounded by the same ball which cut his companion in two.

The conflict of an hour and a half proved that the batteries at Donelson were too strong to be silenced by the gunboats. It was hoped that the fire of the fleet would have been so successful as to have warranted an immediate assault by the whole body of troops on the land side. But, on the contrary, the enemy's fire had been so vigorous that nearly every boat had been more or less disabled, and but twelve guns could be brought to bear upon the foe. Under these circumstances the commodore was compelled to withdraw his boats. This was exceedingly discouraging. It was necessary to take the boats back to Cairo for repairs. And it would seem impossible that General Grant, with his troops buried in the lowlands of the forest, could storm heights where an almost equal number of men were strongly intrenched. General Grant wrote that night, —

" Appearances are that we shall have a protracted siege here. I fear the result of an attempt to carry the place by storm with new troops. I feel great confidence, however, of ultimately reducing the place."

Another night came, cold, dark, and freezing. A furious storm wailed through the tree-tops, sifting down the snow upon the sleepless, shivering host there so nobly battling for the life of their country. General Grant seemed to be insensible to hunger, cold, or weariness. With few words, but with tireless action, he was everywhere. Two hours after midnight, he received the following communication from Commodore Foote, who was on board his flag-ship " St. Louis," severely wounded, and in great pain : —

" DEAR GENERAL, — Will you do me the favor to come on board at your earliest convenience ? as I am disabled from walking, by a contusion, and cannot possibly get to see you about the disposition of these vessels, all of which are more or less disabled."

Before daylight the general was by the side of his wounded friend the commodore, who urged that General Grant should remain as quiet as possible with the land force, until he could return with his repaired gunboats to aid in the bombardment, or in a protracted siege, should that be necessary.

But the enemy — alarmed by the fate of Fort Henry, and by the vigor and devastation of the assaults already made by sea and land, and conscious that re-enforcements would be sent, both of boats and troops, to make the investment perfect — resolved to endeavor, without delay, to cut his way through our lines, and escape. The fire of the gunboats had proved more disastrous to them than was then known.

It will be recollected that McClernand's division occupied the extreme right. The line here did not extend quite down to the river. Upon this point the foe prepared to strike their blow, hoping by the weight of nearly their whole combined force to crush our right, and thus to open an unobstructed road to Nashville. It was a well-devised scheme. It was with tremendous vigor undertaken. With still greater vigor it was defeated.

While General Grant was conversing with the commodore on the flag-ship, in the earliest dawn of the morning, the attack was made. The desperate assault fell first upon General Arthur's brigade. Heroically this handful of troops opposed an army, until compelled to retire with heavy loss. All of McClernand's troops were soon engaged. General Grant was four or five miles distant. It was not safe to weaken any other point of the line, as this might prove but a feint to cover a more impetuous assault elsewhere. General McClernand's men held their ground bravely, until their ammunition was exhausted; then coolly retiring, they passed through the ranks of fresher troops to a spot still within the range of rebel musketry, where they refilled their cartridge-boxes.

Twelve thousand men advanced, in three columns, to cut their way through the national lines. They so arranged it that three or four regiments should attack each regiment of the Union troops.   Slowly, and contesting every inch of ground, the patriots fell back.   General Lewis Wallace was in command of the troops which oc- cupied the centre.   General McClernand called to him for aid.   But he had received orders to protect the centre, that the enemy might not effect a sortie there.   Greatly embarrassed, as he listened to the increasing roar of the battle, he despatched a courier with all speed to the head- quarters of General Grant.   But the general was absent, on the flag-boat of the commodore.   During this delay, another and more urgent appeal came from General Mc- .Clernand.

"I am overpowered," he said: "my flank is turned. My whole division will soon inevitably be cut to pieces. The safety of the entire army is endangered."

General Wallace could delay no longer.   He vigorously brought up the centre to the support of the shattered left wing.   But still the national troops were greatly outnum- bered; and slowly they were compelled to fall back, though fighting with the utmost determination.   Just then, as General Grant was returning to his headquar- ters from the flag-ship, he met an aid galloping up to in- form him of the assault.   His sagacity immediately sug- gested to him the true state of affairs.   ·Shrewdly sus- pecting that the rebels had concentrated nearly their whole force for an attack upon our left, he ordered Gen- eral C. F. Smith to hold his command in readiness for a vigorous assault upon the weakened right of the foe. Then riding rapidly forward, he soon reached the front where our troops were contending, and slowly yielding before fearful odds.

Their ammunition was nearly exhausted.   Very many officers had fallen.   The foe was pressing forward with shouts of victory; and a scene of awful disaster and confusion was presented to the eye. The right wing had been rolled back upon the centre, and seemed almost destroyed. Both parties were so exhausted that there was a moment's lull in the battle. We had taken a few prisoners. General Grant ordered their haversacks to be examined. They contained rations for three days.

"They mean to cut their way out," said the general. "They have no idea of staying here to fight us. Whichever party first attacks now will whip; and the rebels will have to be very quick if they beat me."

He at once despatched orders for General Smith to make his attack with our left wing. He also sent a request to Admiral Foote, saying,—

"·A terrible conflict has ensued in my absence, which has demoralized a portion of my command; and I think that the enemy is still more demoralized. If the gunboats do not appear, it will re-assure the enemy, and still farther demoralize our troops. I must order a charge, to save appearances. I do not expect the gunboats to go into action."

Two of the boats accordingly ran up the river and opened fire, throwing shells at long range into the enemy's camp. Generals McClernand and Wallace were informed of the attack to be made by General Smith upon the enemy's right, and were ordered to renew the battle with the utmost determination, as soon as General Smith should commence his assault. The intelligent soldiers understood the movement, and were re-animated with hope. But so sure at that moment was the rebel General Pillow that he had cut his path of escape through our lines that he telegraphed to Nashville, "*On the honor of a soldier, the day is ours.*"

General Smith rapidly formed his column of attack. It consisted of the Second and Seventh Iowa and Fifty-second Indiana. He led the charge in person. It was one of the most heroic deeds, and one of the sublimest scenes, of the war. The rebels, flushed with victory, were bewildered and astounded to find themselves suddenly assailed by General Smith on their right, by Generals McClernand and Wallace on their left and centre, and by the gunboats in the river. The charging column of General Smith moved forward like the sweep of the tornado. The lines which were to oppose them were weakened; and speedily their shouts announced to their comrades, who were fighting two miles distant on their right, that they were within the intrenchments of the foe.

As the rebels saw the stars and stripes floating over a portion of their bastions, their hearts sank within them. The glad sight seemed to animate the troops under the command of Generals McClernand and Wallace to superhuman efforts. They had rushed so impetuously forward that the two armies were mingled in the greatest confusion, often resulting in a hand-to-hand fight, — the assailants and the assailed seeking the shelter of the same tree.

The conflict continued till night closed it. But everywhere the rebels were driven back. The national troops regained every inch of ground which they had lost. So signal was the victory, that another half-hour of daylight would have enabled General Smith to have passed the outworks, and to have captured the fort.

Thus terminated this day of dreadful battle. General Grant, who had been up all the preceding night, slept a few hours in a negro hut. General Smith, with his command, bivouacked on the frozen ground he had so gloriously won. The battle had swept over an extent of many miles. The wounded, the dying, and the dead were scattered far and wide upon the blood-stained snow. Groans of anguish ascended from the forest and the ravines; and scenes of woe were witnessed over which angels might weep.

There was but little sleep for either army that night. The national troops were in the unsheltered, snow-clad fields, wherever the tide of battle had borne them. A wintry wind swept over their shivering, freezing ranks. The foe was maddened and desperate. At any moment he might again burst forth. Sleepless diligence was requisite.

Consternation reigned within the rebel camp. The morning of victory had passed away into an evening of awful defeat. The rebel leaders at midnight met in council. It was certain that General Grant would renew the assault in the morning. He occupied positions which would surely render the assault successful. Buckner, whose troops were in front of General Smith's command, declared that he could not maintain a conflict of another half-hour with the national troops. The question agitated was whether they should make another desperate endeavor to cut through our lines, or surrender. All admitted that the fort could no longer be held.

It will be remembered that General Floyd was in command. He had been so implicated in the Rebellion, when a member of the United-States Cabinet, that he feared that, if taken, he would be hung as a traitor. He therefore declared, that, in consequence of his past relations with the Federal Government, personal considerations rendered it necessary for him to make his escape. He consequently resigned his command to General Pillow, that he might himself take a boat, and escape up the river.

But General Pillow was in scarcely better repute with the national government than was Floyd. He also was very nervous as to the results of his capture. "There are no two men," said he, "in the Confederacy the Yankees would rather capture than General Floyd and myself." He therefore followed the example of Floyd ; and, that he might escape with him in the boat, surrendered the command to General Buckner.

General Buckner was a soldier, and had some sense of a soldier's honór. He refused to follow the disgraceful example of Floyd and Pillow in deserting his unfortunate comrades in the hour of their calamity. There were two steamers lying at the wharf. Floyd and Pillow, in the darkness of the night, crept down to the steamers ; and, with as many as could be crowded on board, — about three thousand, it is said, in number, — crossed to the opposite shore, and escaped. The soldiers, who stood around in great numbers, as they witnessed this ignominious flight, greeted their fugitive chieftains with hisses and execrations.

The morning had not yet dawned. General Buckner, while these scenes were taking place at the wharf, sent a bugler and a note to General Grant, proposing to surrender. To this despatch, General Grant replied, —

"No terms other than an unconditional surrender can be accepted. I propose to move immediately upon your works."

There was nothing for Buckner but to submit ; and he returned the answer, — which raised a smile throughout the Union, — "The disposition of forces under my command, incident to an unexpected change of commanders, and the overwhelming force under your command, compel me, notwithstanding the brilliant success of the Confederate arms yesterday, to accept *the ungenerous and unchivalrous terms which you propose.*"

Thus fell Donelson. The stars and stripes were unrolled in the morning breeze over its proud bastions. General Grant immediately mounted his horse, and rode to the headquarters of General Buckner. They had been schoolmates at West Point, and comrades in the United-States army afterwards. It was a great victory,—by far the greatest which had then been achieved in the course of the war. Sixty-five guns in battery were taken, over seventeen thousand small arms, an immense amount of provisions and military stores; and fifteen thousand prisoners fell into the hands of the victor. General Grant assured General Buckner that he had no desire to humiliate his captives, and that the officers would be allowed to retain their side-arms.

The Union loss during the siege was a little over two thousand. Of these, about four hundred were killed. The rebel loss is not known. They stated it at twelve hundred; General Grant estimated it at twenty-five hundred. General Halleck co-operated very efficiently in this glorious achievement, by rapidly pushing on re-enforcements to General Grant. These arrived in such numbers that, on the morning of the surrender, twenty-seven thousand Union troops could have been brought forward for the charge. The turning-point of the battle was the magnificent attack made by General Smith upon the enemy's right. When General Buckner congratulated him upon that gallant charge, he replied with truth, and yet with magnanimity characteristic of the man,—

" Yes: it was well done, considering the smallness of

the force that did it. But no congratulations are due me. I simply obeyed orders."

General Grant was introducing a new era into the conflict, — the era of hard fighting. He knew the prominent leaders in the rebel army, and was well assured that there could be no peace until their forces should be destroyed. This sentiment animated him with increasing vigor to the end. It was through stern battling, and not by strategy, that peace was to be obtained.

The secretary of war, Mr. Stanton, immediately recommended Grant as major-general of volunteers. President Lincoln nominated him to the Senate on the same day. The nomination was. instantly confirmed. Mr. Stanton then wrote the following letter, which was read throughout the Union with enthusiastic approval: —

" We may well rejoice at the recent victories; for they teach us that battles are to be won now, and by us, in the same and only manner that they were ever won by any people, or in any age, since the days of Joshua, — by boldly pursuing and striking the foe. What, under the blessing of Providence, I conceive to be the true organization of victory, and military combination to end this war, was declared in a few words by General Grant's message to General Buckner: ' *I propose to move immediately on your works.*' "

From that hour to the termination of the great conflict in the destruction of General Lee's army before Richmond, these two illustrious men co-operated with all their wonderful energies, and with perfect harmony of thought and action.

CHAPTER V.

THE BATTLE OF SHILOH.

Opening of the Tennessee and Cumberland Rivers. — Generals Grant and
Sherman. — Disembarkation at Pittsburg Landing. — The Situation. —
Plan of the rebel General Johnston and its Success. — Valiant Defence. —
General Lewis Wallace unjustly censured. — His Vindication. — Prompt
Action of Colonel Webster.

HE fall of Fort Donelson was the first really important success which the Union arms
had achieved since the commencement of
the war. General Grant had thus suddenly
attained national fame. The results of the
capture were immense. By the fall of Henry and Donelson, the Tennessee and Cumberland Rivers were thrown
open for the range of our rapidly-increasing gun-boat fleet,
through hundreds of miles, into the interior of the rebel
States. The rebel military line had been pierced ; and, as
our troops could now attack both Cumberland and Bowling Green in the rear, the evacuation of both of those
important posts became imperative. Bowling Green was
immediately abandoned ; and, in a fortnight after the fall
of Donelson, the batteries and the garrison had vanished
from the bluff at Columbus. Nashville, the capital of
Tennessee, far up the waters of the Cumberland, was
speedily occupied by our troops.

General Grant was assigned to the new military district

of Tennessee.   Brigadier-General William T. Sherman, whose name was then unknown, but whose renown has since filled the world, was assigned to the command of the district of Cairo.   Generals Sherman and Grant had spent one year together at West Point, General Sherman being in the graduating class as Grant entered the institution.   They had not since met; but General Sherman had rendered Grant efficient aid at Donelson, by vigorously forwarding to him supplies.   A correspondence was then commenced between them; and the hearts of these two noble men, engaged in the same glorious enterprise, at once blended in sympathy.   General Sherman was the senior officer, yet he wrote to General Grant at Donelson on the 13th of February:—

"I will do every thing in my power to hurry forward your re-enforcements and supplies, and, if I could be of service myself, would gladly come, without making any question of rank with you or General Smith."

When Donelson fell, and all the country was ringing with the plaudits of General Grant, for a victory to which General Sherman had so essentially contributed, the latter wrote to the conqueror, warmly congratulating him on his success.   General Grant replied:—

"I feel under many obligations to you for the kind terms of your letter, and hope that, should an opportunity occur, you will earn for yourself that promotion which you are kind enough to say belongs to me.   I care nothing for promotion, so long as our arms are successful."

It makes one proud of human nature to see these men of great achievements, unmindful of all rivalries, bound in the ties of ever-during friendship, remaining faithful to each other under the sorest trials and temptations, and coming off alike victors, sharing together the confidence and gratitude of their countrymen.

Within a week after the fall of Donelson, General Grant sent General C. F. Smith fifty miles up the river, with four regiments, to take possession of Clarkesville. On the 27th, General Grant went to Nashville, which the enemy had abandoned. At this time a slight misunderstanding arose between General Grant and General Halleck, in consequence of the failure of several of General Grant's despatches to reach the headquarters of General Halleck. We have not space for the correspondence; but, when the facts were known, General Halleck exempted General Grant from all blame.

The beautiful city of Nashville, the capital of the State of Tennessee, containing about fifteen thousand inhabitants, is situated on the south side of the Cumberland River, about one hundred and twenty miles from its mouth. It was surrendered to a small Union force without any conflict. A strong union feeling animated the settlers upon the banks of the Cumberland, so that the whole stream, from Nashville to its mouth, was entirely under our control. General Grant now removed his headquarters to Fort Henry, that he might obtain equal control of the Tennessee River. Here he was engaged in fitting out an expedition to ascend that stream.

The enemy was concentrating a large force at Corinth, just across the Tennessee line, in the State of Mississippi. It was their object to enter Kentucky, where they would find many sympathizers, and thousands ready to join their banners. They then intended to cross the Ohio, and thus to carry the war into the Northern States. It was a bold plan, and one which these bold men were well capable of undertaking. It therefore became the great object of General Grant's ambition to destroy this army. Still, he could only act by the consent of his superior,

General Halleck, who was an extremely cautious man. General Grant and Admiral Foote were often greatly annoyed by the restraints which the prudence of General Halleck imposed upon their zeal.

With this object in view, General Grant, taking quite a large force, ascended the Tennessee River as far as Pittsburg Landing. His army consisted of five divisions, commanded respectively by Generals Sherman, Hurlburt, McClernand, Lewis Wallace, and Colonel Lauman. These troops were conveyed up the river in fifty-seven transports, convoyed by gunboats. They were disembarked on the west side of the Tennessee, at Pittsburg Landing, about twenty miles from the intrenched camp of the rebels at Corinth. General Smith, a good soldier and a good engineer, selected the spot. It was very favorable for their contemplated advance upon Corinth, but also exposed them to be attacked in their turn. Here they awaited the arrival of General Buell, who was marching from Nashville to join them with forty thousand men. Impeded by rains and bad roads, and by the constitutional caution of their commander, the advance of these re-enforcements was not as rapid as had been expected.

Thus the army with which General Grant was to operate was divided by the Tennessee River, General Buell with his force being several miles distant on the east, while the troops of General Grant were encamped on the western bank, in a wide ravine or valley near the stream. It was simply a landing, with two log-huts composing its only visible improvement. Streams running into the Tennessee, above and below his encampment, protected his flanks. A good supply of transports, defended by gunboats, secured his communications with

the opposite shore. A country road passed through the
ravine towards the west, with wooded hills rising to a
considerable elevation on the north and the south. A
little back from the river, there was a rolling country, cut
up with ravines, covered with forest, and interlaced with
an inextricable maze of wood-paths. Here the army of
General Grant was encamped, spreading over a space of
several square miles. They were expecting to advance
immediately upon the arrival of General Buell's re-
enforcements, and thus, imprudently, had not protected
themselves with intrenchments.

In consequence of General Grant's misunderstanding
with General Halleck, he had been for a short time out
of command. There is a certain degree of mystery connected with these events which has never yet been fully
explained ; and it is not the duty of the writer to attempt
to investigate those facts which a military commission
failed to elucidate. Neither would it be possible, in the
brief space allotted us, to make intelligible to the reader
all the mazes of that confused and terrible conflict through
which General Grant again, as at Donelson, advanced
from defeat to victory.

Thirty-five thousand Union troops were resting upon
the hillsides and the ravines of Pittsburg Landing. At
a distance of twenty miles from them, there was a rebel
camp strongly intrenched, containing about seventy thousand men. General Albert Sidney Johnston was in command, supported by the most noted chieftains, — Beauregard, Hardee, Bragg, and Polk. General Breckenridge
was in command of the reserve. The advance of the
Union troops was near Shiloh Church ; and thus the first
day's battle, which soon ensued, is frequently called the
battle of Shiloh. General Johnston wisely resolved to

move forward with his whole force, and crush the little army of Grant before Buell could arrive. He was well aware of the valor of the foe he was to assail, and that caution was requisite as well as courage. Each party concealed, as far as possible, from the other its numbers, its position, and its means of attack and defence. Reconnoissances were sent out by the rebels, and several very spirited skirmishes ensued. This put our troops somewhat on their guard ; but it was generally supposed that the rebels, standing behind strong intrenchments which they had been rearing for months, would avail themselves of the great advantage of their forts and ramparts, and there await the assault.

It was General Johnston's plan to burst suddenly into the Union camp in the earliest light of the 5th. But a drenching rain came, the narrow roads were soon trampled into sloughs, and the march was so impeded that the rebel troops did not reach our front till late in the afternoon of that day. Their presence was so concealed by the forest, the underbrush, and the hills that our troops had no consciousness that the whole rebel army was encamped but a few yards from their lines.

.At half-past five o'clock the next morning, Sunday the 6th of April, the rebels in three columns came rushing upon our advanced divisions, which were under the command of Generals Sherman and Prentiss. These troops were three or four miles from the landing. At that early hour they were taken by surprise. The odds against them were terrific. Successful resistance was hopeless. Many of the men were not dressed. The arms were stacked. An awful scene ensued of confusion and terror and blood. A whole army was crushing, annihilating two feeble divisions. A storm of bullets and shell swept through the tents. So sudden was the onset that some were shot in their beds. General Prentiss and General Sherman did all that mortal energy could do to meet the awful crisis.

General Prentiss was speedily overwhelmed, his force dispersed, and himself and three regiments taken prisoners. Both he and General Sherman had anticipated an attack, warned by the vigorous skirmishing of the previous days; but it came at an unexpected hour. The destruction of Prentiss's division now turned the whole force of the rebels upon Sherman. He fought like a lion, and by his own personal valor held his brigades together so as slightly to check the advance of the foe. General McClernand, who was stationed a little in his rear, came promptly to the rescue.

But the two bodies united, with all their combined valor, could do but little to resist so overwhelming an assault. Some broke, and fled back to the river in terror; others stood bravely to their guns and maintained their martial array, resolved to sell their lives as dearly as possible.

When the battle commenced, General Grant, with his staff, was taking an early breakfast, preparing to set off in search of General Buell, whose approach had been announced. The tremendous cannonade, nine miles from the point at which he stood, revealed to him at once the whole truth. He despatched aids in all directions, to hurry up the detached divisions in support of the feeble lines, which were swaying and falling beneath the blows of the foe. A courier was instantly despatched to General Buell with the following note : —

"Heavy firing is heard up the river, indicating plainly that an attack has been made upon our most advanced positions. I have been looking for this, but did not believe the attack could be made before Monday or Tuesday. This necessitates my joining the forces up the river, instead of meeting you to-day as I had contemplated."

General Grant was then at Savannah, nine miles below Pittsburg Landing. He was there to meet General Buell, having received from him, the day before, the following note :—

"I shall be in-Savannah myself to-morrow, with perhaps two divisions. Can I meet you there ? "

General Grant replied :—

" Your despatch just received. I will be here to meet you to-morrow. The enemy at and near Corinth are probably from sixty to eighty thousand."

General Grant was then suffering from a very severe bruise. The day before, he rode out to General Sherman's lines on the extreme front, to confer with him upon the posture of affairs. As he was returning in the darkness of a rainy night, his horse, slipping upon a log, fell upon his rider. This lamed him for a week, and caused him excruciating pain.

On Saturday the 5th, the head of Nelson's column reached Savannah, where General Grant was waiting, in his crippled state, the arrival of General Buell. These troops were immediately sent up the river, to a position about five miles from the point opposite Pittsburg Landing. The transports, protected by the gunboats, were ready at any moment to take them across the stream, to re-enforce the troops upon the other side, in case of need.

A few miles above Savannah, and about four miles below Pittsburg Landing, there was a place called Crump's Landing. Here General Lewis Wallace was stationed with a division of about five thousand men. General

Grant took a transport, under a full head of steam, for the front. He stopped a moment to see General Wallace. This energetic commander had his whole force drawn up, in readiness to move immediately in obedience to whatever orders. The roar of the battle raging but a few miles from him was ringing incessantly in his ears. He was directed by General Grant to hold himself in readiness to march to the support of the main army, should he receive orders so to do; or, should the attack in front prove a feint, to be prepared to protect himself from an assault along the Purdy Road. This interview was held on board the transport. The situation of General Wallace was isolated and exposed. It was apprehended that the enemy might be contemplating an attack upon him.

General Grant then hurried the transport on to Pittsburg Landing, and rode immediately to the front. A scene of disaster here met his eye. Our advance line was abandoned to the enemy. Their encampment was in his hands. The division of General Prentiss was destroyed. The divisions of Generals Sherman and McClernand, though struggling desperately with the foe, were greatly demoralized, and had been driven back two miles. The field was filled with fugitives and stragglers, running back to the river's brink for the protection of the transports and of the gunboats. Still the battle raged hour after hour, as our troops fell sullenly back, and re-formed and advanced anew, behind the lines in their rear. To most, the day seemed hopelessly lost, and the destruction of the army inevitable.

An aid-de-camp was despatched to General Lewis Wallace, urging him to hasten with all possible speed to the front, with his fresh division of five thousand men. Still hour after hour passed, and he did not make his appear-

ance. It was one of the unavoidable casualties of war.
He has been severely, but very unjustly, censured for this
delay. He merits gratitude and applause only for the
heroism and wisdom he displayed on the occasion.

In obedience to orders he remained, chafing as he listened to the tumult of the battle which was ever drawing
nearer, awaiting instructions to move. At eleven o'clock a
courier arrived, directing him to march as rapidly as possible, and join the national army *on their right*. He immediately put his force in motion, by the only road through
which his object could be attained. But, in the meantime, the rebels had driven our lines in so far that a con-
tinuation in that line would bring him far away from our
troops, in the rear of the victorious foe : thus would the
capture of his whole division be inevitable.

An aid from General Grant came galloping up to inform
him of this fact ; and that he must promptly change his
direction, and hasten down to the landing, where the retreating troops were crowded together. But there was
no cross-road through the forest and over the ravines by
which he could possibly march. It was absolutely necessary — there was no escape from it — for him to retrace his
steps, several miles, to the Purdy Road ; there to take the
River Road, which would conduct him to the landing.
This he did with all possible energy, though he was unable to reach the field of battle until after sunset. There
is nothing more cruel than to heap reproaches upon a
gallant soldier, who is perilling life and limb for his country, because he does not perform impossibilities.

At four o'clock in the afternoon, our lines were everywhere broken, and driven back almost to the river's brink.
General Prentiss was a prisoner. General W. H. L. Wallace, one of the most gallant officers, had been borne from

the field mortally wounded. Further retreat of the troops was impossible. Colonel Webster, General Grant's chief of staff, collected a battery of twenty-two pieces, two of which were heavy siege-guns, and from a commanding eminence opened a terrific fire upon the advancing foe. The enemy recoiled before these rapid and deadly discharges of grape and canister and shells. Just then a loud shout was heard rising from thousands of voices, and General Nelson's division of Buell's army was seen upon the opposite bank of the river. The transports speedily conveyed them across. Two of the gunboats, — "The Tyler," and "The Lexington," — now that the foe were brought within their range, opened fire. Their enormous shells — the most terrible missiles then known in war — circled through the air, and, falling in the midst of the dense ranks of the foe, exploded with fearful carnage. The victors were checked. The pursuit was arrested. The enemy drew sullenly back; his fire slackened; and soon night, darkness, and silence enveloped the scene.

The rebels had attained a signal success. Our army had been routed, and a portion of it had been driven two or three miles before the foe. We had lost several thousand prisoners, and the whole field of battle was covered with the dying and the dead. Such were the results of the battle of Shiloh.

The singular absence of rivalry and jealousy between General Grant and General Sherman is remarkably manifested in the despatch which General Grant sent to the government soon after this battle, recommending General Sherman to promotion.

"To General Sherman," he writes, "I was greatly indebted, for his promptness in forwarding to me during the siege of Fort Donelson, re-enforcements and supplies from Paducah.   At the battle of Shiloh, on the first day, he held with raw troops the key-point to the landing. To his individual efforts I am indebted for the success of that battle.   Twice hit, and several (I think three) horses shot under him on that day, he maintained his position with raw troops.   It is no disparagement to any other officer to say that I do not believe that there was another division commander on the field who had the skill and experience to have done it."

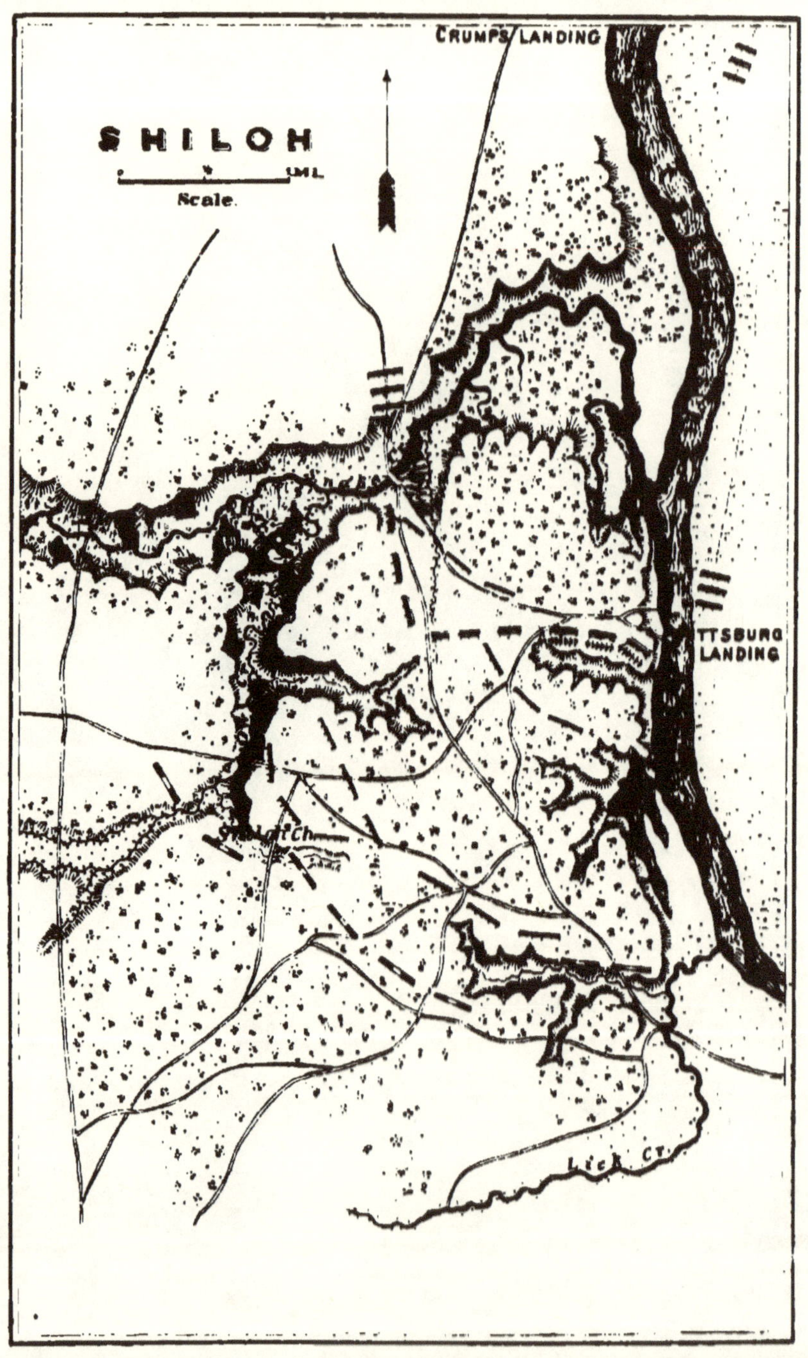
SHILOH
Scale.
1 ML
CRUMPS LANDING
TTSBURG LANDING
Shiloh Ch
Lick Cr.

CHAPTER VI.

THE VICTORY AT PITTSBURG LANDING.

Renewal of the Battle. — Retreat of the Rebels. — General Grant's Charge. — Spectacle of the Battle-field. — Testimony of General Sherman. — Grant's Congratulatory Order. — The Unfavorable Impression. — Speech of Hon. E. B. Washburne. — General Halleck assumes the Command. — The Advance upon Corinth. — The Investment. — Impatience of the Troops.

HE peculiar character of General Grant has never been more signally displayed than in the darkest hours of disaster. The dreadful calamity which the army had encountered at Shiloh seems not to have disturbed in the least his equanimity, or his confidence in the final result of the campaign. His words, his looks, his whole demeanor, inspired all with the assurance that the dawn of the morning would bring victory.

There was little sleep for the national troops that night. The gunboats, with their terrible shells, — which a negro described as " the wrath of God," — kept up through the night an incessant fire. The shattered divisions were re-organized. A new line of battle was formed. General Nelson's fresh troops, eager for the fray, were placed in position. General Lewis Wallace had arrived with his troops, panting for the conflict. General Buell was close at hand with his strong re-enforcements. Generals Mc-

Cook's and Crittenden's divisions of Buell's army, comprising twenty thousand men, which arrived during the night, were ferried across the river, and formed in line of battle. General Grant, confident of victory, visited every division commander, giving to each minute directions, and ordering all, at the earliest dawn, to charge the foe with the utmost possible impetuosity. Each commander was to attack with a heavy skirmish-line as. soon as it was light enough to see, and was then to follow up the attack with his whole command, leaving no reserves. General Grant perhaps relied upon the troops of Buell — now rapidly arriving — for a reserve, should any be needed.

During the night, mercifully, very mercifully, a heavy storm of rain arose. The exploding shells had set the woods on fire. The crackling flames were spreading through the dry grass and stubble in all directions. But for the rain, which thoroughly drenched the two sleepless and unsheltered armies, many of the wounded would have been burned alive. About midnight General Grant, having completed his arrangements, sharing the discomfort of his troops, threw himself upon the ground, and with a stump for a pillow, utterly exhausted by fatigue, slept soundly through the storm.

With the earliest light the battle was renewed. From the left, the centre, and the right, the national army — now in the majority, and with many fresh troops newly arrived — commenced the impetuous charge. The rebel troops were astounded at this sudden apparition of the dense lines of a defiant army rushing with shouts to the assault, when they had expected only to meet routed and fugitive foes. The rebels were exhausted with the tremendous exertions of the preceding day ;. and, though they fought well, they could not resist the impetuosity of the outnumbering national troops. General Lewis Wallace and his men performed prodigies of valor, proving to a demonstration that their delay of yesterday was their calamity only, not their fault. General Buell himself had arrived, — a thoroughly educated soldier, — and handled his troops with the ability which he ever displayed on the field of battle, but which, unfortunately, he did not always exhibit in his slow and cautious marches.

The advance of the patriot troops was resistlessly onward. Everywhere the foe recoiled before them. Step by step the national troops gradually regained every foot of ground they lost the day before. The retreat of the enemy became more rapid, less orderly; though still, like brave and well-officered men as they were, bad as was their cause, they fought with desperation. By night they were driven five miles from the ground which they had occupied in the morning.

Towards the close of this triumphant day, General Grant, who seemed to be everywhere present, met the First Ohio Regiment near a position occupied by the rebels, which it was very important at that juncture to take. He halted the regiment, and placed himself at its head. The troops recognized him with an enthusiastic cheer. General Grant ordered them " to charge ; " and led them in person, as much exposed as any private to the fire of the foe. They would have followed him to the cannon's mouth. An exhausted and retreating regiment, animated by the sight, closed up their wavering ranks, and, with cheers, joined in the charge. The foe was swept pell-mell from the spot; and thus one of the most important positions of the battle-field was gained.

The day was now far spent. The foe was rapidly retreating, to find shelter behind his intrenchments at

Corinth. The national troops, though victorious, were in the extreme of exhaustion; but the zeal of General Grant seemed to be proof against all weariness. He was anxious to pursue the retiring foe; but Generals McCook and Crittenden assured him that pursuit was then impossible, that their troops, brave as they were, would drop in their ranks from sheer exhaustion. They had made a forced march all the day before; they had passed almost a sleepless night; they had fought with tremendous energy during the day; a heavy rain was now falling, the darkness of a stormy night was coming on, and the roads were trampled to mire. Human strength could go no farther; and the weary hosts threw themselves upon the field which they had so grandly reclaimed, and found repose in sleep. The rebels stopped not to look behind until safe in their intrenchments at Corinth.

The attack of the rebels was wisely planned and heroically executed; but, through those casualties of war which no sagacity can fully provide for, it proved an utter failure. They marched from their intrenchments flushed with the confidence of victory: they returned mangled and bleeding, with their ranks broken, their numbers terribly diminished, leaving many of their wounded to fall into our hands, and their dead unburied. General Beauregard reported his total loss, in killed, wounded, and missing, at ten thousand six hundred and ninety-nine. General Grant's estimate of the rebel loss was very much greater. Our burial parties reported the rebel dead at four thousand. This, according to the usual proportion of the wounded, would bring their loss up to twenty thousand. General Grant's loss was twelve thousand six hundred and ninety-nine. Each army had gained a victory: each army had encountered a defeat.

Still, it must be admitted that the advantage on the whole was immensely with the national troops. The rebel army, demoralized and disheartened, had fled to seek protection behind their intrenchments. The national army, animated and emboldened by victory, was eager to pursue the foe, again to strike those blows which were destined eventually to bring the Rebellion to an end.

The field of battle, after the conflict was over, presented a terrible spectacle. For two days it had been swept incessantly by the storms of war. Two large armies had twice surged over it, each struggling in turn with the energies of despair. Scarcely a rod could be seen, for miles over the wide expanse, which did not contain the dead or the wounded. In many places where charges had been made, the dead lay in rows, as if cut down by the scythe of the mower. One tree, not eighteen inches in diameter, was struck by ninety balls within a distance of ten feet from the ground. It would seem that not a bird could have flown over that battle-swept field unscathed. General Grant seemed to bear a charmed life. Not a bullet touched him. A ball passed through General Sherman's hat, another glanced from his shoulder-strap, and a third passed through his hand. Scarcely a twig could be found in the underbrush which had not been struck.

There is a mystery connected with these battles of Shiloh and of Pittsburg Landing which has never yet been fully solved. General Prentiss is reported to have made the following statement: —

" General Beauregard asked me if we had any works at the river. To which I replied, ' You must consider us poor soldiers, general, if you suppose we would have neglected so plain a duty.' The truth is, however, that we had no works at all."

General Grant says, "As to the talk of our being surprised, nothing could be more false. If the enemy had sent us word where and when they would attack, we could not have been better prepared. Skirmishing had been going on for two days between our reconnoitring parties and the enemy's advance. I did not believe, however, that they intended to make a determined attack, but simply to make a reconnoissance in force."

Immediately after the battle, General Halleck arrived at Pittsburg Landing, and assumed the command of the army. It was not supposed that at this time he was very friendly to General Grant; and the country expected a very thorough investigation of the case. The result of that investigation was, that General Halleck exonerated General Grant from all blame. Still the community were left in the dark. In an order to the troops, which was intended as an announcement to the country, General Halleck thanked General Grant and General Buell, with their officers and men, " for the bravery and endurance with which they sustained the general attacks of the enemy on the 6th, and for the heroic manner in which on the 7th they defeated and routed the entire rebel army." Brigadier-General Sherman was particularly commended for the services which he had rendered on the occasion; and it was urged that he be promoted to the rank of major-general of volunteers.

General Sherman wrote, at this time, a very noble letter in defence of General Grant, from which I will make a few extracts. It was addressed to the editor of " The United-States Service Magazine," and was published in January, 1865 : —

" I will avail myself of this occasion to correct another very common mistake, in attributing to General Grant the selection of that battle-field. It was chosen by that veteran soldier, Major-General Charles F. Smith, who ordered my division to disembark there, and strike for the Charleston Railroad. It was General Smith who selected that field of battle, and it was well chosen. On any other we surely should have been overwhelmed, as both Lick and Snake Creeks forced the enemy to confine his movement to a direct front attack, which new troops are better qualified to resist than where the flanks are exposed to a real or chimerical danger. Even the divisions of the army were arranged in that camp by General Smith's order, before General Grant succeeded him to the command of all the forces up the Tennessee, — headquarters, Savannah. If there were any error in putting that army on the west side of the Tennessee, exposed to the superior force of the enemy, also assembling at Corinth, the mistake was not General Grant's. But there was no mistake."

General Grant, in a congratulatory order to the troops, issued on the 8th of April, says, —

" The general commanding congratulates the troops who so gallantly maintained their position; repulsed and routed a numerically superior force of the enemy, composed of the flower of the Southern army, commanded by their ablest generals, and fought by them with all the desperation of despair. In numbers engaged, no such contest ever took place on this continent. In importance of result, but few such have taken place in the history of the world."

It cannot be denied, that, for a time, there was a strong impression throughout the country unfavorable to the conduct of General Grant at Pittsburg Landing; and it must also be admitted that each succeeding development of facts has tended to throw new lustre upon the genius of General Grant, as exhibited on that occasion. But, for a season, he was certainly under the cloud. With characteristic silence he endured the wrong, waiting his opportunity to reply by deeds, and not by words.

The Hon. E. B. Washburne, Member of Congress from General Grant's district in Illinois, in a speech upon this occasion in the House of Representatives, May 2, 1862, said, in reference to the charge of intemperance which was then brought against the general, —

"But there is a more grievous suggestion touching the general's habits. It is a suggestion that has infused itself into the public mind everywhere. There never was a more cruel and atrocious slander upon a brave and a noble-minded man. There is no more temperate man in the army than General Grant. He never indulges in the use of intoxicating liquors at all. He is an example of courage, honor, fortitude, activity, temperance, and modesty; for he is as modest as he is brave and incorruptible. It is almost vain to hope that full justice will ever be done to men who have been thus attacked. Truth is slow upon the heels of falsehood. It has been well said that ' falsehood will travel from Maine to Georgia while truth is putting on its boots.'

"Though living in the same town with myself, General Grant has no political claims on me; for, so far as he is a politician, he belongs to a different party. But to the victory at Pittsburg Landing, which has called forth such a flood of denunciation upon General Grant: as to whether there was or not what might be called a surprise, I will not argue it. But, even if there had been, General Grant is nowise responsible for it; for *he* was not surprised. He was at his headquarters at Savannah when the fight commenced. Those headquarters were established there as being the most convenient point for all parts of his command. Some of the troops were at Crump's Landing, between Savannah and Pittsburg; and all the new arrivals were coming to Savannah. That was the proper place for the headquarters of the commanding general at that time. The general visited Pittsburg Landing, and all the important points, every day. The attack was made Sunday morning by a vastly superior force. In five minutes after the first firing was heard, General Grant and staff were on board a steamboat, on the way to the battle-field; and, instead of not reaching the field till ten o'clock, or — as has been still more falsely represented — till noon, I have a letter before me from one of his aids who was with him, and who says he arrived there at eight o'clock in the morning, and immediately assumed command. There he directed the movements, and was always on that part of the field where his presence was most required, exposing his life, and evincing in his dispositions the genius of the greatest commanders.

" With what desperate bravery that battle of Sunday was fought! What prodigies of valor! Our troops — less than forty thousand — attacked by more than eighty thousand picked men of the rebels, led by their most distinguished generals! After fighting all day with immensely superior numbers of the enemy, they only drove our forces back two and one-half miles, and then it was to face the gunboats and the terrible batteries so skilfully arranged and worked by the gallant and accomplished officers, Webster and Callender, and which brought the countless host of the enemy to a stand ; and, when night came, this unconquerable army stood substantially triumphant on that bloody field. I believe, notwithstanding the desperate fighting on Sunday, and the partial repulse of our troops, that, aided by the fresh troops of the brave Lewis Wallace, that army could have whipped the enemy on Monday without further re-enforcements."

The rebels were again rendezvoused at Corinth, behind a series of intrenchments which they deemed impregnable. General Halleck, who had now assumed the command, superseding General Grant, was a man of decided abilities, but of excessive caution. Though General Grant was left second in command, he was not often consulted by General Halleck, who was a very positive man, and seldom asked counsel of others. The army was largely re-enforced, and divided into three corps. General Thomas was placed in command of the right, General Pope of the left, and General Buell of the centre. The reserve was intrusted to General McClernand.· General Grant still nominally commanded the district of West Tennessee, with Generals Thomas and McClernand as his corps-commanders. His situation was a painful one, as he generally was regarded as in disgrace.

Under the command of General Halleck, the national army moved slowly and cautiously towards Corinth. There was no longer any failure in the use of the spade, and in the throwing up of intrenchments. Wherever the troops halted, ramparts and bastions rose immediately around them; and every precaution was adopted to prevent surprise. The progress, though sure, was necessarily slow. Some of the more impetuous generals chafed under these restraints. Six weeks were employed in advancing sixteen miles.

The Union troops were then nearly within range of the guns at Corinth. It was estimated that General Beauregard had seventy thousand men behind those ramparts, though he reported his numbers at forty-seven thousand. General Halleck had a hundred and twenty thousand bayonets under his control, with a splendid array of artillery and siege-guns. He planted his army in front of the rebel works, rearing counter-works, and preparing to carry the place by siege. General Grant was of the opinion that the enemy's works could, without doubt, be carried by assault. He expressed this opinion to General Halleck ; but the suggestion was repelled by the intimation, " that, when General Halleck needed the advice of General Grant, he would call for it." The modest soldier did not again obtrude his opinions.

The siege of Corinth was now commenced. It was safely prosecuted, according to the established rules of military art. The troops were impatient ; the generals were impatient ;. the country was impatient. The narrative of the mortifying result of the siege must be reserved for the next chapter.

CHAPTER VII.

THE SIEGE OF CORINTH AND THE ADVANCE TO VICKSBURG.

The Secret Evacuation. — Chagrin of the Army. — General Grant restored to his Command. — His Headquarters at Corinth. — Plans of Price, Bragg, and Van Dorn. — The Rebel Batteries at Vicksburg. — The Advance upon Vicksburg. — Failure of the Canal. — The Lake-Providence Enterprise. — The Moon-Lake Enterprise. — The Yazoo Enterprise.

Y the latter part of May, the national army, in vast strength, was gathered around the rebel intrenchments at Corinth ; which were spread over miles of the wild, rugged, solitary country. The rebels had occupied all the important eminences by their batteries, so as to command every approach to their works. The cautious general moved with great circumspection. There were occasional skirmishes and military duels from opposing heights ; but it was very evident that General Halleck had no intention of storming the intrenchments, and that nothing could induce General Beauregard, who was then in command of the post, to emerge from behind his ramparts. Gradually, however, our lines drew nearer to the foe, until we were within two hundred yards of their main intrenchments. It was universally supposed that a tremendous struggle was at hand, and the North contemplated the result with great solicitude.

On the 30th of May a very curious explosion was heard

within the enemy's lines, sounding like volleys of large siege-pieces in repeated explosions of twos and threes; and clouds of smoke were seen ascending from Corinth. This attracted the attention of the whole army, and General Morgan L. Smith's brigade was sent forward cautiously, to ascertain the cause. The brigade approached the first redoubt of the enemy, and encountered no fire. Hesitatingly it pressed on, and entered the redoubt. It was empty. Not a vestige of the foe could be seen. Surprised at this, the brigade pushed on throughout the frowning labyrinth of ramparts and bastions, and found all silent and deserted. The troops entered the streets of Corinth. Nothing met the eye but solitude and desolation. They marched through the town, ascended College Hill beyond; and, as far as the eye could reach, no sign of the enemy could be seen. The rebels had vanished in the night, leaving not a man behind. Indeed, for weeks they had been very shrewdly and secretly conducting their retreat; and the works were all entirely evacuated.

Very adroitly was this movement accomplished. An army of nearly a hundred thousand men, almost within pistol-shot of another hostile army a third larger, had effected its retreat unobserved, almost unsuspected; carrying off its sick, its provisions, its military stores, its *matériel* of war. Nothing of any value was left behind. For more than a month the national army had been held at bay, while this movement was in operation. Thus ingloriously the siege of Corinth terminated.

The troops under General Halleck, and many of their officers, had been anxious to assail the works during the siege, as they felt confident that they could carry them by storm. They were exceedingly chagrined in having the foe thus escape them, and were eager for the pursuit.

The roads were good, the enemy demoralized, and the national troops in the finest condition. But the circumspection of the commander-in-chief held them back. A reconnoitring force was sent out a little way, which returned having accomplished nothing. This mode of conducting warfare was not at all in accordance with the spirit of General Grant. But, in his subordinate position, he could only remain in camp in obedience to orders. He still nominally retained command of the district of Tennessee; and as our army broke up, and retired from Corinth, his headquarters were transferred to Memphis, which had fallen into the hands of the national forces. Soon after, about the middle of July, General Halleck was recalled to Washington, to supersede General McClellan as general-in-chief of the American forces. The command of the army of the Tennessee consequently reverted again to General Grant. He established himself at Corinth, as an important strategic point to command the Mobile and Ohio, and the Charleston and Memphis Railroads, which there crossed.

Here, in the midst of the enemy's country, he had several important points to protect, and was compelled to act purely on the defensive. For eight weeks he was continually threatened by large rebel forces under Generals Van Dorn and Price. The works at Corinth were altogether too extensive to be manned by the small garrison under General Grant's command. He accordingly constructed works nearer the town, which subsequently became of very great importance. Our troops in Virginia were at that time encountering terrible disasters. Both Maryland and Ohio were threatened with invasion. Every man whom Grant could spare was taken from him, and sent to the North. He was thus left to defend himself almost without troops. His despatches at this time testify to the anxieties which oppressed him, to the sleepless vigilance with which he watched his foes, and his resolution to maintain his position to the very last extremity. The rebel General Price siezed Iuka, on the Charleston Railroad, twenty-one miles south-east of Corinth. He intended to traverse Tennessee to re-enforce Bragg, who was marching through Kentucky to invade Ohio. At the same time Van Dorn was threatening Grant at Corinth, designing to effect a junction with Price. Grant wished to strike Price a blow, hoping to crush him before this junction was effected. But he could not safely weaken his little garrison at Corinth, to advance upon Price, as he was already severely threatened by Van Dorn. Such were the cruel embarrassments to which he was exposed.

He sent out a force, however, under Generals Rosecrans and Ord, of about seventeen thousand men, to attack Price at Iuka. There was a bloody battle; but Price succeeded in escaping, and, having united with Van Dorn, marched upon Corinth. General Grant had now established his headquarters at Jackson, as the point at which he could be best in communication with the whole of his extended district. The rebels were in force at La Grange and at Ripley. Jackson and Bolivar were threatened as well as Corinth. It was for some time uncertain upon which point the enemy would strike his concentrated blow.

Suddenly the foe appeared in strength before Corinth. General Rosecrans was then in command there. He had nineteen thousand men in his ranks. The enemy approached with thirty-eight thousand men. Their banners first appeared in front of Corinth on the 2d. Serious fighting commenced upon the 3d. General Rosecrans was driven from his outer defences to the interior works which General Grant had caused to be constructed. These works saved the army and the post. The rebel troops rushed to the assault with their usual bravery. After a fierce battle, in which General Rosecrans greatly distinguished himself, the rebels were repelled with enormous slaughter. Two of the commands alone lost over four thousand men in killed, wounded, and missing. Though our troops fought behind their ramparts, over two thousand were either killed or wounded.

While the battle was raging, General McPherson, with re-enforcements, arrived from Jackson, having been sent by General Grant in aid of the beleaguered garrison. General Grant, confident of the repulse, had also sent a force under Generals Hurlburt and Ord, four thousand strong, to strike the foe in flank upon their retreat. The plan, so sagaciously formed, was entirely successful. As the bleeding and shattered columns of the rebels were crossing the Hatchie River, these troops fell impetuously upon them. The rebel advance was forced back. A battery of artillery and several hundred men were captured, and many were driven into the river and drowned. Had the orders given by General Grant been faithfully followed up, the entire force of Van Dorn would have been destroyed.

But the casualties of war are innumerable; and we are apt to forget that all nerves are not made of steel, and that men utterly exhausted by fighting two days and a night are in a poor condition to pursue through rain and mire a desperate, though retreating, foe. The battles of Iuka and Corinth, both of which General Grant directed until the troops were in presence of the enemy, secured very important results. They relieved West Tennessee from all immediate danger.

The community was slow in giving General Grant credit for the genius he possessed. He was a man of few words: his address was far from imposing. He assumed no airs of greatness. The extreme simplicity of his manners deceived even those who were most familiar with him; so that it was but gradually the community awoke to the consciousness that General Grant was a man who would certainly accomplish whatever he undertook.

In the latter part of October very considerable reenforcements were sent to him; and he suggested to General Halleck that a movement should be made into the interior of Mississippi, to attack the enemy on the bluffs at Vicksburg, where they were erecting a Gibraltar-like fortress to command the Lower Mississippi. The importance of this stream to the United States cannot be exaggerated. Its waters fertilize a valley containing thirteen thousand square miles, being six times as large as the empire of France. Fifty-seven navigable streams pour their floods into the bosom of this father of waters. It is the great river, not only of the United States, but — all things considered — of the world. And yet a little band of rebels in the South had insolently assumed the right of wresting that river from the United States, and taking command of its mouths. Our gunboat fleet had indignantly swept away the obstructions placed below New Orleans, and had restored that grand city to its allegiance.

The rebels had seized upon Vicksburg, which was situated upon a bluff, in a remarkable bend of the river, about four hundred miles above New Orleans. Early in January, 1861, they had commenced throwing up batteries on this spot. After the fall of Island No. 10, their fortifications were greatly enlarged and strengthened. In June, 1862, Admiral Farragut, ascending in gunboats from New Orleans, attempted to demolish these batteries ; but they proved too strong for him. It became evident that they could be carried only by a united land and river force. General Grant now proposed abandoning Corinth, destroying all the railroads in that region, and concentrating his troops at Memphis, which was about sixty miles due west from Corinth, on the east bank of the Mississippi River.

After much correspondence with General Halleck, and various minor movements of detachments of his army, — abandoning some posts and occupying others, here opening new communications and there destroying old ones, — by the close of January, 1863, General Grant was prepared for his great attempt upon Vicksburg. The eyes of the whole continent were fixed upon the enterprise. Here the rebels had concentrated the utmost of their strength. Here the national government was to strike the heaviest of its blows.

The entire force at General Grant's command in the department of the Tennessee amounted to a hundred and thirty thousand men. Of these he took fifty thousand with him for the reduction of Vicksburg. These troops were conveyed down the Mississippi in gunboats and transports, and landed at Milliken's Bend and Young's Point, — two positions on the western bank of the river, a few miles above Vicksburg. Commodore Porter was to co-operate with a fleet of sixty vessels, carrying two hundred and eighty guns and eight hundred men. The guns of Vicksburg, of course, prevented communication between the national forces above and below the batteries.

In Commodore Farragut's unavailing endeavor (to which we have alluded) to destroy the batteries at Vicksburg, he endeavored to cut a canal across the neck of the peninsula, which the very remarkable bend in the river here makes. Could this canal be completed, General Grant could run through with his transports out of range of the enemy's guns, and thus obtain a position in the rear of Vicksburg. The Yazoo River, which ran into the Mississippi north of Vicksburg, and whose banks the rebels had strongly fortified, prevented his attaining this end in that direction.

General Grant's first attempt was to open this canal. For six weeks several thousand hands were incessantly at work upon it, and the whole nation watched with eagerness the result of the enterprise. It does not appear that General Grant had any great confidence in its success. But it was necessary to keep the army employed. He had other plans in view which could not then be executed. For many weeks four thousand soldiers and a large number of negroes were employed upon this work, cutting a trench ten feet wide, six feet deep, and about three miles long. It was supposed that the opening of this trench would turn the current of the river, changing its channel.

The work was nearly completed when, on the 8th of March, there was a sudden rise in the river. The dam at the head of the canal broke away; the water rushed in; and, instead of sweeping through the canal, obstinately chose its own course, and, flowing in all directions, inundated the low and marshy ground and submerged the camps. The troops were compelled to flee for their lives, and many of the horses were swept away and drowned. This disaster, and the fact that the rebels had succeeded in planting heavy guns which enfiladed the canal, caused the enterprise to be abandoned.

At the same time that this work was in progress, General Grant sent a large body of men to a point seventy miles north from Vicksburg, to cut a short canal from the river west to a sheet of water called Lake Providence, which was formerly the bed of the river. This lake was connected, from its southern extremity, with Swan Lake, by a bayou filled with snags and winding through the tangled forest. Swan Lake found an outlet into the Tensas River. Through this stream, boats could pass into the Black River, and thence into the Red River, which entered the Mississippi far below Vicksburg. To open this channel for the passage of the boats through the labyrinth of streams and bayous on the west of the Mississippi, it was apparently only necessary to cut a canal through the morass along a channel which the river formerly occupied, dig out a few shallows, cut away a few snags, sawyers, and windfalls, and thus to open a new Mississippi, parallel to the old one.

Stupendous as this plan appeared, it was by no means irrational. The river is ever changing its old channels, and finding new ones. The region here to be traversed, through pathless morasses and stagnant bayous and tangled forests, was as gloomy as the imagination can conceive. Newspaper correspondents kept the nation informed of all these movements. The progress of the work was watched with the liveliest interest. At last the canal was successfully opened. A few barges entered Lake Providence. Success seemed very hopeful: Experienced engineers and axemen accompanied the pioneer fleet. The puff of the steamer echoed along those silent streams buried in gloom, which even the Indian's canoe had never penetrated. But at last a drought came. There was no depth of water in the lagoons; and the enterprise was of necessity abandoned.

But General Grant was never discouraged. Whatever he undertook, he was bound in some way to accomplish. He now turned his attention to the east side of the river. One hundred and fifty miles north of Vicksburg, and nearly opposite Helena, there is, but a few hundred yards from the eastern shore of the river, what is called Moon Lake. From the southern extremity of this long sheet of water, Yazoo Pass leads into Coldwater River, and this into the Tallahatchie, and this into the Yazoo River, which enters the Mississippi just above Vicksburg. The mouth of the Yazoo was so strongly guarded by rebel batteries that our transports could by no possibility ascend it, to place our troops in a position to gain the rear of Vicksburg. It was deemed possible, that, by cutting a canal into Moon Lake, a way might be opened for the transports, through those clogged and winding streams, into the Yazoo, so far above the rebel intrenchments as to enable them to land troops where they could march upon Vicksburg in the rear.

This route had formerly been used in passing from the Mississippi to the Yazoo. But, as the swellings of the great river often overflowed the very extensive alluvial region found there, the State of Mississippi had constructed a strong levee, which cut off the entrance to the pass. This levee was cut on the 2d of February; and a wide channel opened by the explosion of a mine. The torrent rushed in, cutting a channel so deep and wide that in two days there was a river pouring into Moon Lake through which the largest steamers could pass.

But the rebels, from whom these operations could not be concealed, were busy lower down accumulating vast obstructions. The forest was extremely luxuriant with tangling underbrush and a dense growth of gigantic trees. These trees, consisting of cotton-wood, oak, elm, sycamore, and pecan-wood, were felled in great numbers across the narrow path. Most of this timber was very solid and heavy, and would not float. Filling the stream with their enormous interlacing branches, they formed obstructions of the most formidable nature. These extended for miles. One of these barricades was a mile and a quarter in length, composed of mammoth trees which extended entirely across the stream. Many of these giants of the forest weighed twenty tons. If cut in pieces, they would sink, and still clog the channel. They had therefore to be drawn out by main force. In all this work of obstruction, the rebels found efficient aid in the forced labor of the slaves.

The Union troops were much embarrassed by the fact that nearly the whole country was submerged, leaving only a narrow strip of land forming the banks of the streams. After long and tedious work, the passage was opened from Moon Lake to the Coldwater. But the enemy had, in the meantime, reared still more formidable obstructions, protected by heavy batteries farther below.

On the 24th of February, General Ross entered the pass with twenty-two light transports, conveying forty-five hundred men. The expedition was convoyed by two iron-clad gunboats and several light-armored craft, which could run in very shallow water, and which were significantly called " the mosquito fleet." The naval force was under Lieutenant-Commander Watson Smith. On the 2d of March, the fleet reached the Coldwater.

This river is about one hundred feet wide, and runs through a dense and solitary wilderness a distance of about forty miles, when it enters the Tallahatchie, — a stream so broad and deep that it could not be easily obstructed. The steamers drifted cautiously down upon the swift current, using their paddle-wheels often to retard their speed. To avoid ambuscades, and the many other perils of the unknown navigation, they tied their boats to the shore at night. This romantic navigation of a tortuous, swift, and unexplored river, traversing an unbroken forest, now rippling over sand-bars, now expanding into a lake, now contracted into a narrow channel, was safely accomplished through a distance of two hundred miles.

General Grant, encouraged by this success, hoped to be able to transport his whole army by this route to the Yazoo River, above Haines's Bluff. The round-about distance from Milliken's Bend was about nine hundred miles. First, a single division, under General Quimby, was sent to the support of General Ross; soon after, General McPherson, with his whole corps, was ordered to enter the pass as soon as suitable transportation could be obtained. The Tallahatchie River receives a tributary, called the Yallabusha, at a point near which is found the small town of Greenwood. The two streams united form the Yazoo.

Here the rebels had erected a battery which they called Fort Pemberton. It was placed upon low land, but a few feet above the water; for nothing like a hill can be found in this dreary region. Indeed the battery, which included two heavy guns, and which commanded both the land and the water approaches from the north, was so low in position that it was nearly surrounded by the flood, rendering a land attack impossible.

The iron-clads approached within a range of about eight hundred yards, and opened fire. There was also a small battery placed upon the shore, to co-operate. But the rebel works were found too strong to be carried by any force there at our command.   In the brief battle which ensued, one vessel was disabled, six men were killed and twenty-five wounded.   The rebels lost but one man killed and twenty wounded.

A rise of two feet of water would drown the garrison out.   It was thought that cutting the levee on the Mississippi, three hundred miles distant, might accomplish this purpose.   The majestic river was then rushing to the ocean in the full strength of its spring flood.   The levee was cut, eighteen miles above Helena.   The mighty torrent poured in, and spread over leagues of space; but, refusing to take the line of the Coldwater and the Tallahatchie, left the little garrison at Greenwood still on land elevated two feet above the flood.   In the meantime the rebels were hurrying troops from Vicksburg to Greenwood, and General Grant became alarmed for General Ross's expedition.   His troops were in danger of being surrounded and cut off in the tangled network of forest and bayou through which he was struggling.

To relieve General Ross, and at the same time to gain a position in the rear of Vicksburg, another expedient was adopted.   Our gunboats held the mouth of the Yazoo River for a distance of about seven miles from its entrance into the Mississippi.   Above this rose Haines's Bluffs, frowning with batteries which our boats could not pass.   But just below these bluffs, near the point where the river enters the Mississippi, Steele's Bayou enters the Yazoo from the north.   There was opened here a labyrinthine route, which, after innumerable windings, conducted one into the Yazoo River again, sixty miles above the bluff.   The weird-like passage led from Steele's Bayou to Black Bayou; thence through Deer Creek, the Rolling Fork, the Big Sunflower, and the Sunflower, into the

Yazoo. General Grant accompanied Admiral Porter on a reconnoissance up these streams. The principal obstructions they encountered were from the overhanging trees. Both the general and the admiral concluded that the boats could be sent through by that route. General Grant returned to Milliken's Bend, to press forward the expedition. He said, —

" If we can get boats in the rear of the enemy in time, it will so confuse them as to save Ross's force. If not, I shall feel restless for his fate until I know that Quimby has reached him."

Could this plan have succeeded, the garrison at Fort Pemberton would have found themselves between the two national forces, and would have been compelled to a surrender or to a hasty evacuation. About thirty steamers of the enemy, which had ascended to those higher waters, would also have been captured.

On the 16th of March, General Sherman, with Stuart's division, set out on this enterprise. Admiral Porter led the expedition, with five iron-clads and four mortar-boats. General Grant sent a despatch to General Quimby, informing him of the movement, and urging him to press forward to the support of General Ross. General Sherman's troops ascended the Mississippi in large transports about thirty miles, to Eagle Bend. Here they were landed, and, marching across a neck of land about a mile in width, were received on board the transports, which ascended the bayou to meet them. They were compelled on their march to traverse a swamp, over much of which they could only pass by building floating bridges. Reaching the stream, they found the channel, as they advanced, much obstructed by drift timber. The channel was so narrow, and the turns so short, that it was often with the greatest difficulty that the unwieldy iron-clads could work around the bends. At one time it required twenty-four hours to advance four miles. The gunboats were furnished with very powerful engines; and, though moving slowly, they advanced with apparently resistless power, crushing saplings, bushes, and drift-wood beneath them, and breaking down the gigantic branches of the trees which swept their decks.

"I never yet saw," says Admiral Porter, "vessels so well adapted to knocking down trees or demolishing bridges." At length it was found that the more frail transports could proceed no farther; and the troops were transferred to tugs and coal-barges. Thus they crept slowly along over this blending waste of forest and water, until they approached the Rolling Fork. Here Admiral Porter, on the 20th of March, found his progress impeded by a barricade of heavy trees felled in his front. As he commenced removing these obstructions, the rebels, four thousand in number, opened fire upon him from the swamps around. They had several pieces of artillery, and their sharpshooters were concealed be-hind the trees. They had a large number of negroes with them, whom they compelled, by threats of death, to pile up these obstructions in front and in rear of the boats. Admiral Porter's heavy guns were of but little avail against such an assault. The land-forces were several miles below, laboriously following in the path which the gun-boats had opened. The labor of remov-ing these obstructions, under artillery and musketry fire, was prodigious. But it was unfalteringly pushed on by day and by night.

Admiral Porter sent a despatch to General Sherman, thirty miles below, to hasten to his assistance. This energetic man immediately landed his troops; and, though it was night, led them himself along the narrow bank of the river, which afforded the only practicable path of dry land. They groped through the cane-brakes by lighted torches. General Sherman very speedily, with his light artillery and his infantry, scattered the rebel skirmishers.

But the further prosecution of the enterprise was now found to be impracticable. The enemy was in very considerable strength, both before them and behind them, with a large number of slaves who were compelled to co-operate, or throw up obstructions in front, and also in the rear to cut off their retreat. Hence it became necessary for the expedition to return. The stream was so narrow at this point that the iron-clads were compelled to back down with unshipped rudders, as there was no room to turn. General Sherman, with his land-force, protected them from the skirmishers who were crowding the forest.

On the 27th, the expedition had safely returned to the vicinity of Vicksburg. Generals Ross and Quimby also withdrew from their perilous entanglements in safety; and, by the latter part of March, the Union troops were again concentrated at Milliken's Bend.

CHAPTER VIII.

RUNNING THE BATTERIES.

Bitter Feeling towards General Grant. — President Lincoln approves his Course. — His Movement upon Vicksburg. — Opposition to his Plans. — March to New Carthage. — Self-reliance of General Grant. — Admiral Porter. — Enthusiasm of the Sailors. — Conflict on the River. — Running the Batteries. — Secessionist Revenge.

THE marvellous and heroic attempts to capture Vicksburg by digging canals and traversing bayous was now ended. " What next ? " was the anxious inquiry of the nation. " Nothing," was the response of unbelieving ones in the North. " The works," they said, " are impregnable. There is no power in the national government that can take them." General Grant remained — as usual — silent. He was not in the slightest degree disheartened. He had never placed his main reliance upon any of these undertakings. In anticipation of their not improbable failure, other plans were already matured in his mind. But these, his final plans, could not be consummated until the summer drought should come on, when the marshy land opposite Vicksburg could be traversed by the troops. While waiting for this, General Grant had very wisely engaged in the enterprises we have enumerated. They presented at least a fair chance of success. They occupied the army ;

they interested the whole country, and gave food for its hopes. Had General Grant encamped his troops at Milliken's Bend, and waited inertly through these months, the whole country would have risen in rebellion against him. Had he revealed his ultimate plan, the rebels would have adopted very energetic, and probably effectual, measures to prevent its execution.

General Grant was well aware of the necessity of the most prompt and energetic action; for the country was beginning to be very restless. Multitudes were clamoring for his removal. The president was besieged with petitions, and almost with demands, that General Grant should be laid aside, and some other one assigned to his place. But Abraham Lincoln had a peculiar instinct, which enabled him to judge correctly of men. It is possible, but not probable, that the reticent general had confided to him his plans. At all events, President Lincoln turned a deaf ear to all the clamor raised against General Grant, quietly remarking, "I rather like the man: I think we'll try him a little longer."

The rebels were now exultant, and insolent in their taunts, as they stood at their guns at Vicksburg. Jefferson Davis pronounced the fortress to be the Gibraltar of America. But the Gibraltar was destined soon to fall. General Sherman, ever the noble co-operator with General Grant, was exceedingly anxious in view of the posture of affairs. He rode to General Grant's headquarters, and urged that the only way of attacking Vicksburg was to approach it from the north. "That," replied General Grant, "would require a retrograde movement to Memphis. I am determined to take no backward step. The country would be discouraged by it, and it is in no temper to endure such a reverse."

General Grant's plan, as the time for its execution arrived, was communicated to his staff-officers. It is not known that one of them approved of it. Nearly all opposed it as a fatal error. Perhaps there is not another man in the nation who would have conceived it in its details. Even the president, notwithstanding all his confidence in General Grant, followed his movements with great anxiety and surprise, fearing he had committed an irretrievable fault. The triumphant success of the enterprise has proved its wisdom; for this success was not the result of accident, but of combinations, the efficiency of which all can now comprehend.

The plan which General Grant proposed, which he had thoroughly considered and decided upon, was to have some of the naval fleet run the batteries at Vicksburg. He would at the same time move his army, by a rapid march through the forest on the western banks, to New Carthage, a few miles below the rebel batteries. The boats there would be ready to convey his troops across the river to Warrenton. He would then find good roads, by which he would advance rapidly to the investment of Vicksburg in the rear; while the gunboats, both above and below, would assail the works from the river, in front of Vicksburg.

To this plan nearly all objected. It was opposed with seemingly unanswerable arguments.

"This movement," it was said, "will effectually sunder the army from the North and from all its supplies. An almost impregnable fortress will be between our army and its base. If failure come, there is no retreat; and the ruin will be entire."

General Sherman wrote upon this occasion a letter to General Grant, proposing a different plan, but closing with these words, so characteristic of the magnanimity of the writer : —

"I make these suggestions, with the request that General Grant simply read them, and give them, as I know he will, a share of his thoughts. I would prefer that he should not answer them, but give them as much or as little weight as they deserve. Whatever plan of action he may adopt will receive from me the same zealous co-operation as though conceived by myself."

It is greatly to the honor of General Grant's subordinates, that, as soon as they found that he had definitely settled upon his plan, they, without a murmuring word, gave it the support of their utmost energies.

The whole national force was now concentrated at Milliken's Bend. As soon as the spring flood had so far subsided that the troops could advance by land through the morasses which line the western shores of the river, General Grant ordered a secret and rapid movement of his troops — concealed from observation by the forest — to the little town of New Carthage, about thirty miles below the batteries at Vicksburg. Even then, the water in the river was four and a half inches higher than the road ; which road was only twenty inches above the water in the impenetrable. morass spreading out, apparently without bounds, to the west. It was found needful to construct several bridges across the swollen bayous.

The vast complications involved in these plans seemed all to be easily grasped by the mind of General Grant. His watchful eye was everywhere. While maturing these schemes of an advance upon Vicksburg, he wrote to General Hurlburt, —

"It seems to me that Grierson, with about five hundred picked men, might succeed in cutting his way south, and cut the railroad east of Jackson, Miss. This undertaking would be a hazardous one; but it would pay well, if carried out."

This was probably the first inception of that magnificent raid which has given the gallant little band led by Colonel Grierson world-wide renown. The successful accomplishment of this plan, which was commenced in the middle of April, destroyed for a time the only railroad by which the garrison at Vicksburg held communication with the interior of the rebel States. It operated as a very powerful diversion in favor of General Grant's new campaign. Colonel Grierson with his bold riders swept over a path six hundred miles in length, tore up fifty miles of railroad, broke down telegraph wires, destroyed three thousand stands of arms, and captured five hundred prisoners. His loss was but three killed and seven wounded.

General McClernand, with the Eleventh Army Corps, led the advance through the morass in the march to New Carthage. It was a toilsome and perilous undertaking; but, with able and energetic leaders and devoted soldiers, it was heroically accomplished. The heavy artillery wheels cut through the saturated soil, soon rendering the path an entire slough. Through this mire, horses and men waded knee-deep, and the hubs of the wheels often disappeared from sight. Much of the way, it was necessary to build corduroy roads. It was needful to guard with the utmost care twenty miles of levee, lest it should be cut by the enemy, and the whole country be inundated.

Notwithstanding every precaution, the rebels had got some intimation of the movement; and, as they approached New Carthage, they found the levee cut, and the inrushing flood had spread out into a lake, which, surrounding New Carthage, converted it into an island. But General Grant had inspired his troops with his own silent, indomitable energy. Undismayed by the appalling prospect before them, they pressed on; now creeping along a little elevation of the land, now wading shallow plains, now bridging roaring floods, now constructing miles of corduroy road, till finally they reached their destination. A position was taken at Perkins's Landing, twelve miles below New Carthage.

The army was now south of Vicksburg. That frowning fortress seemed to cut off all its communication with the North. It would be almost impossible for the army to retrace its steps. It would be extremely difficult, if not impossible, to transport provisions and military supplies over the long and pathless marsh through which the army had waded. Was the army ruined? Many said, "Yes." Was it on a sure path to victory? The result will show.

As General Grant stood at Perkins's Landing, looking upon the rushing flood of the Mississippi before him, with no transports to cross the stream, and conscious that the batteries of Vicksburg were strong as rebel skill and strength could make them, he must have had great confidence in his own resources not to have been appalled in view of the peril before him. But he did have that confidence; and no one could discern in his quiet demeanor, or in his placid features, the slightest intimation of a fear or of a doubt.

It was now necessary to attempt to run the batteries with gunboats, and also with barges laden with provisions. The stoutest heart might be excused from recoiling from the dangers of such an adventure.　Fortunately for General Grant, Admiral Porter, whose courage never waned, and whose energy never abated, was not only ready, but eager, to co-operate with the commander-in-chief in his boldest plans.　"I am happy to say," wrote General Grant, " that the admiral and myself have never yet disagreed upon any policy."

There is some little diversity in the accounts which are given of the number and character of the boats which were engaged in this enterprise.　After a careful examination of these narratives, it seems to me that the following account must be nearly accurate: " The Forest Queen," " The Henry Clay," and " The Silver Wave " were heavily laden with military stores.　These were plain, wooden boats.　Speed was essential to their safety ; and also interior capaciousness, for conveying supplies below, and also for transporting the troops across the river.　The boilers were carefully protected by bales of cotton and of wet hay.　The engines were put in the best possible running order, and an ingenious contrivance was adopted to prevent any gleam of the fire from appearing, to guide the guns of the foe.

The undertaking was regarded as so hazardous that it was not thought right to *order* men to engage in it. Volunteers were called for.　So many came forward, eager for the enterprise, that it was necessary for the aspirants to abide the decision of the lot.　The excitement was intense, to see who would be the favored ones. Pilots, engineers, firemen, deck-hands, were clamorous with their proffered services.　A boy, who had drawn what he deemed a prize, was offered a hundred dollars for his chance, and rejected the offer.　He stood exultingly at his post, and passed the batteries in safety.

Eight gunboats and the transports were concealed in a bend in the river, where they were prepared for the trying ordeal. The plan was to select a very dark night, and then to send down the gunboats to take position in front of Vicksburg, and open upon the batteries a terrific fire. Under cover of this fire, and in some degree sheltered by the iron-clads, the transports were to endeavor to run by, with the utmost speed.

The night of the 16th of April was moonless and dark. A little before midnight, all the lights had disappeared in Vicksburg, and silence and gloom reigned undisturbed over both the river and the land. One after another the huge, shadowy masses emerged from their concealment, and as cautiously as possible steamed down the river. Admiral Porter led the way with " The Benton." The other iron-clads followed in a line. The three transports then crept along, keeping as near as possible to the western bank. General Grant took his stand in a transport in the middle of the river, to watch the operation. The portion of the patriot army remaining at the bend, some upon the shore and others upon the boats, watched with breathless silence the heroic little fleet as it glided away into the impenetrable darkness.

Nearly three-quarters of an hour elapsed, when a brilliant flash was seen, followed by a roar which shook the hills. The rebels had opened fire. In another instant the whole line of the bluff was ablaze with meteoric flashes, followed by battle's loudest thunders. The iron-clads were soon all in position, and vigorously responded. Under cover of the smoke, the darkness, and the tumult of the contest, the transports — hugging the Louisiana shore — rushed on at the top of their speed.

But, suddenly, new gleams of light appeared; and immense piles of rubbish and combustibles, prepared for such an event, burst into flame, converting night into day. The whole plan was now revealed, and the batteries turned many of their guns upon the transports. "The Forest Queen" soon received two shots, which so disabled her that she floated helpless down the stream. But one of the gunboats took her in charge, and towed her safely to New Carthage. "The Henry Clay" was struck by a shell, which set her cotton on fire. She was soon enveloped in a blaze, and floated down the rapid river a mountain of flame. The crew took to the boats, and escaped to the Louisiana shore. Here they concealed themselves behind the levee during the cannonade, and the next day made their way back through the submerged swamps to their camp. It is said that General Sherman, who was watching the bombardment in a small boat, picked up the pilot as he floated from the wreck.* "The Henry Clay" was burned to the water's edge. "The Silver Wave" fortunately escaped untouched. And the whole of the eight iron-clads maintained their battle, and passed the batteries without incurring any serious injury.

For an hour and a half the conflict raged. The batteries lined the bluff for a distance of eight miles. As the little fleet, with the loss of but one transport, passed beyond the range of the guns, silence and darkness again ensued. The midnight tempest of battle, which had so suddenly burst forth, as suddenly subsided. And the dark river flowed by the beleaguered city, as calm, as peaceful, as if its echoes had never been awakened by the pealing thunders of war. The slight injuries which the boats had received were speedily repaired by volunteer mechanics stepping forth from the ranks.

* Military History of General Ulysses S. Grant.

"It is a striking feature," says General Grant, "so far as my observation goes, of the present volunteer army of the United States, that there is nothing which men are called upon to do, mechanical or professional, that accomplished adepts cannot be found for the duty required, in almost every regiment."

General McClernand had led the advance to Perkins's Landing, where he was awaiting with intense anxiety the result of the attempt to run the batteries. The first indication the troops had of the fate of the fleet was in the smouldering wreck of "The Henry Clay" drifting down the stream. A rich old rebel, whose magnificent estate was near by, was so jubilant that he could not repress his exultation. Rubbing his hands with delight, he came to General McClernand, and said, —

"Where are your gunboats now? Vicksburg has put an end to them all."

But scarcely had the morning dawned ere the whole little fleet, one boat after another, appeared around a bend in the river. They were greeted with as heartfelt cheers as ever burst from human lips. The Yankees now in turn inquired of the crest-fallen secessionist, "Where now are our gunboats? Has Vicksburg destroyed them?" The miserable old man, obdurate in his rebellion, was so chagrined that in his rage he declared that the Yankees should never take shelter in his house. With his own hands he applied the torch. In an hour the splendid mansion, with all its surrounding buildings, was in ashes.

None but those who witnessed these scenes can imagine how dreadful the desolation caused by this war, so wantonly provoked by those who were crushed by its footsteps. The utter ruin of this man's magnificent estate may be given as an example of the fate which overwhelmed thousands of others.

" His plantation was one of the loveliest in Louisiana. High enough to be secure from inundation, it overlooked the meanderings of the Mississippi for nearly fifty miles. Wide savannas teemed with the wealth of the corn and the cotton plant, while the spacious lawns were clad in all the charms of precocious summer in this balmy clime. Japan plums and fig-trees grew in the open air, and groves of magnolia and oleander bloomed. The softness of the atmosphere, redolent with unfamiliar fragrance, and the aspect of the landscape, brilliant with blossoms and verdure, enchanted the soldiers. ' Here at last,' they cried, ' we have found the sunny South.' But desolation and destruction fell like a storm-cloud over the scene. In a few hours a blackened pile was all that remained of the stately mansion. The broad plantation became a camping-ground. The venerable trees in which it was embosomed were hewn down for fire-wood, and the secluded fields were speedily transformed into a confused and bustling bivouac." *

The success of this experiment in running the batteries was so gratifying, that, a few days after, six more transports were sent down the stream, towing twelve barges, loaded with forage. One of these transports, " The Tigress," received a shot below the water-line, and sunk on the Louisiana shore. The rest, with one-half of the barges, got through with but trifling damage. The army was now prepared to move, General Grant intending mainly to supply its wants from the agricultural abundance of the country through which he was to march.

---

* Military History of Ulysses S. Grant, by Adam Badeau.

CHAPTER IX.

THE MARCH TO THE REAR.

Bombardment of Grand Gulf. — Crossing at Bruinsburg. — Friendly Ne-
groes. — Advance upon Port Gibson. — The Battle.— Repulse of the Foe.
— Flight and Consternation. — Grant's Despatches. — His Caution and
Danger. — Personal Habits. — Testimony of General Badeau.

 FEW miles below Perkins's Landing, where
the Union army was gathered, there is the
town of Grand Gulf, on the eastern bank of
the Mississippi. The great object now was
to cross the river. The rebels were watching with great diligence to oppose this movement. The
troops were marched down the west banks of the river
to a place oddly called Hard Times. They were now
seventy miles below Milliken's Bend. About ten thousand of the troops were taken down the river in transports. Thorough reconnoissances were made of the eastern shore, to find a suitable place for the landing of the
troops. It was decided that Grand Gulf was the spot
most feasible for this purpose. The rebels were aware
of this, and had erected strong batteries to prevent the
operation. The plan was for the gunboats to silence the
batteries, and immediately the troops were to be landed
from the transports at the foot of the bluff, and carry the
works by storm. Ten thousand soldiers were crowded
into the transports, and conveyed to a point in the river

nearly opposite Grand Gulf, but just out of range of its guns. There they awaited impatiently the result of the bombardment. General Grant directed the minutest details of these movements, anticipating every obstacle, and providing for every emergence. The difficulties to be surmounted were immense ; and no one can read General Grant's despatches without being impressed with that comprehensiveness of mind which could grasp and master them all.

On the morning of the 29th of April, Commodore Porter commenced the bombardment with seven iron-clads and one ordinary gunboat. The rebels had thirteen heavy guns in battery, supported by a series of rifle-pits. For five and a half hours a very vigorous fire was kept up on both sides. General Grant, who anxiously watched the battle from a tug in the middle of the stream, says, —

"Many times it seemed to me that the gunboats were within pistol-shot of the enemy's batteries."

The attempt, however, proved unsuccessful. The guns of the enemy were in so elevated a position that all the valor and energy of Commodore Porter's fleet were unavailing in the attempt to silence them. Not one gun was dismounted. The fleet, however, did not experience any serious injury. The idea of attempting to land the troops in the face of these unsilenced batteries was not to be cherished for a moment. But General Grant was prepared for the casualty. He had previously decided what to do, should the gunboats fail in accomplishing their purpose. Grant, like Napoleon, so matured his plans that he had always decided just what to do in case of defeat, however confident he might be of victory.

A previous reconnoissance had disclosed to him, that

there was a good landing about six miles below, at Bruinsburg. With his accustomed promptness he requested Commodore Porter, that very night, again to attack the batteries. Under cover of this fire, all the transports succeeded in running the batteries. At the same time the troops on shore marched down to the appointed rendezvous, where the gunboats soon joined them. They were immediately ferried across the river. General Grant was the first one to step upon the bank. The landing of the whole force at Bruinsburg was effected without the loss of a single man.

We cannot refrain from mentioning here an incident illustrative of the unjust obloquy to which military men are often exposed. The incident also remarkably develops the magnanimity of those truly great men, Generals Grant and Sherman.

When General Grant was about to make an attack upon Grand Gulf, he wished to distract the attention of the enemy at Vicksburg, to prevent him from sending re-enforcements to the batteries below. General Sherman was then in command of the troops still left at Milliken's Bend. General Grant wrote to him, stating the advantage which would accrue from a threatening movement upon Haines's Bluff. In the letter, he said, —

" A vigorous demonstration in that direction would be good, so far as the enemy is concerned ; but I am loth to order it, because it would be so hard to make our own troops understand that only a demonstration was intended, and our people at home would characterize it as a repulse."

General Sherman, who had already suffered very severely from newspaper assaults, regardless of his own reputation if he could serve his country, nobly replied, —

"I believe a diversion at Haines's Bluff is proper and right ; and I will make it, let whatever report of repulses be made."

He did make the attack, with ten regiments and eight gunboats. The troops were landed. Reconnoissances were sent out. Ostentatious dispositions of the troops were made for the mock battle. The enemy was greatly alarmed. His troops were hurriedly moved to and fro. General Sherman, having accomplished his purpose, withdrew without the loss of a man to Milliken's Bend ; and his enemies shouted over his defeat. He then marched rapidly down the river with his command, to join his comrades in their march towards the rear of Vicksburg.

Scarcely had General Grant landed at Bruinsburg, in a country almost entirely unknown to him, ere friendly negroes gathered around, giving much valuable information, and offering to pilot him by a good road to Port Gibson, a small town in the rear of Grand Gulf, a distance of twelve miles from Bruinsburg. This was the direct route to Vicksburg. The capture of Port Gibson would compel the evacuation of the batteries at Grand Gulf. The enemy was now fully alive to the momentous issues at stake. They were concentrating their troops from all quarters, to assail the audacious invaders who were thus penetrating the very heart of rebeldom. Not a moment was to be lost, lest the rebels should gather in strength for the defence of Port Gibson.

General McClernand was immediately despatched with the advance, with three days' rations in their haversacks. They had not a tent or a wagon. General Grant required no greater sacrifices of his troops than he was ready to make himself.

"He took with him," says the Hon. Mr. Washburne,

of Illinois, who accompanied the expedition, " neither a horse, nor an orderly, nor a camp-chest, nor an overcoat, nor a blanket, nor even a clean shirt. His entire baggage for six days was a tooth-brush. He fared like the commonest soldier in his command, partaking of his rations and sleeping upon the ground with no covering but the canopy of heaven."

By the feint which General Sherman had so effectually made against Haines's Bluff, the foe was prevented from sending re-enforcements to join the garrison at Grand Gulf. At three o'clock in the afternoon of the 30th of April, — the very day on which the troops landed at Bruinsburg, — General McClernand, with the advance, commenced his march. The road led first, for a couple of miles, along the levee; then, turning to the east, it wound through a hilly country covered with forest, — broken, precipitous, and rugged. It was the spring of the year; and, in that almost tropical clime, the weather was excessively warm. The region was surpassingly beautiful. Flowers bloomed all around, and bird-songs and fragrance filled the air. The gorgeous military array, winding through the valleys and climbing the hills, added much to the picturesque impressiveness of the scene.

The night was serene and brilliant; and, being so much cooler than the day, the troops pressed joyously on until two o'clock in the morning. Here they came in sudden contact with a rebel battery which frowned from an eminence directly before them. It was composed of a part of the garrison from Grand Gulf, who had stationed themselves there, hoping to check the advance until re-enforcements should arrive from Vicksburg. General Bowen, in command, had about eleven thousand men in line of battle. It was necessary to wait until morning before commencing the attack. With the earliest dawn the position of the rebels was carefully examined. Here, again, the ever-friendly negro came to our aid. General McClernand was informed that the rebels had seized upon a point where the road forked; but, the two roads running nearly parallel, each conducted along narrow ridges to Port Gibson. The ravines on either side of these roads were tangled with forest and under-brush, protecting from a flank attack the rebels, who occupied both of the roads. The only alternative for General McClernand was to retreat or to cut his way through. He was the last man to think of a retreat, and made immediate preparations for the assault. The position of the rebels was impregnable. By a direct attack General McClernand, with the re-enforcements which soon arrived, could bring nineteen thousand men into the battle. But, notwithstanding his superiority in numbers, the commanding position occupied by the rebels gave them the decided advantage.

General McClernand in person led the assault upon the right, aided by Generals Hovey, Carr, and Smith. General Osterhaus, aided by a division of McPherson's corps, under General Logan of Illinois, attacked upon the left. A battle — a desperate, prolonged, and bloody battle — ensued. · About ten o'clock General Grant arrived, and took the command. Late in the afternoon, by a vigorous combined charge, the entire line of the enemy was broken and swept away; and they retreated precipitately towards Port Gibson, leaving their dead and wounded on the field.

The Union troops impetuously pursued till the darkness of night arrested their steps. They were then within two miles of Port Gibson. It was not deemed prudent to advance farther in an unknown country, and in the dark, lest they should fall into some ambuscade. General McClernand led in the pursuit. The enemy, as night closed in, seemed to be rallying for another stand. General Grant, however, thought it probable that under cover of the night they would again attempt to effect their retreat. His directions to General McClernand were, —

"Push the enemy with skirmishers well thrown out until it gets too dark to see him. Then place your command on eligible ground, wherever night finds you. Park your artillery so as to command the surrounding country, and renew the attack at early dawn. If possible, push the enemy from the field, or capture him. No camp-fires should be allowed, unless in deep ravines and in rear of the troops."

By the moonlight of his bivouac the tentless general sent his despatch to the government, announcing his victory. Our loss, he stated at about a hundred killed and five hundred wounded. He estimated the loss of the enemy as about equal to his own; the foe having also lost six hundred and fifty who were takén prisoners, and six field-guns which were captured.

The consternation with which the rebels were now seized may be inferred from the following telegram sent that night by the rebel General Pemberton to his superior officer, General Joseph E. Johnson : —

"A furious battle has been going on since daylight just below Port Gibson. Enemy can cross all his army from Hard Times to Bruinsburg. I should have large re-enforcements. Enemy's movements threaten Fort Jackson, and, if successful, cut off Port Gibson and Port Hudson."

In the night, as General Grant had supposed, the rebel

troops again retreated, and in the morning were no-where to be seen. They rapidly retired across the two forks of the Bayou Pierre, destroying the bridges behind them. The garrison at Grand Gulf, dismayed in finding themselves thus outflanked, precipitately abandoned their intrenchments, spiking their guns and destroying their ammunition. Our fleet immediately took possession of the deserted works, and Grand Gulf became an important base for our supplies.

General McClernand's troops, flushed with success, early the next morning entered Port Gibson, and immediately employed a heavy force in rebuilding the bridge across the south fork. Other troops, while this work was in operation, forded the bayou, and, led by General Logan, pursued the flying enemy. Re-enforcements were now pressing forward to the aid of our advance guard, and the onward movement was pushed with great vigor. General McPherson, General Logan, and General Crocker were now all chasing, by different routes, the flying foe, who was retreating, thoroughly demoralized, and without ammunition. He was driven, without a moment's respite, through Willow Springs, and across the Big Black River.

With all this audacity and impetuosity of movement the utmost caution was observed, to guard against reverses. Every possible contingency seems to have been considered and provided for. The soldiers now received the tidings of Colonel Grierson's successful and magnificent raid. It filled the rebels with consternation, and animated the Union soldiers with renewed zeal. General Grant had a fine army under his banners,— thirty-five thousand men, made doubly-strong from its enthusiastic confidence in its leader.

" My army," he wrote, " is composed of hardy and disciplined men, who know no defeat, and are not willing to learn what it is."

It is said, that, during all the fatigues of this campaign, General Grant practised total abstinence from all intoxicating drinks. This is the testimony of those who were constantly with him.

An officer of his staff, who must have been acquainted with his daily habits, wrote some time after this, —

" If you could see the general as he sits just over beyond me, with his wife and two children, looking more like a chaplain than a general, with that quiet air so impossible to describe, you would not ask me if he drinks. He rarely ever uses intoxicating liquors. He is more moderate in his habits and desires, and more pure and spotless in his private character, than almost any man I ever knew. He is more brave, has more power to command, and more ability to plan, than any man I ever served under; cool to excess when others lose nerve, always hopeful, always undisturbed, never failing to accomplish what he undertakes." *

In this connection, the following extracts from the pen of Major Penniman will be read with interest : —

" I have seen him in the familiarity and seclusion of camp-life, and I know perfectly well what his personal habits are. He messes with his staff as he would with his own family. No intoxicating liquors are on the table at dinner or at any other time. It is not his habit to use them, nor does he encourage it in others. No man of all the hundreds of thousands he has commanded ever heard General Grant use profane language. One

---

* General Grant and his Campaigns. By Julian K. Larke, p. 466.

of his highest meeds of praise consists in the fact, that, through all his commands to his present elevated post, he has had no jealousies, bickerings, or quarrels among his officers.   He has the rare faculty of selecting the right man for the right place."

All who know General Grant will testify alike to the remarkable purity and spotlessness of his personal character.   All will remember the playful remark of President Lincoln when, soon after the capture of Vicksburg, some one alluded to the rumor that General Grant used intoxicating drinks to excess.

" What kind of whiskey does he drink ? " inquired the president, with a peculiar twinkle of the eye.   " Is it Bourbon, or Monongahela ?   For, if it makes him win victories like this at Vicksburg, I should like to send a demijohn of the same kind to every general in the army."

General Grant had come to the full conviction that the only way to conquer the Rebellion was to destroy its armies, and exhaust its resources.   He had therefore resolved to support his troops, so far as possible, from the abundance of the regions he traversed.   To most persons, the position of General Grant even now must have seemed very perilous.   Many of his officers so regarded it.   Under any ordinary commander, the situation would have been quite hopeless.   The frowning batteries of Vicksburg were before him.   Nearly sixty thousand men were gathered there, and along the line of the Vicksburg and Jackson Railroad.   General Pemberton reported his numbers 59,411.   Another rebel force, under General Gregg, was hurrying down from the north-east to strengthen the already formidable array assembled for the protection of Vicksburg.

General Grant was in the heart of the enemy's country, with but thirty thousand men under his banners. The rebel army was much scattered, for it had long lines and important points to defend. General Grant's troops were concentrated, and could move almost with the impetus and momentum of a shell, ready at any moment to explode, and carry devastation far and wide. He decided first to hurl the whole weight of his columns upon Gregg, and crush him before he could effect a junction with Pemberton. The soldiers were provided with three days' rations, trusting to the country for forage. The utmost celerity and secrecy were essential. He did not confide his plan even to the general-in-chief at Washington. In fact, the authorities there were appalled in view of his boldness. General Grant assumed the responsibility. There is something sublime in this solitary energy, unsustained by a single word of encouragement.

" So Grant," says General Badeau, " was alone. His most trusted associates besought him to change his plans, while his superiors were astounded at his temerity, and strove to interfere. Soldiers of reputation and civilians in high place condemned in advance a campaign that seemed to them as hopeless as it was unprecedented. If he failed, the country would concur with the government and the generals. Grant knew all this, and appreciated his danger, but was as invulnerable to the apprehensions of ambition as to the entreaties of friendship or the anxieties even of patriotism. That quiet confidence which never forsook him, and which amounted indeed almost to a feeling of fate, was uninterrupted. Having once determined in a matter that required irreversible decision, he never reversed, nor even misgave; but was steadily loyal to himself and his plans. This absolute and implicit faith was, however, as far as possible from conceit or enthusiasm. It was simply a consciousness,— or conviction rather, — which brought the very strength it believed in ; which was itself strength ; and which inspired others with a trust in him, because he was able thus to trust himself." *

General Howard also has alluded to this strong conviction, on the part of General Grant, that success would crown his endeavors. It is stated in a paragraph in "The New York Times" of February 18, —

" General Howard says that General Grant is strictly a temperate man and religious. His marked characteristic is a wonderful faith in his success, amounting almost to the fatality in which Napoleon so strongly believed. General Howard can be relied on."

* Military History of Ulysses S. Grant, p. 222.

CHAPTER X.

IT is impossible to convey to the reader an idea of the innumerable thoughts and plans and anxieties which must have crowded the mind of General Grant. In military combinations, very much depends upon the faithful performance of all the details. Here there was to be a feint; there, a direct assault. At one point, the enemy was to be deceived by a false movement. Again, scattered divisions were to be suddenly concentrated upon some given position. Colonel Grierson's raid was a part of General Grant's campaign. Admiral Porter's expedition to the Red River was another act in the great drama. In this brief narrative it is impossible to trace out the complicated mazes of these movements, which, guided by one master-mind, were working out the grand result. It is almost bewildering to read the innumerable despatches rapidly issued by General Grant, and embracing the most multiplied and varied combinations.

The rebels, defeated at Port Gibson, had retreated

across the Big Black River, where they made another stand and gathered re-enforcements. General Grant deceived them into the belief that he intended to follow and attack them there. He had now within call forty-three thousand men and a hundred and twenty guns. The rebel army was divided. A portion was on the right bank of the Big Black, gathering in strength to oppose the passage of General Grant's troops. General Joe Johnston was assembling another army at Jackson, the capital of the State of Mississippi, — a very important strategical point, at the junction of two railroads. Here the rebels had also accumulated a large magazine of supplies.

Instead of crossing the Big Black, General Grant turned suddenly to the right, and marched rapidly along the eastern bank of the river. He cut loose entirely from his communication with Grand Gulf, and depended for supplies upon the country, and such stores as he could take with him. As he thus cut loose from his base, and plunged into the midst of his foes, he telegraphed to the government at Washington, " You will probably not hear from me for several days." The Union army, in two divisions, advanced by roads nearly parallel. Generals Sherman and McClernand took the right; while General McPherson had command of the left, keeping close to the river, and threatening the railroad between Jackson and Vicksburg. Great precautions were adopted to conceal, as far as possible, his movements from the enemy.

It was General Grant's object to seize Jackson, destroy or disperse the rebel army assembled there, and capture the supplies. He would then turn with his whole force upon Vicksburg, and crush the army intrenched there. His plan was wisely conceived and magnificently accomplished. On the 12th of May, General Logan, of McPherson's division, encountered the foe within a few miles of Raymond, on the direct road to Jackson, and but about fifteen miles from that city. The rebels were about five thousand strong, advantageously posted in a piece of timber, with two batteries of artillery, which swept both the road and a bridge over which it was necessary for McPherson to pass.

The battle was immediately opened with great vigor. Our troops, outnumbering the foe, speedily drove him from his position. Still it was a hard-fought battle, in which we lost, in killed, wounded, and missing, four hundred and forty. The loss of the enemy in killed and wounded was four hundred and five. We took also four hundred and fifteen prisoners, two pieces of cannon, and quite a quantity of small arms.

The rebels fled through the streets of Raymond, hotly pursued by the Union troops. They retreated along the road which led by Mississippi Springs to Jackson. The country was rough, wild, and densely wooded. General Grant had so deceived the rebels, that Pemberton had massed his forces at Edwards's Station, on the railroad running from Jackson to Vicksburg, confidently expecting the attack there. But, by adroitly turning our troops to the right, General Grant had avoided a battle with this strong force, had dispersed an important division of the enemy, and had opened an almost unobstructed path to Jackson.

All the difficulties which our troops encountered and triumphantly surmounted cannot well be imagined. General McClernand reports that his corps subsisted for thirteen days on six days' rations, and such scanty supplies as the country could afford. They were wholly without tents, regular trains, and almost without cooking utensils. Yet not a murmur was heard from the lips of his troops. They seized all the flour-mills on the way, grinding the corn found in the storehouses, and using the ambulances for ammunition-wagons.

Jackson was strongly fortified. It was an exceedingly important position. The rebels were now fully aware of its peril, and began to rush for its protection. General Johnston hastened there the day after the battle of Raymond, and took the command with an estimated force of eleven thousand men. As many more were near by, marching upon the double-quick to re-enforce him. Johnston, in his alarm, telegraphed Pemberton, who was at Edwards's Station, to fall with his whole force upon the rear of Grant. But Grant was advancing so rapidly, and was so deceiving the foe by the mysterious movements of his army divisions, that the rebel leaders were bewildered, and knew not upon what point to concentrate their forces, either for attack or for defence.

Generals McPherson and Sherman were at Raymond, marching along the southern road to Jackson. General McClernand was threatening Edwards's Station, his pickets being within two miles of the rebel troops, who were massed there in numbers sufficient to overwhelm him, had they but known his weakness. Very skilfully McClernand deluded the foe into the belief that he was about to make an attack, even when he was withdrawing his troops to join the Union force at Raymond. Intense activity now prevailed. General Grant ordered all the details of the movement. All the divisions were concentrating in rapid march upon Jackson. Sherman and McPherson met before the city, by different roads, at the same hour of the 14th.

The rebel outposts were driven in, and the rebel lines were encountered, strongly intrenched in battle array a short distance outside of the city. The conflict immediately commenced with artillery. As the hostile batteries were thus exchanging shots, General Grant carefully examined the ground, and posted his troops for the decisive attack. We will not attempt to describe the tactics of the battle. For an hour it was delayed by a shower, in which the windows of heaven seemed to be opened, and both armies were drenched by the flood. No man could open his cartridge-box, lest it should be instantly filled with water.

As the rain abated, the battle commenced, with the incessant rattle of musketry and the roar of artillery. Both parties fought with fierceness, with desperation,— the one to destroy our government, the other to maintain it ; the one to banish free institutions from the earth, the other to defend the sacred rights of man. There were charges and counter-charges, the rush of onset, the confusion of retreat, shouts of victory, and cries of agony, and groans of death. There were many boys in the rebel ranks,— boys who scarcely knew for what reason they had been dragged from the sides of their mothers, and forced into this cruel war. The pitiless missiles of destruction, undiscriminating, tore them limb from limb. There were many boys in the Union ranks,— boys who in the free and intelligent North had been instructed in the principles of liberty. They fully comprehended their mission. The prayers of their mothers accompanied them. Cheerfully they perilled life and limb for their country and humanity.

And here these boys stood, firing bullets into each other's bosoms, sometimes even grappling in the deadly struggle, and their blood mingling in death. Alas for man! Even the victories over which he rejoices send mourning and despair to thousands of homes. After a conflict of three hours, the enemy fled, having lost about nine hundred in killed, wounded, and prisoners. General Crocker led the final charge,— General Crocker, whom Grant classed with Sherman and Sheridan, as one of the best division commanders he had ever known.

The rebels were intrenched upon the crest of an eminence over which the road passed, their guns commanding the plain below. The Union troops advanced, in the final and decisive charge, across this plain and up the hill with as measured tread as if on dress-parade, while the rebel fire was piercing their ranks. Our troops returned no answering fire until within thirty yards of the foe. Then a well-aimed, deadly volley was poured into the rebel lines; and with fixed bayonets, and making the welkin ring with their cheers, the troops rushed forward in the impetuous onset. The opposing troops wavered, broke, fled; and the path was open to Jackson. General Grant, with his staff, was the first to enter the enemy's works. His son, a lad of thirteen years, accompanied him upon this campaign. As they approached the town, the boy galloped ahead, and was the first to enter the capital of Mississippi.

General Grant allowed himself not a moment to repose upon his laurels. Indeed the rebels were all around him, and the utmost activity and vigilance were requisite to secure himself from disaster. The troops marched into the streets, and the national banner was proudly unfurled from the State House. The intrenchments and rifle-pits outside of the city were occupied by the Union troops. General Grant took possession of the house which General

Johnston had occupied the night before. The victorious army was immediately employed in destroying the railroads in every direction from the city, for a distance of twenty miles. Bridges, factories, and arsenals were blown up and burned. Every thing which could be of military service to the rebels was destroyed.

General Johnston had retreated north by the Canton Road, and had intrenched himself about fifteen miles from the city, where he anxiously awaited the co-operation of re-enforcements. Pemberton on the west at Edwards's Station, and Johnston on the north, were now operating for a junction. It was a matter of the utmost moment to prevent this concentration. General Grant, with inferior numbers, contrived to be superior on every field of battle. His troops had acquired such perfect confidence in him, as he led them so invariably to victory, that they obeyed his orders with alacrity, regardless of sleeplessness, hunger, and fatigue. His subordinate officers were also very able men, who performed the tasks allotted to them with the utmost promptitude.

Immediately upon entering Jackson, Generals McPherson and McClernand were ordered to wheel around their columns, and to march rapidly west towards Edwards's Station, to attack Pemberton before he could be re-enforced by Johnston. Pemberton, informed of their approach, had selected his field of battle with skill, which he had acquired at West Point, at the expense of the government he was now seeking to destroy. There was a long ridge of land with quite a precipitous front, called Champion Hill, over which the road passed which the Union troops must necessarily traverse. In front of this ridge, there was an open plain; and the road which led over that plain from east to west, as it reached the hill, turned suddenly. south, and diagonally ascended the ridge. Here Pemberton stationed and intrenched his troops, — twenty-five thousand in number. General Grant was informed of his movements, and collected all the force at his command to meet the crisis. He immediately hastened in person to the front, and sent the following despatch to Sherman : —

" Start one of your divisions on the road at once, with their ammunition-wagons, and direct the general commanding the division to move with all possible speed until he comes up with our rear beyond Bolton. It is important that the greatest celerity should be shown in carrying out this movement, as I have evidence that the entire force of the enemy was at Edwards's Depot at 7, P.M., last night, and was still advancing. The fight may, therefore, be brought on at any moment."

At the same time he sent a despatch to Blair, who was some miles to the south, but also on a road that led directly to Edwards's Station.

" The enemy," said he, " have moved out to Edwards's Station, and are still pushing on to attack us with all their force. Push your troops on in that direction as rapidly as possible. If you are already on the Bolton Road, continue so ; but, if you still have a choice of roads, take the one leading to Edwards's Depot. Pass your troops to the front of your train, except a rear guard, and keep the ammunition wagons in front of all others."

As General Grant rode to the front, it was rather an appalling spectacle which met his eye. Champion Hill rose before him about seventy feet above the plain. Its summit was bald, affording an admirable position for the artillery of the foe. The sides of the hill were covered with an impenetrable growth of forest and of underbrush, through which it was almost impossible to penetrate. Upon this eminence stood twenty-five thousand determined men, with an ample array of cannon, and commanded by an able general.

The battle commenced with musketry and artillery, as soon as our troops came within range of the enemy's guns. Round shot and shell from their batteries pierced our ranks, while incessant volleys of musketry were flashing from the forest, where no foe could be seen, and into which it seemed useless to direct our fire. Many of our soldiers were veterans who had been in many battles, and who had witnessed the deadly strife at Donelson, at Shiloh, and at Pittsburg Landing. They testified that they had never, upon any field, seen the fusilade from this hillside surpassed.

The centre of our line was under command of General Hovey. For a time he held his men firm under the tremendous fire of the foe. At length they were compelled gradually to retire, though in perfect order. The battle was long, and for a time seemed doubtful. General Quimby was sent to the support of the centre. Other dispositions were made to attack the foe in flank, and to threaten their rear. General Logan succeeded in gaining a very important position on their left. Order was then given for a simultaneous charge, while the massed artillery concentrated its fire upon the heart of the foe. There was an hour of terrific struggle which covered the hillsides with the mangled remains of the dying and the dead, when the enemy — vanquished, bewildered, despairing — turned, and fled over the brow of the hill.

It was now about four o'clock in the afternoon. This was the hardest fought battle of the campaign thus far. The victory cost us over two thousand four hundred men in killed, wounded, and missing. As our men had been necessarily massed for the charge in ascending the hill, the fire of the enemy's infantry was for a short time deadly in the extreme. The enemy lost, however, in killed, wounded, and prisoners, nearly six thousand men, and thirty pieces of cannon. The heroes slept on the field they had won so dearly. The mangled bodies of men and horses, dismounted cannon, and all the wrecks of the battle, were scattered around in wild confusion. The dead slept peaceful and silent, side by side, enemies no more. Did their spirits ascend together to the judgment to answer for the passions and the struggles of the hour? Four thousand must have appeared suddenly together before that tribunal, slain by each other's hands. The soldiers called the spot "The Hill of Death."

At eight o'clock that evening, a portion of the army had advanced, and taken possession of the encampment at Edwards's Station, through which the foe had precipitately retreated. General McClernand was despatched in hot pursuit of the routed army. General Grant and his staff accompanied the advance until late in the night. He then threw himself down upon the porch of a house, which had been used as a rebel field-hospital, and took a few hours of repose, while the groans of the wounded and the dying blended with his dreams. It is a curious fact, that, the very night of this great victory, General Grant received a despatch from General Halleck ordering him to abandon the campaign upon which he had entered, and to go back to co-operate with General Banks for the capture of Port Hudson.

But General Grant could now very safely disregard these orders. The President, General Halleck, Congress, and the whole nation were in a few days electrified with the tidings of his marvellous achievements, and with undivided voice they all bade him God speed. Early the next morning, — the 17th, — General McClernand, who had energetically resumed the pursuit at half-past three o'clock, overtook the foe at Big Black River. They had crossed the stream, and taken possession of the bluffs which lined the western shore. The eastern shore was low and flat, and completely commanded by the artillery on the bluffs. Both the railroad and the turnpike crossed the river here upon bridges, side by side. There was also a bayou which, in the form of a semi-circle, composed a natural ditch or moat twenty feet wide and about three feet deep, emerging from the river above the bridges, and, after a circuit of about a mile, entering it again below.

A better position for defence, art could scarcely have created. Pemberton availed himself of it, determined to maintain himself there at all hazards till re-enforcements should arrive. Trees and bushes fringed the banks of the bayou; and many of these had been felled, forming an abatis to obstruct the advance. The bayou was defended by twenty pieces of artillery and four thousand men. The remaining rebel force — four thousand strong — had taken position upon the bluffs, on the western banks of the river. To carry this position it was necessary for the Union troops first to pass over the open plain in face of the enemy, then to bridge or wade the bayou while exposed to the fire of the batteries and of four thousand infantry, sweeping their ranks with grape-shot and bullets. Having accomplished this feat, and having driven the enemy from the line of the bayou across the river by the bridges which would be destroyed behind them, they were then to force the passage of the river, and charge the whole concentrated foe upon the bluffs, and carry the position by storm. To one sitting by the fireside it seems impossible that such an achievement could have been accomplished. But it was accomplished heroically and speedily.

General McClernand brought up his artillery, and opened a well-aimed and deadly fire, which staggered the foe. Under cover of this fire General Lawler succeeded in advancing unobserved, concealed by the bushes and the nature of the ground, with eleven hundred men, to a position on the left of the rebel works. The soldiers threw off their blankets and their knapsacks, and rushed through the waters of the bayou. A murderous fire of shot and shell was instantly turned upon them, which crimsoned the stagnant pool with their blood. But still the impetuous troops pressed on, crossed the bayou, and rushed upon the rebels in flank and rear. The enemy, bewildered by so unlooked-for an assault, in great numbers threw down their arms and surrendered. In a few moments seventeen hundred and fifty-one prisoners, with eighteen pieces of cannon and a large supply of small arms and ammunition, fell into the hands of the victors. This brilliant feat, accomplished by McClernand's corps, was effected at a loss of twenty-nine killed and two hundred and forty-two wounded. General Osterhaus was unfortunately wounded at the commencement of the fight. The panic-stricken rebels, abandoning their guns almost without a struggle, fled across the bridges, and set them on fire even before half of the fugitives had escaped. Thousands of men were now running up and down the banks in despair. Some with sinewy arms succeeded in swimming across. Many others in the unavailing attempt were drowned. Others still, threw down their arms and surrendered.

General Grant was now in possession of the entire eastern bank of the river. It is very evident that the enemy was bewildered, and to a very considerable degree terrified, by this resistless march and these uninterrupted victories of General Grant. Pemberton's army was quite demoralized. Stragglers in large numbers were abandoning it. He feared that Grant might cross the river above or below, and by a flank movement interpose between him and Vicksburg. Thus both the garrison and his own army would be at the mercy of the victor. From this point of the Black River it was scarcely fifteen miles to Vicksburg Bluffs. General Pemberton accordingly abandoned his position, and retreated to take refuge behind the intrenchments of Vicksburg. He thought that he should enjoy a few hours' respite from pursuit, since it would require, he supposed, twelve hours at least for General Grant to bridge anew the deep and rapid stream.

CHAPTER XI

THE CAPTURE OF VICKSBURG.

Crossing the Big Black. — Singular Interview between Grant and Sherman. — The Investment of Vicksburg. — Magnitude of the Achievement. — Progress of the Siege. — Johnston's unavailing Endeavors. — Explosion of the Mine. — Distress of the Besieged. — The Capitulation. — Rebel " Chivalry." — Letter from President Lincoln.

HE Big Black River was now to be bridged for the passage of an army. Speedily General Grant's engineers accomplished the work. The battle of Black-River Bridge, as it was called, was terminated about ten o'clock on the 17th. Before eight o'clock of the next morning, thousands of the Union troops were on the western banks, ready for battle or for the march. General Grant, while the bridges were being constructed, sent a cavalry reconnoissance back to ascertain the movements of Johnston. He sent a despatch to Sherman, saying, —

" Secure a commanding position on the west bank of Black River as soon as you can. If the information you gain, after crossing, warrants you in believing you can go immediately into the city, do so. If there is any doubt in this matter, throw out troops to the left, after advancing on a line with the railroad bridge, to open your communication with the troops here. We will then

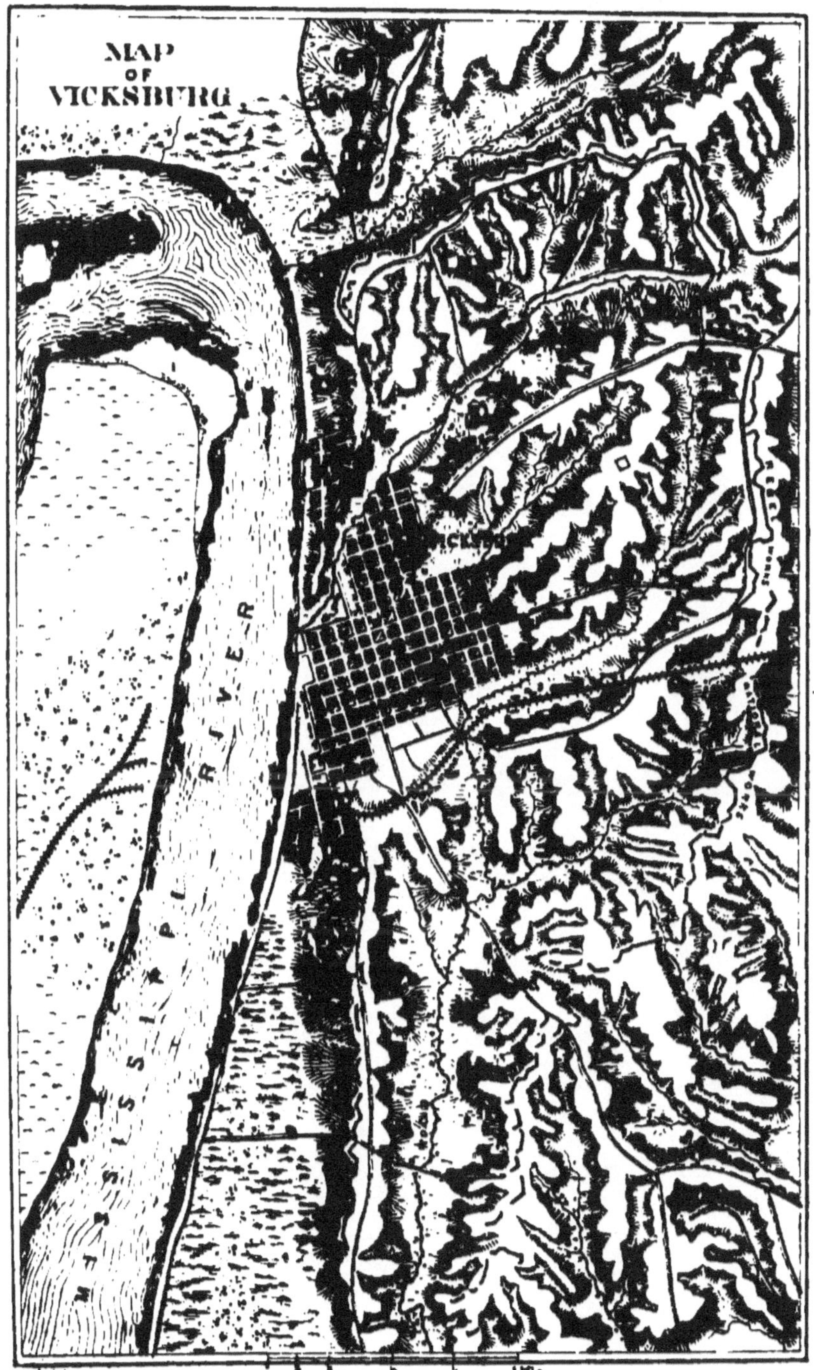

MAP
OF
VICKSBURG
MISSISSIPPI RIVER

move in three columns, — if roads can be found to move on, — and either have Vicksburg or Haines's Bluff to-morrow night. The enemy have been so terribly beaten yesterday and to-day that I cannot believe that a stand will be made, unless the troops are relying on Johnston's arriving with large re-enforcements ; nor that Johnston would attempt to re-enforce with any thing at his command, if he was aware at all of the present condition of things."

By half-past nine o'clock of the 18th, the energetic General Sherman was within three miles and a half of Vicksburg, where the head of his column entered the Benton Road. He now commanded the rear of both the rebel garrisons, at Vicksburg and at Haines's Bluff. His soldiers halted for the remainder of the command to come up. Here General Grant joined Sherman. Together these two distinguished men rode to the summit of one of the Walnut Hills, from which they could look down upon the Yazoo River, and upon those bluffs on its southern banks in front of which, but a few months before, General Sherman had met a bloody repulse.

Silently, for a few moments, they gazed upon the scene around them. At last Sherman turned abruptly, and said to General Grant, —

" Until this moment I never thought your expedition a success. I never could see the end clearly until now. But this is a campaign. This is a success, if we never take the town."

General Grant, the most taciturn of men, as usual said nothing. He probably felt as certain then of the capture of Vicksburg as he did on the morning when General Pemberton surrendered to him his sword. Before night General Sherman had placed his troops within nearly musket range of the intrenchments of Vicksburg. Early the next morning he seized several of the out-works of the foe, and captured a number of prisoners.

General McClernand pressed forward, and invested the doomed city on its southern side. General McPherson followed with his corps, and filled up the gap in the cen-tre. Thus, by Tuesday morning of the 19th, the city was invested both by river and by land. The Union lines extended in a long circuit of nearly twenty miles, from Haines's Bluff, on the Yazoo above the city, to Warren-ton on the Mississippi below. The rebel army was shut up in its fortress, having no communication with the outer world, and with scarcely a possibility of escape.

Precipitately the foe had abandoned Haines's Bluff, and a small Union force was sent to occupy it. Indeed, the navy had taken possession of the port before the arrival of the troops. They found fourteen guns, which the foe had left behind in his sudden flight. This was made the base of our supplies. Every thing we needed could be brought safely down the river from the north. Good roads were built, and the beleaguering army was abundantly supplied with every thing it could need for its efficiency and its comfort. The fall of Vicksburg was now certain. The only question was, how many days it would be able to hold out.

But three weeks had passed since General Grant com-menced this campaign. He had marched in that time over two hundred miles, had fought five battles, in which over twelve thousand rebels had been either killed, wounded, or taken prisoners. He had seized the capital of the State of Mississippi, and destroyed the railroads leading to it for a distance of more than thirty miles around. He had started upon this enterprise without baggage wagons, and with an average of but two days' rations in the soldiers' haversacks. His losses in all — killed, wounded, and missing — were but four thousand three hundred and thirty-five. As the crowning result of all this, he had invested the city and garrison of Vicksburg so that their fall was inevitable. The fall of Vicksburg insured the evacuation of Port Hudson. Thus the Mississippi would be open to the nation from Cairo to its mouths. Surely such a campaign will favorably compare with the most brilliant recorded in ancient or modern story.

The whole line of forts, bastions, and ramparts on the east of Vicksburg, which the rebels had reared to protect themselves from attack on the land side, was about eight miles in length. The detached works were connected by a continuous line of rifle-pits. Trees had been felled in front of the whole line, presenting an entanglement of branches through which it was almost impossible to penetrate. Vicksburg was thus a vast intrenched camp. Behind these works, which were armed by nearly two hundred cannon so placed as to sweep every possible avenue of approach, General Pemberton now stood with nearly forty thousand men.

He knew that it was impossible for General Grant to take the works by storm. As General Grant had ventured into the very heart of the rebel States, General Pemberton was confident that he would be able to defend the works until General Johnston could rally an overwhelming army, and fall upon the rear of the Union troops and crush them. Thus General Grant was under the necessity of looking vigilantly every day in two directions, — upon General Johnston behind him, and upon the desperate garrison at bay before him. He was not, however, at that time aware of the real strength of the garrison. He supposed it to be much less than it actually was.

The energy of General Grant, and the ardor of his men, are manifest from the fact, that, at half-past ten o'clock of the first day of the investment, a very vigorous though unavailing attempt was made to carry the place by assault. Again, two days after, another still more heroic and determined effort was made. All the energies of the army were upon this occasion called into requisition. The soldiers were so sure that they could carry the works that they would not have willingly toiled in the trenches until they had made the trial. No one in the Union army was then aware that the garrison in Vicksburg was so strong in numbers. It subsequently appeared that General Pemberton had absolutely more men behind these intrenchments — which were about as strong as nature and art could rear — than General Grant could bring to the assault. Both of these charges were repelled, with heavy loss to the Union arms.

It was now evident that the strong works of Vicksburg could only be carried by siege. A formidable army was in the meantime gathering in General Grant's rear. He ordered every available man in his district, who could possibly be spared, to be sent to his aid. He wrote to General Prentiss, " To watch the enemy, and to prevent him from collecting a force outside near enough to attack my rear. I require a large cavalry force. Contract every thing on the line of the route from Memphis to Corinth, and keep your cavalry well out south there. By this means you ought to be able to send here quite a large force."

Johnston was collecting his shattered bands at Canton,

a little north of Jackson, and was calling loudly upon the Confederacy to send him re-enforcements. To hold him in check, it was necessary for General Grant, while conducting the siege, to defend the line of the Big Black River, that Johnston might not be able to cross. General Halleck co-operated with all his great energies in sending forward re-enforcements, to enable General Grant to meet his varied and complicated wants. His confidence in General Grant was now fully established, and he rendered him the most constant and efficient aid.

By the 23d of May, General Grant had forty thousand men at his command. The full energies of every man were every day called into requisition. Many thousands were busy with the pickaxe and the spade. Others were at work at the guns, throwing an incessant storm of shot and shells inside of the intrenchments. The fleet co-operated in this work, harassing the foe from the river's side with their terrible bombs. Sharpshooters often drove the rebels from their guns, striking with the bullet every head or hand which appeared above the parapets. Camps were established in the woods and ravines, and the most vigorous measures were adopted to promote the health and comfort of the troops. Roads were opened, and streams and gullies were bridged, to aid in the rapid transmission of all supplies. The most vigorous military police was established, that there should be no disorder. Of necessity an army is an absolute monarchy. There is nothing which can test a man's ability more severely than to be the monarch of such an organization, in the midst of all the turmoil and peril and vast responsibilities of war. Mere bravery, mere fighting qualities in the commander, under such circumstances, amount to but little. The most varied and highest qualities with which the human mind can be endowed are then called into requisition.   General Grant displayed wide-reaching intelligence and administrative ability of the highest order.

We have not space to describe the operations of the siege.   From its commencement to its close, it was almost one continued roar of battle, through which,— and constantly exposed to the fire of the foe,— works of the siege were incessantly pushed forward. Many negroes came within the lines.   General Grant employed all who came, paying them fair wages; and they rendered very efficient aid.   The amount of labor performed cannot be described, and can scarcely be imagined. Opposite the works of Vicksburg, corresponding works of equal magnitude rose rapidly.   Twelve miles of trenches were dug. Eighty-nine batteries were reared.   By the last of June, there were two hundred and twenty guns in position.

The enemy endeavored to blow us up with mines, to drive us back by sorties, to impede our works by shot and shells.   There were some very severe conflicts between the rebel batteries and the gunboats. The defence was conducted with as much determination as the assault was pressed.   On the 25th of May, General Grant had written to General Banks,—

" I feel that my force is abundantly strong to hold the enemy where he is, or to whip him if he should come out.   The place is so strongly fortified, however, that it cannot be taken without either a great sacrifice of life or by a regular siege.   I have determined to adopt the latter course, and save my men.   The great danger now to be apprehended is, that the enemy may collect a force outside, and attempt to rescue the garrison."

On the 31st, he again wrote, " It is now certain that Johnston has already collected a force from twenty thousand to twenty-five thousand strong, at Jackson and Canton, and is using every effort to increase it to forty thousand. With this, he will undoubtedly attack Haines's Bluff, and compel me to abandon the investment of the city, if not re-enforced before he can get here.".

One of the important events of the siege, which may be mentioned simply as characteristic of the nature of the conflict, was the explosion of a mine on the 25th of June. A gallery was dug under an important part of the enemy's works. In this mine, two thousand two hundred pounds of powder were placed. Its explosion was to be the signal for a simultaneous attack from every gun on the land and in the fleet. Through the gorge cut by the explosion, several thousand men were to rush to gain an advance position.

It was three o'clock in the afternoon of a pleasant summer's day. The troops were withdrawn to a safe distance. Perfect silence reigned. The match was applied to the fire. A little white puff of smoke rose along the trenches through which the fuse was laid; and the fire crept rapidly — and yet it seemed very slow — along under the ground towards the buried magazine. The thousands looking on held their breath in suspense. Then came the phenomenon of the upheaving of a mountain, a flash, a thunder-peal as if the archangel's trump were sounded; and the air was filled with the volcanic eruption of earth and rocks and timber and guns, and the blackened, mangled forms of men hurled a distance of from eighty to a hundred feet into the air; and all this enveloped in a cloud of smoke and dust which moved solemnly and sublimely away before the gentle breeze.

Instantly, over a line twelve miles in length, battle's

fiercest tempest burst forth. An eye-witness says, "The scene at this time was one of the utmost sublimity. The roar of artillery, rattle of small arms, the cheers of the men, flashes of light, wreaths of pale blue smoke over different parts of the field, the bursting of shells, the fierce whistle of solid shot, the deep boom of the mortars, the broadsides of the ships of war, and, added to all this, the vigorous replies of the enemy, set up a din which beggars all description."

The troops rushed in at the gorge, which was large enough to hold two regiments. The rebel troops with equal desperation rushed forward to meet them; and thus the struggle continued, not only until the sun went down, not only until the twilight disappeared, but far into the hours of the night. Such were the scenes through which the siege of Vicksburg was conducted.

At every point the rebels found that General Grant had anticipated them, and that their plans were thwarted. Ere long it became evident to General Pemberton that he would be compelled to surrender, unless he could contrive some way to escape. His provisions were nearly exhausted. Seven days more would consume them. He conceived the design of building a large number of flat-boats, and of escaping with his army by night across the Mississippi. The materials for his boats were to be obtained by tearing down the houses of Vicksburg. General Grant was informed of this by a deserter. The gun-boat fleet redoubled its diligence, and the plan was frustrated.

The position of the Union troops was still deemed quite perilous. General Grant was between two powerful armies. While besieging one, he was in constant danger of assault from the other. If both should combine in a simultaneous attack, it seemed not improbable that the garrison at Vicksburg might escape. The rebels no longer deemed it possible to save Vicksburg. The last of May, General Johnston wrote to General Pemberton, —

"I am too weak to save Vicksburg; can do no more than attempt to save you and your garrison. It will be impossible to extricate you, unless you co-operate."

Famine was now consuming the garrison. The troops were living upon half-rations. The inhabitants of the city were burrowing in holes in the hillsides, to escape the bombardment. Flour was a thousand dollars a barrel in Confederate currency, molasses twelve dollars a gallon, beef two and a half dollars a pound. There was scarcely a house in the city which had not been struck by shot or shells, and many had been entirely demolished. A number of women and children had been killed. Shells were continually exploding in the streets. Thousands were in the hospitals, in extreme suffering, deprived of almost every comfort. Those in the trenches were in almost an equally pitiable condition.

And all this these guilty men had brought upon themselves by rebellion, — by rebellion against the best government in the world. And the only excuse which even they assigned for this crime was that the National Government would not prove recreant to every principle of true democracy, and aid them to enslave their brother man.

It is said that General Grant was one day riding round his lines, when he stopped for water at the house of a rebel woman. She asked him tauntingly if he expected ever to get into Vicksburg. He replied, —

" Certainly. I cannot tell exactly when I shall take

the town; but I mean to stay here till I do, if it takes me thirty years."

In the admirable "Military History of General Grant," by General Adam Badeau, we have the following extracts from despatches sent by General Grant to his subordinate officers, which will give the reader some idea of the multiplicity of cares which must have engrossed his mind: —

To Parke: "I want the work of intrenching your position pushed with all despatch. Be ready to receive an attack, if one should be made; and to leave the troops free to move out, should the enemy remain where he is."

To Ord: "Get batteries as well advanced as possible, during the day and night."

To Parke, directing him to join Sherman: "An attack is contemplated, evidently by way of Bear Creek, and that within two days. Move out four brigades of your command, to support your cavalry; and obstruct their advance, as near Black River as possible, until all the forces to spare can be brought against them. Travel with as little baggage as possible, and use your teams as an ordnance and supply train to get out all you may want from the river."

To Dennis: "An attack upon you is not at all impossible. You will therefore exercise unusual vigilance in your preparations to receive an attack. Keep your cavalry out as far as possible, to report any movement of the enemy; and confer with Admiral Porter, that there may be unanimity in action."

To Parke: "Certainly use the negroes, and every thing within your command, to the best advantage."

To Herron: "Be ready to move with your division at

the shortest notice, with two days' cooked rations in their haversacks."

To McPherson: "There is indication that the enemy will attack within forty-eight hours. Notify McArthur to be ready to move at a moment's notice on Sherman's order. The greatest vigilance will be required on the line, as the Vicksburg garrison may take the same occasion for an attack also."

Such were the daily toils and cares of General Grant, allowing him but little time for food or sleep. By the 1st of July, his works, at ten different points, were within a few hundred feet of the rebel defences. The time for final assault had now come. It was understood in both armies that it would take place on the 4th of July. General Pemberton was well aware that he could not repel the charge, and that he could not cut his way through the lines now drawn so closely around him. His humanity recoiled from the awful carnage which must necessarily result from the capture of the place by storm. He called a council of war, and it was agreed to capitulate.

On the morning of the 3d, Pemberton sent a note under a flag of truce to General Grant, proposing an armistice, that terms of capitulation might be arranged, stating that it was his wish to save further effusion of blood. General Grant replied, —

"Your note of this date is just received, proposing an armistice for several hours for the purpose of arranging terms of capitulation through commissioners to be appointed. The useless effusion of blood you propose stopping by this course can be ended at any time you may choose, by the unconditional surrender of the city and garrison. Men who have shown so much endurance and courage as those now in Vicksburg will always challenge the respect of an adversary, and, I can assure you, will be treated with all the respect due to prisoners of war. I do not favor the proposition of appointing commissioners to arrange the terms of capitulation, because I have no other terms than those indicated above."

General Bowen, who brought the note from Pemberton, urged that General Grant should have a personal interview with General Pemberton. To this request General Grant returned a verbal answer, that, if General Pemberton desired it, he would meet him between the lines, in General McPherson's front, at three o'clock that afternoon.

At the appointed time and place, the two generals met, each accompanied by several officers of his staff. The conference was held on a gentle eminence, beneath an oak-tree, not two hundred feet from the rebel lines. The works on both sides were crowded with soldiers enjoying the temporary lull of the storm of war, gazing with intensest interest, but with very different emotions, upon the simple yet sublime spectacle.

The two generals, though both Northern men, had never met before. Courteously they shook hands. Pemberton inquired what terms of capitulation would be allowed him. General Grant replied, "Those which have been expressed in my letter of this morning." The rebel general was irritated, and evidently regarded the terms "ungenerous and unchivalrous;" for he turned upon his heel, saying, "If this is all, the conference may terminate, and hostilities be resumed immediately." "Very well," was General Grant's reply; and he turned away as if about to retire to his lines.

General Bowen, of Pemberton's staff, ventured to interpose, and entered into conversation with some of the officers of General Grant's staff; while the two chieftains, stepping a little aside, conversed for a moment together in low tones which were not overheard. General Bowen then proposed that the rebel garrison should be permitted to march out of Vicksburg with the honors of war, carrying with them their muskets and their field guns. General Grant smiled at this proposition, and declared it to be utterly inadmissible. Finally, it was agreed that both parties should return to their lines; that the truce should continue; and that General Grant, having conferred with his officers, should transmit in writing the terms he would accept. These terms General Pemberton was to submit to his officers, and return a prompt reply.

General Grant withdrew to his headquarters, and held — it is said for the first time in his life — a council of war. They all, with one exception (General Steele), suggested terms which Grant was unwilling to propose. He firmly adhered to his original proposition of " unconditional surrender," and sent the following letter to General Pemberton : —

" In conformity with agreement of this afternoon, I will submit the following proposition for the surrender of the city of Vicksburg, public stores, &c. On your accepting the terms proposed, I will march in one division, as a guard, to take possession, at eight o'clock, A.M., to-morrow. As soon as rolls can be made out, and paroles signed by officers and men, you will be allowed to march out of our lines, — the officers with their side-arms and clothing; and the field, staff, and cavalry officers, one horse each. The rank and file will be allowed all their clothing, but no other property. If these conditions are accepted, any amount of rations you may deem necessary can be taken from the stores you now have, and also all the necessary cooking utensils for preparing them. Thirty wagons also, counting two horse or mule teams as one, will be allowed to transport such articles as cannot be carried along. The same conditions will be allowed to all sick and wounded officers and soldiers, as fast as they become able to travel. The paroles for these latter must be signed, however, while officers are present authorized to sign the roll of prisoners."

These terms were submitted that night by General Pemberton to a council of war, and accepted. A little after midnight, an answer was returned as follows:—

" I have the honor of acknowledging the receipt of your communication of this date, proposing terms of capitulation for this garrison and port. In the main, your terms are accepted. But in justice both to the honor and spirit of my troops manifested in the defence of Vicksburg, I have to submit the following amendments, which, if acceded to by you, will perfect the agreement between us:—

" At ten o'clock, A.M., to-morrow, I propose to evacuate the works in and around Vicksburg, and to surrender the city and garrison under my command, by marching out with my colors and arms, stacking them in front of my present lines; after which you will take possession. Officers to retain their side-arms and personal property, and the rights and property of citizens to be respected."

To this an immediate answer was returned by General Grant in these words : " I have the honor to acknowledge the receipt of your communication of the 3d of July. The amendment proposed by you cannot be acceded to in full. It will be necessary to furnish every officer and man with a parole signed by himself, which, with the completion of the roll of prisoners, will necessarily take some time.

" Again : I can make no stipulations with regard to the treatment of citizens and their private property. While I do not propose to cause them any undue annoyance or loss, I cannot consent to leave myself under any restraint by stipulations. The property which officers will be allowed to take with them will be as stated in my proposition of last evening ; that is, officers will be allowed their private baggage and side-arms, and mounted officers one horse each.

" If you mean by your proposition, for each brigade to march to the front of the lines now occupied by it, and stack arms, at ten o'clock, A.M., and then return to the inside and there remain as prisoners until properly paroled, I will make no objection to it. Should no notification be received of your acceptance of my terms by nine o'clock, A.M., I shall regard them as having been rejected, and shall act accordingly. Should these terms be accepted, white flags should be displayed along your lines, to prevent such of my troops as may not have been notified from firing upon your men."

General Pemberton immediately sent back the reply, " I have the honor to acknowledge the receipt of your communication of this day, and, in reply, to say that the terms proposed by you are accepted."

We have given a more full detail of these events, as they show so conclusively that General Grant is not merely a soldier, — that he is endowed with a mind of broad comprehension equal to the most difficult emergencies. The wisdom and the firmness, combined with the humanity and the modesty, displayed in these eventful hours, are worthy of all admiration.

The energy and tireless activity of General Grant's mind has perhaps in no case been rendered more conspicuous than that, so soon as he had received General Pemberton's first note, he sent a despatch to Sherman, to be ready immediately to march to attack and disperse, or destroy, the army under General Johnston.

"There is little doubt," said he, "but that the enemy will surrender to-night or in the morning. Make your calculations to attack Johnston, and destroy the road north of Jackson."

Generals Steele and Ord were also directed to be in readiness to march in co-operation with Sherman the very moment the surrender was effected. "I want," he wrote, "Johnston broken up as effectually as possible. You can make your own arrangements, and have all the troops of my command, except one corps."

At ten o'clock on the 4th of July, 1863, white flags rose all along the rebel lines, announcing the surrender of the city. Thus Vicksburg was reclaimed from foul rebellion. Our troops, with loud cheers, marched into the streets and into the forts to gain which they had so long and so valiantly contended. The stars and stripes rising proudly over the fortress announced to the fleet the glad tidings of the surrender. Every vessel was soon in motion; and but an hour or two elapsed ere seventy steamers or barges lined the levee, and the city suddenly emerged from the death of rebellion to life and activity. It is said that this surrender was the most important recorded in the annals of war. At the capitulation of Ulm, hitherto considered without a parallel, thirty thousand prisoners were surrendered and sixty pieces of cannon. Thirty-one thousand six hundred men surrendered at Vicksburg, with one hundred and seventy-two cannon.

General Logan's division, which was in the advance, first entered the works. General Grant, with his staff, rode at the head of the troops. The rebel soldiers gazed upon their conqueror in silence. He rode at once to the headquarters of General Pemberton. There was no one to receive him. He dismounted, and entered the porch. General Pemberton sat there with his staff. These men then very conspicuously developed their novel ideas of " chivalry." Though each one wore his sword through the generosity of General Grant, not one rose in courteous greeting of the valiant and magnanimous soldier. Pemberton was especially sullen and discourteous.

The day was hot, and the trampling of the armies had filled the air with clouds of dust. General Grant, heated and thirsty, asked for a glass of water. He was brusquely told that he could find it inside. He groped his way through the passages till he found a negro who gave him a cup of water. Returning, he found no seat, and remained standing in the presence of his vanquished foes, who were seated, during an interview of half an hour.

In the following terms, General Grant announced his victory to the government : " The enemy surrendered this morning. The only terms allowed is their parole as prisoners of war. This I regard as a great advantage to us at this moment. It saves, probably, several days in the capture, and leaves troops and transports ready for immediate service. Sherman, with a large force, moves immediately upon Johnston, to drive him from the State."

President Lincoln immediately wrote General Grant the following characteristic letter, dated at the Executive Mansion, Washington, July 13, 1863 : —

"MY DEAR GENERAL,— I do not remember that you and I ever met personally. I write now as a grateful acknowledgment for the almost inestimable service you have done the country. I wish to say further, when you first reached the vicinity of Vicksburg, I thought you should do what you finally did,— march the troops across the neck, run the batteries with the transports, and thus go below; and I never had any faith, except a general hope that you knew better than I, that the Yazoo Pass expedition and the like could succeed. When you got better, and took Port Gibson, Great Gulf, and the vicinity, I thought you should go down the river and join General Banks; and, when you turned northward, east of the Big Black, I feared it was a mistake. I now wish to make a personal acknowledgment that you was right, and I was wrong.

"Yours very truly,
"A. LINCOLN."

CHAPTER XII.

THE PERIL AT CHATTANOOGA.

Results from the Fall of Vicksburg. — Humanity of General Sherman. — Peril of the Army in East Tennessee. — Disaster at Chattanooga. — General Grant placed in Command. — His Wonderful Energy. — Opening Communications. — The Pontoon Bridge. — Movement of Hooker and Howard. — The Repulse of the Rebels.

HE fall of Vicksburg rendered it necessary for the rebels to evacuate Port Hudson. Thus every barricade of the Mississippi was swept away, from Cairo to the Gulf; and the Father of Waters rolled — to use an expression of President Lincoln — " unvexed to the sea." General Grant did not allow himself one moment to rejoice over his great victory. On the night of the 4th, Generals Sherman, Ord, and Steele were on the move with forty thousand men, retracing their steps towards Jackson. " Drive Johnston," said General Grant, " from the Mississippi Central Railroad. Destroy the bridges as far north as Grenada with your cavalry, and do the enemy all the harm possible. I will support you to the last man that can be spared."

Grenada is about one hundred miles north of Jackson. Such were the orders General Grant issued, and the operations he put in movement, on the very day in which he was receiving the surrender of Vicksburg. Johnston, who was on the eastern banks of the Big Black, recoiled before the approach of Sherman's army, and fell back upon Jackson.   The Union troops pressed the rebels closely, and drove them behind the intrenchments. Cavalry raids were sent in all directions, extending even sixty miles, destroying every thing which could be of service to the enemy.   General Johnston, with his desponding troops, soon again fled, and by night; crossing the Pearl River, and burning the bridges behind them.   The inhabitants of Jackson were found in such a state of destitution and misery, that General Sherman humanely fed them from the army stores, and did what he could to relieve the wide-spread woe which this wicked rebellion had brought upon them.

Leaving, with General Grant's approval, a large supply of food for the starving inhabitants of Jackson and Clinton, he returned with his troops to Vicksburg.   It was not deemed wise to pursue the fugitive foe, under the blaze of a July sun, through a region quite destitute of water.   The result of the campaign of Vicksburg has been carefully summed up as follows : —

The enemy was defeated in five battles outside of Vicksburg.   Jackson, the capital of the State, was taken ; and Vicksburg fell, surrendering its whole garrison and all its munitions of war.   The enemy lost, in killed, wounded, missing, and prisoners, fifty-six thousand men. General Grant's loss was but twelve hundred and forty-three killed, seven thousand and ninety-five wounded, and five hundred and thirty-five missing. One-half of the wounded were but slightly hurt, and were soon again in the ranks.

These were marvellous achievements.   They could not be the result of any fortunate series of accidents.

They would have shed renown upon the most celebrated captains of antiquity. The war had at length developed our most able military mind. The country was overjoyed, and rang with applause. The government conferred upon the hero the rank of major-general in the regular army. He had struck the Rebellion blows from which it never recovered.

General Grant recommended Generals Sherman and McPherson for promotion to the rank of brigadier-generals in the regular army. The communication in which he urged this reveals his own purity and nobility of character.

"The first reason for this," he wrote, "is their great fitness for any command that it may ever become necessary to intrust to them. Second, their great purity of character, and disinterestedness in any thing except the faithful performance of their duty, and the success of every one engaged in the great battle for the preservation of the Union. Third, they have honorably won this distinction upon many well-fought battle-fields. The promotion of such men as Sherman and McPherson always adds strength to our army."

Immediately after the president's proclamation of emancipation, on the 1st of January, 1863, General Grant fell in cordially with his plan of organizing and arming the negroes. He wrote to an adjutant-general the 11th of July, —

"I am anxious to get as many of these negro regiments as possible, and to have them fully and completely equipped. I am particularly desirous of organizing a regiment of heavy artillerists from the negroes to garrison this place, and shall do so as soon as possible." Soon after, he wrote, "The negro troops are easier to preserve discipline among than our white troops, and, I doubt not, will prove equally good for garrison duty. All that have been tried have fought bravely."

The rebels refused to recognize these colored troops, and threatened to hang all such as were taken, and also to hang their white officers. It was reported that some negro soldiers and their white captain, captured at Milliken's Bend, had been hung. General Grant immediately wrote to General Taylor, then in command of the rebel troops in Louisiana, as follows : —

" I feel no inclination to retaliate for the offence of irresponsible persons ; but, if it is the policy of any general, intrusted with the command of troops, to show no quarter, or to punish with death prisoners taken in battle, I will accept the issue.

" It may be you propose a different line of policy towards black troops, and officers commanding them, to that practised towards white troops. If so, I can assure you that those colored troops are regularly mustered into the service of the United States. The government, and all officers under the government, are bound to give the same protection to these troops that they do to any other troops."

This letter accomplished its purpose, in putting an end to those acts of barbarism which the rebels had inaugurated. General Grant was now anxious to move immediately upon Mobile, from New Orleans, by Lake Pontchartrain. Stunned as the rebels were by the blows which they had received at Vicksburg, there can be but little doubt that the enterprise would have been crowned with immediate success. General Grant was so thoroughly convinced of this that he urged the plan quite zealously. It will probably now be admitted that it was a mistake that General Grant's plans were, in this respect, overruled. His splendid army was, by direction of General Halleck, divided and dispersed. Some were sent to Banks, in Louisiana; some to Schofield, in Arkansas; some to Burnside, in East Kentucky.

General Grant was ordered to co-operate with General Banks in a movement upon Texas. Accordingly, on the 30th of August, he left Vicksburg for New Orleans. While in that city he was thrown from his horse at a review, and very severely injured. For twenty days he was confined to his bed, upon his back, unable to move; and, for two months afterwards, he could only walk with crutches.

General Rosecrans was then in East Tennessee, with an army of sixty thousand men. He had taken Chattanooga, but was in great peril, as the rebels in great force, under General Bragg, were moving upon his rear, threatening his long line of communication with Nashville. The rebels were pressing forward all their possible re-enforcements to the aid of Bragg. The country trembled for the fate of General Rosecrans's army.

General Halleck sent despatches, which were unfortunately delayed ten days in their transmission, directing General Grant to push forward with the utmost speed all the troops which could possibly be spared to the aid of General Rosecrans. Upon receiving this despatch, General Grant immediately sent the troops, in transports, up the river to Memphis; from which point they marched across the country, by the way of Corinth, Tuscumbia, and Decatur. General Sherman was intrusted with the command of this expedition.

In the mean time the enemy concentrated all his available force upon General Rosecrans. To leave him in possession of his positions there, was to surrender to the Union arms the entire command of East Tennessee. It is estimated that the combined rebel force amounted to eighty thousand men. General Rosecrans had but fifty-five thousand, and was far removed from his base of supplies. One of the most terrible battles of the war was fought. Equal desperation inspired both armies; and the carnage on both sides was awful. Our troops were driven back from the line of the Chickamauga River to the city of Chattanooga, where they were besieged behind their intrenchments. The patriot loss, in killed, wounded, and missing, in this desperate battle of two days' continuance, was estimated at sixteen thousand. The rebel loss was probably from sixteen to twenty thousand. They justly claimed the dear-bought victory; for the Union troops were driven from the battle-ground back to Chattanooga. Their lines of communication were entirely cut off, and they were in imminent danger of destruction. This disaster, occurring about the middle of September, caused profound anxiety throughout the country.

The crisis demanded very energetic action. General Grant was appointed to a new command, called the Military Division of the Mississippi. He was invested with nearly dictatorial powers. All the forces west of the Alleghanies were subjected to his almost absolute control. In fact, nearly all the armies of the West were combined under his command, and subject to his single will. The responsibility thus placed upon him was immense. Never before had our government intrusted such vast powers to any one. But the exigency was great, and it called for heroic measures. General Rosecrans, placed in the most difficult situation, far from his base of supplies, and overwhelmed by superior numbers, had fought with skill and energy which entitles him to a high rank in the affections of his countrymen.

On the 23d of October, General Grant arrived at Chattanooga, which is situated on the south side of a bend in the Tennessee River. The straggling town of but about four thousand inhabitants is but four miles from the Georgia line, and a hundred miles below the city of Knoxville. Two and a half miles south there is a ridge, or range, rising two thousand four hundred feet above the river, called Lookout Mountain. Parallel to this, and a little west of it, there is another similar ridge, called Raccoon Mountain. Lookout River meanders through the valley between the two. East of Lookout there is another elevation, of the same general character, called Missionary Ridge, about four hundred feet high.

The rebels commanded these three elevations, upon which they had planted their batteries, which were protected by earthworks. It would seem scarcely possible for any human power to scale these mountains to attack the batteries in the face of a foe. And yet these works effectually encircled the town from the river above to the river below.

Chattanooga was thus virtually invested. The rebel batteries commanded the railroad and the river. Communication could be maintained with Nashville only by a rough and mountainous wagon-road of over sixty miles. An army, now numbering forty thousand men, could by no possibility be long supplied by that route. The foe, from his commanding eminences, could look down as from a balloon into Chattanooga, and could throw his shells into portions of the Union camp. The whole command was on half-rations; and there were three thousand sick and wounded in the hospitals, destitute of all comforts. Even the horses were allowed but· one-half forage, and so many had died that there were not enough left to drag the artillery and the baggage-wagons; and thus retreat was impossible. There was only ammunition enough left to supply the army for one short battle. Rebel cavalry were triumphantly scouring the country to cut off our trains. They had just captured a very important one containing ordnance stores and medical supplies.

Such was the condition of the army of the Cumberland when General Grant assumed the command. It was the last of October. The nights were cold. The soldiers had no overcoats, many of them not even a blanket. General Bragg, in command of the rebel troops, did not deem it necessary to make an assault, as he said that starvation was fighting his battle for him as efficiently as he could desire.

General Grant was not in the habit of calling upon the government for re-enforcements. He recognized fully the military ability of General Halleck, and consequently only kept General Halleck clearly informed of his condition. He knew that General Halleck could judge, as well as he, whether re-enforcements were needed. And he had full confidence in the zeal and patriotism of his efficient co-operator. It was a proud stand which General Grant instinctively took, that he could not stoop to beg even for re-enforcements. Had he distrusted the military knowledge and judgment of General Halleck, his course might have been different. General Halleck never failed him.

General Thomas, who had won immortal renown at the battle of Chickamauga, saving the army by his individual heroism, was placed by Grant in command at Chattanooga until he could arrive. On the 19th of October he telegraphed Thomas, " Hold Chattanooga at all hazards. I will be there as soon as possible." The character of General Thomas may be read in his prompt reply, " I will hold the town till we starve."

It was midnight of the 20th when General Grant reached Nashville, coming from Louisville by rail. His noiseless, quiet energy seemed to accomplish miracles. General Burnside, at Knoxville, was telegraphed to place his post in such a position that it could be defended with the least number of men possible. Admiral Porter was telegraphed at Cairo to send some gunboats up the Tennessee to co-operate with General Sherman. General Thomas was telegraphed to employ working parties to construct a road, outside of the range of the rebel batteries, from Chattanooga to Bridgeport, about thirty miles down to the river, to which point supplies could be brought by rail and by river. General Rosecrans, with magnanimity and unselfish patriotism worthy of all praise, cordially greeted the officer sent to supersede him, and did every thing in his power to assist General Grant in attaining a correct knowledge of the posture of affairs. Marshal Ney was a brave man and a splendid officer, though no one would claim for him equality with Napoleon. We had in our army many very noble officers who are entitled to the undying esteem and love of their countrymen, though the war developed but one General Grant. The commissary at Nashville was telegraphed to send, as quick as possible, vegetables for the army.

When General Grant, with his party, arrived at Bridgeport, they could advance no farther either by river or by rail, as both routes were swept by the rebel batteries.

They therefore took horse, and traversed rough mountain roads, which were inundated by recent rains. The defiles were enclosed by precipitous cliffs strewed with the wrecks of wagons, and the carcasses of horses and mules. It was often necessary to dismount, and to lead their horses over difficult and dangerous places. General Grant, who was still lame from the effects of his fall, was carried over these spots in the arms of his soldiers.

The energies of his mind were intensely aroused, and he was continually sending despatches in all directions. He had three armies under his control, for whose safety and success he was responsible,—the army of Chattanooga, under General Thomas; that of Knoxville, under General Burnside; and the troops who were struggling along through Tennessee, under General Sherman. In the evening of a dark, cold, rainy day, Oct. 23, General Grant —drenched, hungry, and exhausted — reached Chattanooga. It was a gloomy night; but the gloom of difficulty and peril which enveloped the beleaguered host seemed more-dense and impenetrable than the atmospheric darkness.

The general course of the Tennessee River, just at this point, is from east to west. The rebels held the southern shore, with the exception of the town of Chattanooga, where our troops were cooped up. We held the northern shore, though annoyed by rebel raiders. The first object to which General Grant directed his attention was to find means of conveying supplies to his army. Unless this could be done, and immediately, ruin was inevitable.

He first constructed a pontoon bridge across the river, about nine miles below Chattanooga, at a place called Brown's Ferry. The enterprise was very bravely and adroitly accomplished, in the presence of a vigilant and victorious foe. The night of the 27th was dark and . foggy. Sixty pontoon boats, which had been secretly prepared, each containing thirty men, pushed from their concealment, and floated down the swollen and rapid stream, hugging the northern bank. Not a loud word was spoken, no oars were used; and thus the boats drifted down the stream undiscovered by the rebel pickets. They landed on the south side of the river; and, after a slight skirmish with the rebel pickets, in which none of the Union troops were killed, and but four or five wounded, they seized some hills which commanded the ferry.

At the same time, a supporting force marched down the northern bank of the river; and, before the morning dawned, the whole force was safely upon the south shore. They threw up intrenchments, planted their batteries, and cut down the trees for an abatis, and in a short time were prepared to defend themselves from attack. By ten o'clock the bridge — and a very excellent one — was completed.

While this important movement was in progress, General Hooker crossed the Tennessee at Bridgeport, about twenty miles below, with the Eleventh Corps under General Howard, and the Twelfth under General Geary; and, driving before him such of the enemy as he met, went into camp, and strongly intrenched himself in the vicinity of the party at Brown's Ferry.

This movement alarmed the rebels. They comprehended all its important consequences; and General Longstreet was sent, it is said with his whole corps, to regain, if possible, the vital point. A fierce battle ensued, which continued into the night, raging through the ravines by the light of a brilliant moon. The rebels were effectually repulsed. General Hooker had seven thousand men engaged. His loss in killed and wounded was four hundred and sixteen. The loss of the rebels was estimated at fifteen hundred. Our troops now so strengthened themselves as to be safe from any future attack. General Grant had thus the command of Lookout Valley.

There were speedily two good lines of transportation provided from Bridgeport, — a wagon-road on the north side of the river of about thirty miles; and a good road of but eight miles from Brown's Ferry, which point could be reached by the river. Our communications with Nashville were now safe, and supplies and re-enforcements could be forwarded without danger. Such is the power of genius. In five days General Grant had wrought this marvellous change. There was no longer any fear for the army at Chattanooga. A door was now open — and one which the rebels could not close — for the arrival of re-enforcements and supplies.

This was but the first step. With unabated zeal General Grant now pressed forward in endeavors to prepare his army to resume offensive operations. Two corps were speedily added to its strength. And General Hooker, already renowned for his splendid martial qualities, was threatening the rebel position on Lookout Mountain. A change, as by magic, had come over the whole scene. The river was alive with steamers bringing supplies; horses and ammunition arrived, and both man and beast rejoiced again in full rations. The spirits of the army were wonderfully revived. Even the sick in the hospitals felt the inspiring influence, and, abandoning their couches, hastened back to the ranks.

"If the rebels," said General Grant, on the 28th, "will give us one week more, I think all danger of losing territory now held by us will have passed away, and preparations may commence for active operations."

CHAPTER XIII.

PREPARATIONS FOR BATTLE.

Extent of General Grant's Command. — March of Sherman. — Chagrin of the Rebels. — Characteristics. — Peril of Burnside. Anxiety of Grant. — Grandeur of the Military Movements. — Grant's Despatches. — Position of General Thomas. — Arrival of Sherman. — Meeting of Sherman and Howard. — Assuming the Offensive.

ENERAL GRANT was now in command of a military division extending a thousand miles, from Natchez on the Mississippi to Knoxville on the Tennessee, and embracing two hundred thousand soldiers. All this region he was to protect, and for all the varied wants of these troops he was to provide. General Burnside, one of the most gallant and devoted soldiers the Rebellion had developed, was at the city of Knoxville, a hundred miles farther up the Tennessee River. He had an army of about twenty-five thousand men at that important post. They were in need of every thing. The only way in which supplies could be forwarded to them was to send them up the Mississippi from St. Louis to the Ohio River, thence up the Ohio to the Cumberland, and then up the Cumberland to the mouth of the Big South Fork. Thus far Admiral Porter, with his gunboats, could convoy them. To that point, one hundred miles from Knoxville, it was necessary for General Burnside to send a guard

to protect the train from cavalry raids and guerilla bands. By this route, — which General Grant arranged, even in its details, — General Burnside received supplies.

General Sherman was on a march of four hundred miles, with the Fifteenth Army Corps. He was traversing the whole breadth of country from Memphis, on the Mississippi, to Chattanooga. Though General Sherman was one of the most sagacious and energetic of men, it was necessary for General Grant, in the vast combinations which he was now forming, to direct the route, to decide upon the points which were to be reached on particular days, and to see that supplies should meet the troops where needed. The march was through the enemy's country. The rebels watched in guerilla bands to attack the trains. Sharpshooters infested the river banks and the defiles. Railroads were torn up, and bridges burned, to impede the march. There is something very beautiful in the manly affection and esteem which seems ever to have existed. between these two illustrious men, Grant and Sherman. When General Grant sent General Sherman north, after the capture of Vicksburg, he said to him, —

"I hope you will be in time to aid in giving the rebels the worst, or best, thrashing they have had in this war. I have constantly had the feeling that I shall lose you from this command entirely. Of course, I do not object to seeing your sphere of usefulness enlarged; and I think it should have been enlarged long ago, having an eye to the public good alone. But it needs no assurance from me, general, that, taking a more selfish view, while I would heartily approve such a change, I would deeply regret it on my own account."

The rebels were quick to perceive that a master-mind

was at work at Chattanooga. Their plans were all thwarted, and the tide of war was turning strongly against them. "The Richmond Enquirer" complained that General Bragg had allowed the Union troops to recover from the defeat at Chickamauga; that the occupation of Lookout Valley by General Grant enabled him to take the initiative, always important in military movements; that General Grant was assuming the offensive in the front, and "under the very nose of General Bragg;" that the Union troops had turned upon their pursuers, and were occupying a threatening position on the flanks of the victors. "The enemy were," adds "The Enquirer," "outfought at Chickamauga, — thanks to the army! — but the present position of affairs looks as though we had been outgeneraled at Chattanooga."

A short time before the arrival of General Grant, Jefferson Davis visited the encampment at Lookout Mountain. As he stood upon that eminence, and looked down upon our bleeding, emaciate army cooped up in Chattanooga, he rubbed his hands complacently, exclaiming, "I have the Yankees now in just the trap I set for them."

There were many Union families in that part of Tennessee. Indeed, the majority of the inhabitants were favorable to the national cause. These families were exposed to every kind of outrage from the Secessionists and the rebel soldiers. Their houses were plundered and burned, their persons were maltreated, their families were insulted. General Grant issued a decree, that, for every act of violence to an unarmed Union citizen, a Secessionist would be arrested, and held as a hostage; that, for every dollar's worth of property taken from such citizens, or destroyed by raiders, an assessment should be made upon Secessionists of the neighborhood, and collected by military force. Wealthy Secessionists were also assessed in money and provisions for the support of Union refugees who had been driven from their homes and into our lines. Such was the vigor with which General Grant grappled with the Rebellion.

To a very eminent degree he possessed that quality, so conspicuous in the first Napoleon, — an almost instinctive judgment of the qualifications of men for any special duty. He thus surrounded himself with the very best subordinates the country afforded for the accomplishment of his plans. Sherman and Thomas and Sheridan, — he selected each for his individual service; and the unanimous voice of the country has ratified the wisdom of his choice. But for this ability to judge of character, he never could have accomplished his great achievements. Had his subordinates failed him, all would have gone to ruin.

" Grant has ever displayed greatness of soul that never yet went with littleness of mind. Who has said as much as he in praise of Sheridan, Sherman, McPherson, Thomas, Meade ? Remember how he lay with his gallant army before Petersburg, in the fall of 1864, when popular impatience in vain goaded him to attack, when the press and the people began to demand his dismissal, and to stigmatize him as ' the butcher;' how then, when Sheridan won his great victories in the valley, and every cap went up for ' Little Phil,' Grant capped the whole by telegraphing that he regarded him as among the first of living generals; how then, when Hood invaded Tennessee, the lieutenant-general gave Thomas all the men he could, and all the means, and contributed in every way to the splendid success at Nashville, yet scrupulously refrained from doing any thing to take the glory from Thomas, as he might have done by simply going on in person ; how then, when Sherman had gone —

'From the centre all round to the sea,'

Grant gave him a brother's welcome, tenderly covered his sad mistake at diplomacy, and presented him to the nation as the great strategist of the war."*

General Sherman, at several points on his march, encountered severe opposition. It was not without hard fighting he repelled these determined foes. About the middle of October, he struck the Tennessee River at Eastport. Here he found ample supplies awaiting him, provided by the forethought of Grant, and steamers to ferry the army across the stream. At this point the river is nearly a mile wide.

With great solicitude, General Grant kept his eye upon Sherman's columns during every mile of their march. They were imperatively and immediately needed, to enable him to strike the enemy a stunning blow. Bragg had sent Longstreet with a sufficient force, as he supposed, to annihilate Burnside's little army at Knoxville. It was not possible to send General Burnside any re-enforcements. It was known that that gallant soldier would hold out to the last possible moment. But there was, apparently, no way in which he could be saved from destruction but by assailing Bragg so fiercely that Longstreet would have to be recalled. This assault could not be made until General Sherman should arrive. Though General Sherman was straining every nerve upon the march, it was feared that before he reached Chattanooga General Burnside would be crushed, and that thus Knoxville

* Springfield Republican.

would fall into the hands of the foe. On the 24th of October, General Grant telegraphed Sherman, "Drop every thing east of Bear Creek, and move with your entire force towards Stevenson until you receive further orders."

By the 1st of November, General Sherman, at the head of his columns, was at Florence. Again Grant telegraphed, on the 7th, "The enemy have moved a great part of their force from this front towards Burnside. I have to make an immediate move from here towards their lines of communication, to bring them back if possible. I am anxious to see your old corps here at the earliest moment."

It is noticeable that General Grant, immediately upon his arrival at Chattanooga, anticipated this movement on the part of the rebels; for he, on the 26th of October, telegraphed General Burnside, —

"Do you hear of any of Bragg's army threatening you from the south-west? Thomas's command is in a bad condition to use, for want of animals of sufficient strength to save his artillery, and for want of rations. If you are threatened with a force beyond what you are able to compete with, efforts must be made to assist you. Answer."

The hours flew swiftly by. Longstreet was on the march to overwhelm Burnside. Sherman, struggling through the miry roads, rebuilding bridges, and often fighting his way, was painfully delayed. Ruin threatened Burnside. The loss of his army and of Knoxville would prove one of the severest calamities. The anxiety which oppressed General Grant, though concealed, must have been dreadful. The peril of General Burnside had become so great that at last Grant decided to attack

Bragg's army without waiting the arrival of Sherman. On the 7th of November, he issued the following orders to General Thomas: —

"The news is of such a nature that it becomes an imperative duty for your force to draw the attention of the enemy from Burnside to your front. I deem the best movement to attack the enemy to be an attack on the north end of Missionary Ridge with all the force you can bring to bear against it; and, when that is carried, to threaten and attack even the enemy's line of communication between Dalton and Cleveland. Rations should be ready to issue, a sufficiency to last four days, the moment Missionary Ridge is in our possession; rations to be carried in haversacks.

"Where there are not horses to move the artillery, mules must be taken from the teams, or horses from ambulances, or, if necessary, officers dismounted and their horses taken. Immediate preparations should be made to carry these directions into execution. The movement should not be made a moment later than to-morrow morning."

At the same time General Grant telegraphed General Burnside of the measures he was adopting for his relief. But it turned out that so many of the horses had perished that it was not possible to obtain enough to move the artillery. Thus they were compelled to await the arrival of Sherman. He needed no urgency. Fully aware of the exigence, he was straining every nerve of energy to its utmost tension. Of course the greatest anxiety was felt for General Burnside. No re-enforcements could be sent to him; and, if they could be sent, there were no means then of feeding them. Rebel forces from different directions were marching upon him; and it was apprehended that he must fall before assaults which no skill or valor could resist. General Grant, however, had great confidence in General Burnside.

"The continent shook with the tramp of advancing armies. Bridges were built in Eastern cities for these soldiers to march over. Engines were brought from Western towns to transport their supplies. The greatest rivers of the republic, the Tennessee and the Cumberland, the Mississippi and the Ohio, were crowded with steamers bringing clothes and shoes to those who were wearing out their garments in mighty marches, and ammunition and food to replace what had already been expended in the campaigns for Chattanooga.

"Over half the territory in rebellion, through these great mountain ranges and by the side of these rushing streams, along the desolated cornfields and amid the startled recesses of the primeval forests, the bustle and the stir of war were rife. Two hundred thousand soldiers were concentrating from the East and the West, either in motion for this one battle-field, or guarding its approaches, or bringing up supplies, or waiting anxiously for those who were, with them, to fight the battle of Chattanooga. And over all these preparations, and all these armies, the spirit of one man was dominant." *

General Grant was by no means despairing. He had so much confidence in General Burnside's soldierly qualities that he believed that he would maintain his position until relief should come. The result proved that he was not deceived in his judgment.

On the 14th of November, General Grant telegraphed Burnside, " Sherman's advance has reached Bridgeport. His whole force will be ready to move from there by

* Military History of Ulysses S. Grant.

Tuesday at furthest. If you can hold Longstreet in check until he gets up, or by skirmishing and falling back can avoid serious loss to yourself and gain time, I will be able to force the enemy back from here, and place a force between Longstreet and Bragg that must inevitably make the former take to the mountain passes, by every available road, to get to his supplies. Sherman would have been here before this, but for high water in Elk River, driving him some thirty miles up that river to cross."

On the 17th, he again telegraphed Burnside, " Your despatch received. You are doing exactly what appears to me to be right. I want the enemy's progress retarded at every point all it can be, only giving up each place when it becomes evident that it can no longer be held without endangering your force to capture. I think our movements here must cause Longstreet's recall within a day or two, if he is not successful before that time. Sherman moved this morning from Bridgeport with one division. The remainder of his command moves in the morning. There will be no halt until a severe battle is fought, or the railroads cut supplying the enemy."

The greatest activity was now exercised in bringing Sherman's army to the extreme right of the enemy's line, where an attack was least expected, and where the defences were weakest. By marching his troops in the rear of the hills, the movement was concealed from the enemy ; and, by keeping up a large number of camp-fires at Whiteside, where the command first rested, Bragg was deceived into the belief that the whole of General Sherman's force was concentrated there. It was, however, all soon gathered in a concealed camp about two miles west of Chattanooga.

Nothing great is ever accomplished in this world without encountering and triumphing over great obstacles. The very elements seemed to conspire against these army movements. Drenching rains fell; the bridges were carried away; the roads were cut up into sloughs.

General Thomas's line was directly in front of Chattanooga, about a mile from the town. His position was strongly intrenched; and, upon a slight elevation in his most advanced point, he had constructed a very effective redoubt, called Fort Wood. A deserter from the rebels stated that Bragg was secretly preparing for a retreat. But Grant had no idea of allowing Bragg to retire unassailed. He ordered Thomas immediately to ascertain the truth or falsehood of the report. Twenty-seven heavy guns protected his line. About a mile beyond him was the first rebel line.

Thomas ordered out the Fourth Corps, under General Granger, and advanced to develop the strength of the enemy. General Howard's corps was massed behind Granger's centre. All the arrangements for the advance were completed by two o'clock in the afternoon. The sun shone brilliantly upon an army of twenty thousand bayonets in line. The rebels from their heights looked with admiration upon the splendid pageant, regarding it as merely a parade. At a given signal the whole line advanced. The enemy from their batteries, and from musketry in the woods, opened a vigorous fire. But our advance was so rapid that two hundred of the enemy were captured in their rifle-pits, and in fifteen minutes the rebels were driven from their whole advanced line. We thus secured a very important eminence, called Orchard Knoll, and our line was advanced a mile. The new position was during the night strongly fortified, and artillery placed in battery.

The rebels began now fully to realize that the tide was turning against them. Their troops became despondent. The army of the Cumberland was jubilant. About five miles above Chattanooga, the North Chickamauga River enters the Cumberland from the west. Here a hundred and sixteen pontoons were constructed and hidden, to float a portion of General Sherman's troops down the river, and land them upon the other side of the Tennessee, to co-operate in the attack upon Missionary Ridge. Seven hundred and fifty oarsmen were selected as the motive power of this squadron. Sherman's army was marched up to this place, under cover of the forest and the hills.

At midnight of Nov. 23d, these pontoons, loaded with Smith's brigade, swept silently into the Tennessee. The night was dark, and they floated down the river so noiselessly that even the national pickets did not observe their passage. The troops were safely landed just below the mouth of the South Chickamauga, which enters the Tennessee from the east. The boats returned for another load. Before morning ten thousand men were landed upon that point. Before the sun rose, a substantial bridge was floating nearly across the river, a strong *tête de pont* had been erected, and a strong artillery force from General Thomas's army was in position to defend the operation. There were ten thousand troops on the northern shore still to cross. Eighty boats, each capable of carrying about forty men, were rapidly transporting them across. Engineers were at work at both ends of the bridge, and the ends would soon meet in the middle of the stream. In the distance, a column was seen winding over the western hills, approaching the river. The spectacle, as beheld in the rays of the morning by the rebels, from the heights of Missionary Ridge, must have been sublime, and yet somewhat appalling.

General Sherman stood at the head of the bridge as it was being pushed out into the stream from the northern shore. General Howard arrived,—advanced to the head of the bridge which was in construction from the southern shore. There was now but a small chasm to be filled. Across this chasm General Howard introduced himself. We think that this was the first meeting of these illustrious men, afterwards united in so many of the most brilliant achievements which history has recorded. As soon as the last boat was in its place, bridging the gulf, Sherman sprang across, and the two generals clasped hands. It was a pledge of that fraternal union which blended the two armies of the Cumberland and of the Tennessee, and which grew stronger and more sacred every day, until our armies, having trampled rebellion everywhere beneath their feet, raised the shout of victory over a nation saved.

At noon the bridge was completed, and Sherman's division, men, horses, and artillery, were on the southern shore. At one o'clock, in three columns, they were marching *en echelon* from the river, following the general course, eastward, of the South Chickamauga.

Clouds had gathered in the sky. A drizzling rain was falling, and the misty atmosphere kindly veiled the movements of the troops from rebel eyes. Our lines now extended along the south banks of the Tennessee, from Hooker's Station below, at Wauhatchie, to Sherman's position on the Chickamauga, a distance of nearly thirteen miles. Thus at last, after these herculean exertions, General Grant was prepared to throw down the gage of battle.

CHAPTER XIV.

THE BATTLE OF MISSIONARY RIDGE.

Lookout Mountain.—General Hooker's Advance.—The Battle in the Clouds.—Retreat of the Foe.—Position of the Armies.—Plan of the Battle.—Characteristics of General Grant.—Movements of Sherman; of Hooker.—The Decisive Charge by Thomas.—The Victory.—Sheridan's Pursuit.—Activity of General Grant.—The great Ability he displayed.

HE rebels were well aware that an immediate assault was at hand. Strong as they were upon their mountain heights, they deemed it scarcely possible that their works could be stormed. General Sherman, advancing in three columns from the river, gained the top of the hill at the northern extremity of Missionary Ridge. He had attained this point almost unobserved by the enemy. An attack was at once made, but it was repelled with but little loss; and, as night came on, Sherman was left to fortify himself in the important position which he had gained. He found, to his disappointment, that he had still a gorge to descend, and another difficult eminence to climb, before he would be fairly upon the plateau of Missionary Ridge. But for this, probably, his assault the next day would have proved an entire success.

All through the night, heavy details were at work upon the intrenchments, while a dense river-fog aided in concealing his movements. Towards morning the vapors were dissipated, the stars came out brightly, and Sherman's camp-fires revealed to thousands of eager eyes in Chattanooga, and even to the rebels on the distant heights of Lookout Mountain, that the Union troops were in position on Missionary Ridge. Hooker, with the Eleventh Corps, was still several miles below, in Lookout Valley, facing the extreme left of the rebel lines. Thomas, with the Army of the Cumberland, was in front of the enemy's centre.

No description can convey to the mind of the reader a correct idea of the multiplied evolutions in the great battle which ensued. Wellington said that one might as well attempt to describe the positions, ever changing, of the dancers in the mazes of the most complicated cotillion, as to describe the evolutions of a great battle. We can only give the prominent features and the grand result. The vast battle-field extended through forests, and over mountains and valleys, for a distance of thirteen miles.

On the 24th, Hooker made a very gallant advance upon Lookout Mountain, fighting all day and late into the hours of the night. When it is remembered that this mountain is two thousand feet high, its sides covered with an almost impenetrable forest, rugged, gullied, encumbered with enormous bowlders and precipitous cliffs, while thousands of armed men, with infantry and artillery, occupied every important position to resist the ascent, it may be imagined how great must have been the difficulty of its capture.

General Hooker marched down Lookout Valley to attack the head of Lookout Mountain, which composed the southern extremity of the rebel line. The rebels occupied the crest in great force, their intrenchments extending down the front and slope of the mountain to its base. The first thirty feet of descent from the summit presents a perpendicular wall of rock. A narrow road, which was often a path along which but one individual could walk, ascended the south-western face of the mountain. General Hooker pushed his columns through the concealment of the forest until he gained a favorable point for ascending the hill. At the same time, to engage the attention of the enemy, his batteries opened a terrific fire, to which the rebels vigorously replied; and the whole mountain seemed to shake beneath the heavy explosions. The summit was soon hid from view in Chattanooga by the cloud of smoke which settled around it. The flashes of the guns and the thunderings from the cloud reminded the beholder of the awful scenes of Sinai.

The rebels, finding themselves suddenly attacked in flank and rear, were thrown into dismay. Effectual resistance was impossible, and from those cliffs retreat was very difficult. Gradually they drew back, yielding position after position, and fighting step by step. Our victorious troops with cheers pressed on, driving the foe before them from west to east.

About two o'clock in the afternoon, the enemy was encountered in strength, and a terrible battle ensued. It was the severest struggle of the day; but the foe was driven back, and Hooker's indomitable host pressed on. The day was now spent: darkness came to arrest the conquerors, and to aid the vanquished in their flight. General Hooker's camp-fires proclaimed to his friends below the glorious victory he had achieved. Lookout Mountain had been carried by storm, and the victors were reposing upon its summit. During the night the foe fled down the rough road which wound along the eastern side of the mountain. They crossed Chattanooga River, and joined their already disheartened confederates on Missionary Ridge. Thus terminated the second day of this great conflict. We had captured Lookout Mountain and two thousand prisoners. The rebels were all now concentrated upon Missionary Ridge, and we were in position to assail them to advantage in front, flank, and rear. Sherman, Thomas, Howard, Hooker, were the able chieftains who led the troops through whose bravery and energy these great achievements had been accomplished; but the imperial mind which had conceived and directed all was that of General Grant. His wonderful combinations, his far-reaching foresight, — anticipating every peril, and providing for every emergence, — and his extraordinary administrative ability, had evolved these results, which were overwhelming the foe with despair, and electrifying the nation with joy.

While these sublime scenes were being enacted, General Grant might be seen — a plain man, in plain dress, with no badge of distinction — limping, from the effects of his fall, alone through the post of Chattanooga. No parade surrounded him; no brilliant staff followed his footsteps; no bustle accompanied his movements. His voice was calm and low and gentle. Not an impassioned word escaped his lips. No sign of impatience could be seen in gesture or countenance. The absorption of his soul in the mighty enterprise was too deep to admit of those ebullitions of pride and passion too often witnessed on similar occasions. Such are the lineaments of one of Nature's noblemen.

The morning of Nov. 25 dawned cold and raw, though the sun rose brilliantly in a cloudless sky. The foe was concentrated in his strong intrenchments on Missionary Ridge, which, it will be remembered, was seven miles long, and rose to the height of four hundred feet from the plain. General Sherman had gained possession of some heights on the north of the ridge, facing the enemy's extreme right. General Thomas had spread out his intrenched lines in both directions, north and south from Orchard Knob, and was thus prepared to assail the foe in his centre from the west. General Hooker, having carried Lookout Mountain, was ready to follow the retreating foe, and assail him upon his extreme left, on the south end of Missionary Ridge.

General Grant, in preparation for the great struggle, had taken his position on Orchard Knoll, from which point the whole field of battle was displayed. Bragg's headquarters were plainly visible on the summit of the ridge. " Trees, houses, fences, all landmarks in the valley, had been swept away for camps ; and the two antagonists, each from his high position, looked down upon the board where the great game was playing."

The plan was, for General Sherman to make a vigorous assault upon Missionary Ridge from the north ; at the same time, Hooker was to assail it from the south. Bragg would thus be compelled to weaken his centre to send re-enforcements to the menaced points. Thomas was then to push forward his whole force from the centre,. and carry the ridge by storm. The plan proved a perfect success.

Before the dawn, General Sherman was in his saddle ; and, as the sun rose, his bugles sounded the advance. The rebel works were attacked with great vehemence, Sherman's troops advancing to within pistol-shot of their lines. General Grant, from Orchard Knoll, watched the progress of the fight.

In the mean time, General Hooker was advancing with his triumphant band from the heights of Lookout. He had descended the north-eastern brow of the mountain, crossed the valley, and was now in the rear of the rebel line, making the ascent of Mission Ridge. All the troops in that vicinity were concentrated there to resist his advance.

Bragg, finding his lines sorely pressed by Sherman, despatched a large force from his centre to strengthen his right wing. As Grant stood upon Orchard Knoll, he had the satisfaction of seeing a massive column of Bragg's forces marching, regiment after regiment, two or three miles to the north, to meet the shock of Sherman's impetuous assault. This was the very movement which Grant had been manœuvring to accomplish. He had thus, as it were, taken command of Bragg's troops.

The decisive moment had now arrived. The assaulting troops of Thomas's army were concealed in four columns behind Orchard Knoll, held like hounds in the leash. "Now, boys, onward!" exclaimed Grant cheerfully, as six guns gave the signal for the charge. These four divisions were led by Johnson, Sheridan, Wood, and Baird. The distance to the first line of rebel rifle-pits was from four to nine hundred yards. The Union troops emerged from their concealment, and advanced upon the double-quick. A tremendous fire from the batteries on the cliff was instantly opened upon them.

"I happened," said Sheridan, in describing this scene to a friend, "to be in advance of my line as it charged." We cannot help remarking, in passing, that General Sheridan very often *happened* to be just in that position in the perilous hour of assault. "Looking back," he continued, "I was impressed with the terrible sight of approaching bayonets.   The men were on a run, and the line had become almost a crowd ; and the rebels appeared unable to resist the effect upon their imagination, or their nerves, of this waving, glittering mass of steel."

This line of rebel rifle-pits ran along near the foot of the ridge.   Not a gun was fired by our troops as they rushed onwards, the bristling line of steel glittering in the rays of the afternoon sun.   The rebels were taken so by surprise, that, after a few random discharges of their rifles, they abandoned themselves to despair.   Some threw themselves prostrate in the trenches as our troops rushed over them.   A thousand were thus in a moment taken prisoners, and ordered to the rear.   Others endeavored to escape by clambering the hill.

Thirty pieces of artillery opened upon them with canister and grape ; and a storm of bullets from musketry swept their ranks, as the Union troops laboriously and yet impetuously pursued the fugitives up the steep acclivity.   Step by step the advance was made.   Five or six color-bearers were shot down in succession, bearing a single flag.

About half-way up the hill, another line of rifle-pits was encountered.   This was also carried as was the first. There was still another line of rifle-pits upon the summit, crowded with sharpshooters, and blazing with an incessant fire of musketry.   But undismayed, unbroken, still onward pressed this line of heroes.   They reached the crest.   With shouts which rose above the roar of artillery and the rattle of musketry, the Union troops rushed, like a living tide, into the rebel works.   So resistless and sudden was the movement that crowds were taken in the trenches.

A scene of tumult, confusion, and terror ensued, which

cannot be imagined. The roar of battle continued,—
sixty explosions of cannon each minute. The victors
and the vanquished, in numbers which could not be
counted, were blended upon the ramparts and in the
trenches. There were thirteen thousand in the assault,
eight thousand behind the intrenchments. Shouts of
victory and cries of despair deafened the ear. Whole
regiments threw down their arms ; others fled wildly,
pelted by bullets. In the hot pursuit, the victors often
had not time to reload their guns, but assailed the fugitives with stones. The very batteries with which the
rebels had just been dealing death into our lines were
turned against the disordered masses. The field was won.
The stars and stripes rose,—waved triumphantly over
the rebel redoubts. Their army was cut in twain. Nothing now remained for them but a precipitate retreat, or
destruction.

Just then, General Grant appeared upon the summit
of the hill. At the sight of their beloved chieftain, who
was now to inscribe " Chattanooga " upon the banner
already blazoned with the glorious names of " Donelson "
and of " Vicksburg," they raised a shout which reached
the ears of the rejoicing thousands in the city below, and
which added new speed to the footsteps of the fugitives,
who in the most rapid flight alone could hope for safety.

" There is nothing in this world," said the Duke of
Wellington, " more dreadful than a great victory, except
a great defeat." This victory cost four thousand Union
men, in killed and wounded. Who can tell the anguish
which these tidings conveyed to thousands of homes !
The rebels also were sons, husbands, fathers. Many of
them had been forced into the fight. The amount of
their loss can never be known. The hill was covered

with heaps of their dead, in every form of mutilation. Seven thousand prisoners were driven into our rear. Ten thousand stand of arms and fifty-two pieces of artillery were captured.

In fifty-five minutes this great achievement was consummated. Bragg was in despair. He had considered his position impregnable, and had not the slightest idea that the Union troops could drive him from it. The attempts he made to rally the fugitives to form another line in the rear were entirely unavailing. The disaster was irreparable. A panic had seized both officers and men, and they could no more be arrested in their flight than the torrent of Niagara could be stopped in its plunge. Thomas was in front, Sherman on their right, and the thunders of Hooker's advancing columns were heard approaching them on their left.

Fortunately for the vanquished, night now came. The rebels were familiar with the roads; and, as they had fought from behind their trenches, they were not much fatigued. The Union troops, from the impetuosity of their charge, and from the toil of clambering the hill, were greatly exhausted, and were in no condition to pursue, — groping their way in the dark, through unknown roads, over a strange country.

Still the impetuous Sheridan pressed forward, during the twilight, upon the heels of the fugitives. He came near capturing Bragg himself. A large wagon-train was seen a half-mile before him in the valley below, with several pieces of artillery, flying over the roads, the horses goaded to their utmost speed.

Sheridan urged his troops forward, eager for the prize. The rebels planted a battery upon an eminence, to beat him back. It was charged in front, flank, and rear. "It was now dark; and, just as the head of one of these columns reached the summit of the hill, the moon rose from behind, and a medallion view of the column was disclosed, as it crossed the disk of the moon, and attacked the enemy. Outflanked on right and left, the rebels fled, leaving the coveted artillery and trains. Those who escaped capture were driven across Chickamauga Creek, where they burned the bridges almost while they passed." *

At half-past seven o'clock, that evening, General Grant sent the following modest telegram to General Halleck : —

" Although the battle lasted from early dawn till dark this evening, I believe I am not premature in announcing a complete victory over Bragg. Lookout Mountain-top, all the rifle-pits in Chattanooga Valley, and Missionary Ridge entire, have been carried, and are now held by us. I have no idea of finding Bragg here to-morrow."

That night General Grant wrote to General Sherman, who had so signally contributed to the success of the day by drawing the heaviest blows of the enemy upon himself, —

" No doubt you witnessed the handsome manner in which Thomas's troops carried Missionary Ridge this afternoon, and can feel a just pride, too, in the part taken by the forces under your command, in taking, first, so much of the same range of hills, and then in attracting so much of the attention of the enemy as to make Thomas's part certain of success. The next thing now will be to relieve Burnside."

At the same hour he wrote to Wilcox, " The great defeat Bragg has sustained in the three days' battle, terminating at dusk this evening, and a movement which

* Military History of General Grant.

I shall immediately make, I think will relieve Burnside, if he holds out a few days longer. I shall pursue Bragg to-morrow, and start a heavy column up the Tennessee Valley the day after."

A few other of the despatches which were sent off this night, after these three days of terrible excitement and fatigue, we will give, as illustrative of the wide scope of General Grant's cares, and the tireless energies of his mind : —

"I have heard from Burnside to the 23d, when he had rations for ten or twelve days, and expected to hold out that time. I shall move a force from here on to the railroad between Cleveland and Dalton, and send a column of twenty thousand men up the south side of the Tennessee, without wagons, carrying four days' rations, and taking a steamer loaded with rations, from which to draw on the route. If Burnside holds out until this force gets beyond Kingston, I think the enemy will fly, and, with the present state of the roads, must abandon almost every thing. I believe that Bragg will lose much of his army by desertion, in consequence of his defeat in the last three days' fight."

This great victory pierced the heart of the Rebellion. It rescued Burnside from his perils. Kentucky and Tennessee were delivered from rebel thraldom. Georgia and the South-west were threatened in the rear ; and the glorious victory of Chattanooga was added to the list of those which already honored the name of Ulysses S. Grant.

CHAPTER XV.

THE PURSUIT.

Night-Scene. — Grant's Despatches. — The Pursuit. — Destruction of Chattanooga Depot. — Speech of Jefferson Davis. — The Contest at Ringgold. — The Campaign and the Great Battle. — Lincoln's Proclamation and Letter. — Halleck's Report. — Movements for the Relief of Burnside. — Grant's Despatches.

HOUGH the rebel army was broken and dispersed, it was still a powerful organization. General Grant wished to destroy it as effectually as possible. At daylight, the next morning, the troops were pushed forward in a vigorous pursuit. Everywhere they encountered evidences of the tremendous disaster which had overwhelmed the enemy. Abandoned guns, broken wagons, and fragments of small arms, everywhere strewed the road. The disheartened fugitives often seemed not unwilling to be taken captive. They were gathered up by hundreds. Sometimes whole regiments, when they caught sight of our advancing columns, threw down their arms, and dispersed in all directions, leaving their wounded in our hands.

During the night, the country for miles around was illumined by the blaze of huge fires. The rebels had gathered an abundance of the materiel of war in their encampment, which they supposed no foe could assail.

They were now applying the torch to every thing which they could not carry away. The flight of the routed army was in a south-east direction, towards Ringgold and Dalton. All the roads were clogged with the tumultuous mass, infantry, artillery, baggage-wagons, and swarms of fugitives who had lost their regiments, all blended in vast confusion. The rebels burned the bridges behind them, and felled the forest trees into the roads, to impede the pursuit of the avenging host pressing upon their rear. General Grant said to Sherman, —

" We will push Bragg with all our strength to-morrow, and try if we cannot cut off a good portion of his new troops and trains. His men have manifested a strong desire to desert for some time past, and we will now give them a chance. Move the advance force on the most easterly road taken by the enemy."

To Thomas he gave directions, " You will start a strong reconnoissance in the morning, at seven, A.M., to ascertain the position of the enemy. If it is ascertained that the enemy are in full retreat, follow them with all your force, except that which you expect Granger to take to Knoxville. Four days' rations should be got up to the men between this and morning, and also a supply of ammunition. I shall want Granger's expedition to get off by the day after to-morrow."

Generals Hooker and Palmer pursued, the next morning, along the Atlanta Road towards Ringgold. General Grant was with the most advanced pursuing column. These troops soon reached the Chickamauga Depot, easily dispersing a small force stationed upon a hill to repel them. The scene of ruin presented at the depot was one of the most desolate pictures of the war. The rebels had accumulated here, in a position which they

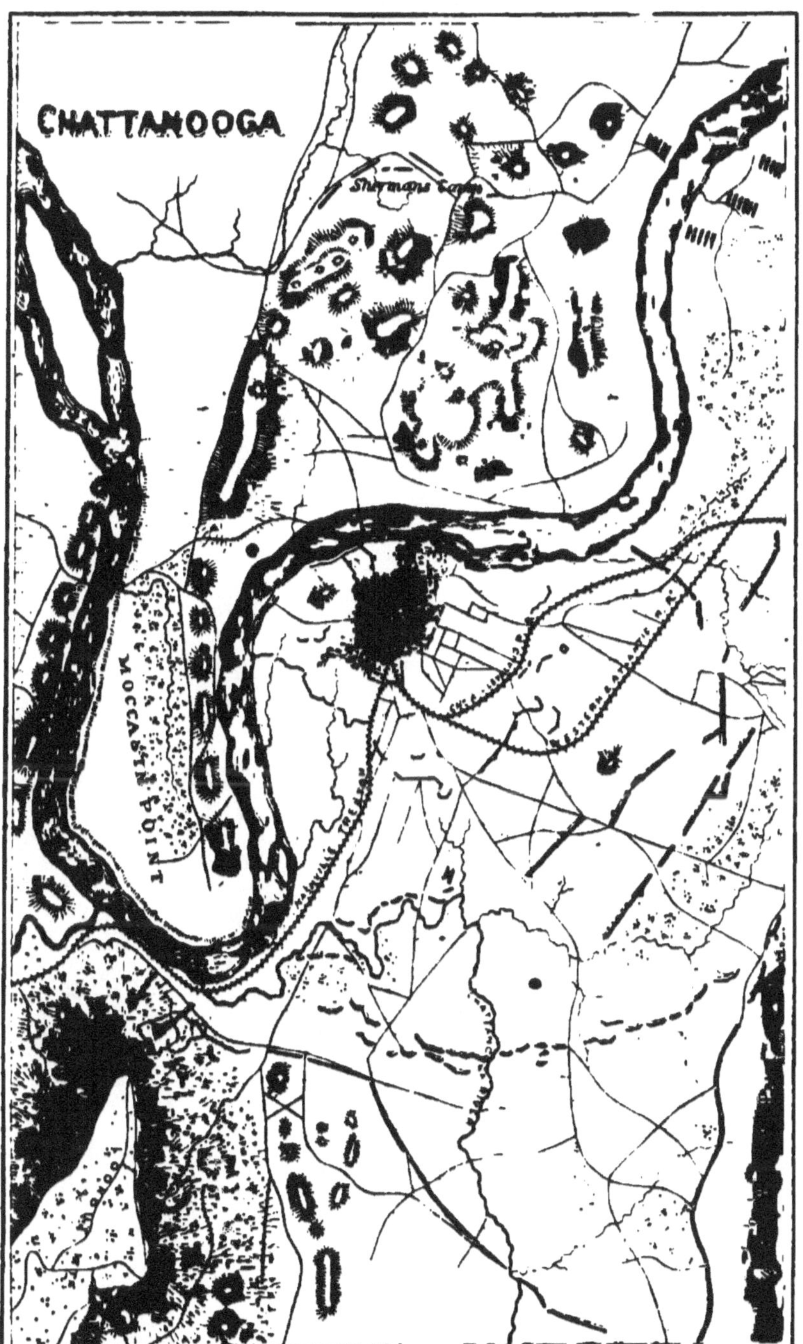

CHATTANOOGA
Sherman's Camp
MOCCASIN POINT

considered unassailable, provisions and ordnance stores for a vast army. In the dismay which their sudden rout created, they, in the darkness of the night, threw as many of these stores as possible upon their teams, and hurried them off. But as the dawn approached, and they heard the tramp of our advancing columns, they applied the torch to every thing that would burn, and fled with the utmost precipitation.

As a brigade of General Sherman's command, under Jefferson C. Davis, came up, the depot was found in flames. There were immense piles of burning corn-meal and bacon. Barrels and boxes were scattered around in the wildest confusion. Pontoon-boats, gun-carriages, wagons, were piled together in smouldering ruin. Food of all kinds — tea, coffee, sugar, flour, molasses — was mingled with cartridge-boxes, broken muskets, and small arms of every kind, — strewing the ground. There were boxes of ammunition here and there, — some broken open, with sparks flying all around them. There were shells and round shot, and caissons and limber-chests, and broken wheels and tongues of wagons, and tents, — every thing, indeed, which an army of a hundred thousand men could need for an almost permanent encampment.

The flight of the enemy had been so precipitate that he had not been able to destroy one-third of his commissary, quartermaster, and ordnance stores. And still it is estimated that the flames consumed property to the amount of fifty thousand dollars. Our troops succeeded in rescuing from the general destruction a pontoon-train of fifteen boats, two sixty-four-pounder rifled siege-guns, twenty army-wagons, sixty thousand rations of shelled corn, fifty thousand rations of corn-meal, four hundred gallons of molasses, one thousand pounds of bacon, together with a considerable quantity of ordnance stores, artillery, and small-arm ammunition.

All the day long, by several roads, the enemy fled: all the day long, by as many roads, the victors pursued. Our troops often marched through the camp-fires of the foe, still blazing upon the Chickamauga hills. The instigators of this infamous rebellion had cruelly deceived the ignorant masses at the South. It is stated on good authority, that Jefferson Davis, in a public speech at Memphis, in 1861, urging the deluded " poor whites " to rebellion, said, —

" You need not fear to cast off your allegiance to the General Government. There will be no war. The Yankees will never fight. One Southern man can at any time whip five Northern men, if he can only run fast enough to catch them."

This was the prevailing spirit in the South. There was need of Vicksburg and Chattanooga to undeceive them. There could never have been true alliance between the North and the South until the Southern people were disabused of these sentiments of ignorance and conceit. The war has proved that both parties are equally *brave:* upon any field where the numbers arrayed against each other are equal, the superior *intelligence* of the North comes in as a makeweight, and turns the scale in its favor.

The rebels ran : the patriots chased them. The route was strewed with the evidences of the precipitation of their flight. Wherever there was a brief conflict, the rebel dead were left unburied, and all the nameless *débris* of a routed army covered the ground for miles. Many prisoners were picked up by the way. Just at night, as

General Sherman, in the advance, was emerging from an extended swamp, he came upon the rear-guard of the foe. Quite a sharp battle ensued, which was soon terminated by the darkness. The town of Ringgold was but five miles distant. Just beyond this town, there was a gap, or gorge, through one of the mountain ranges with which this section of country abounds.

Ringgold was a small town, upon the Western and Atlantic Railroad, containing about twenty-five hundred inhabitants. It was situated just in front of the defile to which we have alluded. This gorge, through which the road passes, is scarcely a hundred yards in breadth at its widest point. The cliffs on either side rise to the height of four or five hundred feet. This gap is about half a mile long. Here the rebels prepared for a very desperate resistance, until their trains, and the main body of their army, could reach a safe distance on the other side of the ridge. Upon the summit of these hills they planted their batteries. They posted their sharpshooters and lines of infantry in the forest which fringed their sides. A battery was also placed in the mouth of the gap, supported by four lines of infantry. Four thousand troops were left to guard this pass, where it would seem that a few hundred men might long hold an army in check.

Here the enemy made quite a desperate stand. Our advance troops, under General Osterhaus, were driven back, being assailed from the front and on both flanks. This transient success quite animated the enemy, who were for the moment, and at that point, numerically far superior. They closely followed our retiring troops, pouring into their bosoms volley after volley with deadly effect. In this brief repulse, the Seventh Ohio, of Geary's division, lost all of its officers. Our men were exceed-

ingly reluctant to retire, even before the most overwhelming odds of a foe whom they had recently so signally
beaten.   Soon a couple of batteries came up to the
protection of our sorely-pressed troops, and, taking commanding positions, opened upon the enemy on the right
and the left.   They were thus thrown slightly into disorder, when a charge was made, and again they fled in great
confusion.   General Grant, as usual, was found at this
post of difficulty, and directed the battle.   The rebels
were driven through the gap, and our troops pursued them
into the valley beyond.   In this brief but desperate fight,
the foe lost a hundred and thirty in killed, who were
left dead upon the field.   We also took two pieces of
artillery and two hundred and thirty prisoners.   Our loss
was sixty killed and three hundred and seventy wounded.
The enemy was driven out of Tennessee into Georgia.
General Grant now retraced his steps, and sent General
Granger to march as rapidly as possible to the relief of
General Burnside.   A reconnoissance was, however,
made by General Hooker, in the direction of the flying
foe, for several miles.   Their line of retreat was found
strewn with broken caissons and wagons, and the bodies
of dead and dying men,—an awful picture of the miseries
which war engenders.

The campaign of Chattanooga was now virtually terminated.   As a campaign running through several months,
it was one of the most memorable in the world's history.
The battle of Chattanooga, occupying several days, will
ever be classed as among the most memorable in the
annals of war.   General Grant hurled his columns of
sixty thousand men, upon a field of battle thirteen miles
in extent, against forty-five thousand men apparently as
strongly intrenched as they could be by the united force
of the works of nature and of art.

The victory was not the result of accident. It was not to be attributed even to the marvellous gallantry of the soldiers, without which all plans are unavailing. No amount of courage could have carried those works, — behind which one man, by the rules of war, is considered equal to five before them, — but for the sagacity with which General Grant made all the arrangements, and guided every movement. In the military history of General Grant, it is well said, —

" Few battles have ever been won so strictly according to the plan laid down. Grant's instructions in advance would almost serve as a history of the contest. Hooker was to draw attention to the right, to seize and hold Lookout Mountain ; while Sherman, attacking Missionary Ridge on the extreme left, was still further to distract the enemy ; and then, when re-enforcements and attention should be drawn to both the rebel flanks, the centre was to be assaulted by the main body of Grant's force, under Thomas. Every thing happened exactly as had been foreseen.

" Each event proceeded regularly according to the calculation. Each subordinate carried out his part exactly as he had been ordered. Each army, brought from a distance, came upon the spot intended, crossed a river or climbed a mountain at the precise moment ; and even the unexpected emergencies of the fight contributed to the result as if anticipated and arranged. In this respect, Chattanooga was one of the most notable battles ever fought."

A woman who resided upon the plateau of Missionary Ridge said to one of our generals, " Before you all came up here, I asked General Bragg, ' What are you going to do with me, general ? ' He says to me, ' Lord !

madam, the Yankees will never dare to come up here.' And it was not fifteen minutes till you were all around here."

This victory was regarded as so signal as to call for national thanksgiving. President Lincoln issued the following proclamation : —

" Reliable information having been received that the insurgent force is retreating from East Tennessee, under circumstances rendering it probable that the Union forces cannot hereafter be dislodged from that important position, and esteeming this to be of high national consequence, I recommend that all loyal people do, on receipt of this information, assemble at their places of worship, and render special homage and gratitude to Almighty God for this great advancement of the national cause."

In reference to this campaign, General Halleck said, in his annual report, " Considering the strength of the rebel position, and the difficulty of storming his intrenchments, the battle of Chattanooga must be considered the most remarkable in history. Not only did the officers and men exhibit great skill and daring in their operations on the field, but the highest praise is due to the commanding general, for his admirable dispositions for dislodging the enemy from a position apparently impregnable. Moreover, by turning his right flank, and throwing him back upon Ringgold and Dalton, Sherman's forces were interposed between Bragg and Longstreet, so as to prevent any possibility of their forming a junction."

Upon the widely-extended battle-field of Chattanooga, General Grant lost five thousand six hundred and sixteen in killed, wounded, and missing. The loss of the enemy has never been ascertained. But General Grant captured six thousand one hundred and forty-two prisoners, forty pieces of artillery, sixty-nine artillery carriages and caissons, and seven thousand stand of small arms. It is supposed that the rebel army must have lost, in all, not less than fifteen thousand men.

General Burnside at Knoxville, a hundred miles distant, rendered very efficient aid towards the great victory at Chattanooga. He fell back gradually from his advanced positions, luring Longstreet on farther and farther from Bragg, so as to render his return to aid Bragg impossible. Indeed, he threw such obstacles in the way of the foe as to compel Bragg to send additional troops to Longstreet.

By the 17th of November, General Burnside had concentrated all his forces behind his intrenchments at Knoxville. The rebel army, pressing him closely, invested the city. The old fortifications were strengthened, new ones were erected, and preparations were made for the most determined resistance. Rifle-pits were dug, abatis of felled trees formed, and every thing done which skill could suggest to repel an assault or to sustain a siege. The great foe to be dreaded was famine.

General John G. Foster was on the way from Washington, to take with him a re-enforcement from Cumberland Gap. But the city was so closely besieged that he could not force his way through the enemy's lines. On the 28th, just after the termination of the pursuit of the rebels at Ringgold, General Grant telegraphed General Foster, —

" The fourth corps, Major-General Granger commanding, left here to-day, with orders to push with all possible speed through to Knoxville. Sherman is already in motion for Hiawassee, and will go all the way, if necessary. Communicate this information to Burnside as soon as possible, and at any cost, with directions to hold to the very last moment ; and we shall not only relieve him, but destroy Longstreet."

The next day he sent a despatch to Granger, urging him to press forward with the utmost expedition. In this he wrote, " On the 23d instant, General Burnside telegraphed that his rations would hold out ten or twelve days. At the end of this time, unless relieved from the outside, he must surrender or retreat. The latter will be an impossibility. You are now going for the purpose of relieving this garrison. You see the short time in which relief must be afforded, or be too late, and hence the necessity for forced marches. I want to urge upon you, in the strongest possible manner, the necessity of reaching Burnside in the shortest possible time."

General Grant's anxiety for General Burnside was sleepless. He knew that that gallant soldier would do every thing which mortal courage and endurance could achieve. But famine is a resistless foe. So great was General Grant's anxiety that he became dissatisfied with General Granger for not pressing forward more impetuously. On the 29th, he sent General Sherman, the most energetic of men, to supersede General Granger.

At the same time, he sent in duplicate the following despatch to the officer in command at Kingston. He was directed to be sure and let one of them fall into the hands of the enemy. The other was to be forwarded to General Burnside at all hazards, and at the earliest possible moment. The despatch was as follows : —

" I congratulate you on the tenacity with which you have thus far held out against vastly superior forces.

Do not be forced into surrender by short rations. Take
all the citizens have, to enable you to hold out yet a few
days longer. As soon as you are relieved from the presence of the enemy, you can replace to them every thing
taken from them. Within a few days, you will be relieved. There are now three columns in motion for
your relief, — one from here, moving up the south bank
of the river, under Sherman; one from Decherd, under
Elliott; and one from Cumberland Gap, under Foster.
These three columns will be able to crush Longstreet's
forces, or drive them from the valley, and must all of
them be within twenty-four hours' march of you by the
time this reaches you, supposing you to get it on Tuesday the 1st instant."

CHAPTER XVI.

THE RELIEF OF KNOXVILLE.

The Siege of Knoxville. — Preparations for Defence. — Rebel Attack upon
Fort Sanders. — Bloody Repulse. — Flight of Longstreet. — Arrival of
Sherman. — Grant's Congratulatory Order. — His Energy. — Testimony
of the Indian Chief. — National Testimonials. — Speeches in Congress.
— Medal. — Sherman's Raid. — Exploring Mountain Passes. — Visit to
St. Louis.

NOXVILLE is situated on the north bank
of the Holston River. On the south it is
protected from assault by the stream. The
rebels crossed the river, to attack the city
from the north, and invested it in a circu-
lar line of earthworks from the river above to the river
below the city. In various ways, intelligence was kept
up with General Grant; and occasionally a forage-train
ran in with a small supply of food.

The beleaguered soldiers heard, with great exultation,
of the prosperous state of affairs at Chattanooga. The
beleaguering host received the same tidings with dismay.
Longstreet understood full well that relief would be immediately despatched to Burnside, should success crown
our arms at Chattanooga. He could consequently no
longer rely upon the slow operations of a siege. His
only chance of capturing Knoxville was to take it by
immediate and direct assault. Indeed, he found sud-

denly his own condition to be one of extreme peril. He was in danger of being cut off from all possibility of retreat, and of being destroyed, or captured, with his whole command.

General Burnside's line of defence closely surrounded the city. On the north-east corner of that line, there was a heavy swell of land, upon which he planted a battery protected by effective earthworks. The post was named Fort Sanders, in honor of the distinguished patriot general who fell in the early part of the siege. As the possession of that eminence would enable the enemy to command the city, the position had been fortified with the utmost care. A dense forest covered the sides of the hill. These trees were felled, presenting an abatis of timber and sharpened branches through which it would be very difficult for the foe to penetrate.

Between this network of forest-trees and the fort, a space had been cleared, two or three hundred yards in width, so as to afford free range for grape and canister. Across this open space, wires had been stretched, so as to be imperceptible to the eye. When Longstreet heard of the defeat of Bragg, he felt the necessity of immediate and desperate action, as his only escape from ruin. Accordingly, he ordered this work to be stormed.

It was Saturday night, Nov. 28. The perilous task was assigned to four brigades of picked regiments. In the night, these men, with heroism which we cannot but admire, deeply as we condemn their cause, worked their way painfully through the abatis until they reached the clearing at its edge. Here they slept upon their arms, awaiting the dawn of the morning which would consign many of them to a sleep from which there would be no earthly waking. They were then almost within rifle-range of our works. Their sharpshooters were pushed forward in the darkness some rods in advance, where they hastily dug rifle-pits for their protection.

Our watchful troops were prepared for the onset. With the first light of the sabbath morning, the enemy opened a furious fire upon the fort with his artillery, hoping to disable our guns. The fire was continued for nearly half an hour, without producing any serious effect. Our batteries remained silent. The men were waiting for the assault, when every discharge would surely accomplish its mission. After the bombardment, the signal for the charge was given. A heavy column, which had been concentrated for the purpose, emerged from the abatis upon the cleared space, at the full run. A scene ensued of carnage and of desperate courage unsurpassed during the war.

As the rebels rushed across the open space, our batteries opened upon them, at point-blank range, in rapid, deadly discharge of grape and canister, while the infantry kept up an incessant fire of well-aimed bullets. Not a shot was thrown away. It was an awful slaughter. Those in the front of the column were tripped up by the concealed wires. But the weight of the column was such, pressed forward by the frenzy of battle, that those who were thrown down by the wires, or who fell torn by the bullet or the shell, were trampled beneath the heels of their comrades, who were pressed onward by those behind. It was an awful scene for a peaceful sabbath morning. The thunders of artillery, the rattle of musketry, the explosion of shells, and the whiz of Minie balls, blended with the half-delirious shouts of onset, the shrieks of the wounded trampled upon, and the groans of the dying.

But Pity must close her eyes and deafen her ears upon

the field of battle. Over the dead and over the wounded the trampling column swept on. They reached the ditch. They swarmed through it, endeavoring to climb the parapet. Hand-grenades were thrown into the midst of the struggling mass, exploding with horrible effect. The cannon opened upon them with triple rounds of canister. The infantry shot, or with the butts of their muskets knocked down, every head which appeared above the parapet. One rebel reached the summit, and planted upon it the Confederate flag. A yell of triumph burst from the lips of his comrades. The next moment he fell a corpse, and the rebel flag followed him into the ditch. Not a rebel entered the fort alive. Hundreds lay dead before it.

A cross-fire now swept the foe and the whole space over which they had advanced and by which alone they could retreat. Nearly all who entered the ditch were killed. Five hundred, finding it impossible to escape over an open field swept by our cannon, surrendered. The ground between the fort and the rebel line was strewn with the dead, more than a thousand having fallen in that hour of carnage. General Burnside lost but thirteen men. The reason for this great disparity is to be attributed, first, to the admirable system of defensive works constructed by the engineers, Generals O. M. Poe and O. E. Babcock; and, secondly, to the genius and heroism of Lieutenant Samuel Benjamin, who commanded the fort, and who inspired the men with his own spirit in conducting the defence. He had less than three hundred men and but eleven guns. He was assailed by four brigades of Longstreet's corps, besides two of Buckner's division, which were held as reserves.

It was but half an hour after this terrible repulse, when

Longstreet received a despatch from Jefferson Davis, the rebel president, informing him of the entire discomfiture of Bragg's army, and directing him to hasten to his support. But Longstreet sagaciously decided that the best way to help Bragg was to remain where he was. Should Grant continue to pursue the fugitive army, in a few days more Burnside would be starved out, and his whole army of fifteen thousand men would fall into the hands of the victor. This would be quite a solace for the loss of Chattanooga. On the other hand, should General Grant feel constrained to hasten to the relief of Burnside, then it would be necessary for him to relinquish the pursuit of Bragg, and the fugitive army might escape.

Sherman was now upon the impetuous advance. Longstreet was cut off from his supplies, and was compelled to subsist off the country already ravaged by the pillage and desolations of war. Just then the despatch, which Grant had designed for him, fell into his hands. It told him that he had not a moment to lose. He therefore hurriedly raised the siege, and commenced his march towards the north-east, to take refuge with the rebel bands in Virginia. On the 5th of December, Sherman and Howard reached Marysville, within a day's march of Knoxville. Here they received the information that Longstreet had raised the siege of Knoxville, and was in full retreat towards Virginia. Sherman sent the following note to Burnside : —

"I am here, and can bring twenty-five-thousand men into Knoxville to-morrow. But, Longstreet having retreated, I feel disposed to stop; for a stern chase is a long one. But I will do all that is possible. Without you specify that you want troops, I will let mine rest to-morrow, and ride to see you."

He rode over to Knoxville the next morning, and held an interview with General Burnside. It must have been a happy hour for both of these illustrious men, sharing in the joys of victory as they had alike shared the perils, toils, and privations of the conflict. But the great struggle was not yet terminated. Scarcely an hour could be given to repose. The vanquished rebels were still malignant and determined. Weary months of stern campaigning were yet before these chieftains ere the blessed hour of peace could dawn.

In this interview, arrangements were made for General Granger, with his command, to enter Knoxville, and garrison the works there. General Burnside was to pursue Longstreet on his retreat, and annoy him in every possible way. Sherman, with the rest of his army, was to return to Chattanooga. There was some apprehension that Bragg, emboldened by the absence of so large a force from the Union army, might turn, and assume the offensive. Two days after, on the 8th, General Grant received from President Lincoln the following despatch : —

"Understanding that your lodgment at Chattanooga and at Knoxville is now secure, I wish to tender you, and all under your command, my more than thanks, my profoundest gratitude, for the skill, courage, and perseverance with which you and they, over so great difficulties, have effected that important object. God bless you all !"

It is difficult to over-estimate the importance of these great achievements. The nation recognized the fact that it was to the genius of General Grant that we were indebted for them. The whole of Tennessee was liberated from rebel thraldom; the rebel army, which from the heights of Lookout Mountain had been menacing the North, was driven, stripped, hungry, and humiliated, into the extreme South; the rebel line of communication between the Atlantic and the Mississippi was hopelessly sundered. The most sanguine could not dream of recovering that which had been thus lost. The mountain fastnesses upon which they had relied as impregnable had been captured. The majestic rivers, flowing through the heart of the territory, which had been so insolently claimed by the Confederacy, were ploughed by our gunboats. The fields upon whose inexhaustible fertility the rebels had relied for the support of their armies had now become the granaries of the Government. The rebels no longer fought animated by hope: their only impulse was the inspiration of despair.

General Grant, on the 10th of December, issued the following congratulatory order to his troops: —

"The general commanding takes the opportunity of returning his sincere thanks and congratulations to the brave armies of the Cumberland, the Ohio, and the Tennessee, and their comrades from the Potomac, for the recent splendid and decisive successes achieved over the enemy. In a short time you have recovered from him the control of the Tennessee River, from Bridgeport to Knoxville. You dislodged him from his great stronghold upon Lookout Mountain; drove him from Chattanooga Valley; wrested from his determined grasp the possession of Missionary Ridge; repelled, with heavy loss to him, his repeated assaults upon Knoxville; forced him to raise the siege there, driving him, at all points utterly routed and discomfited, beyond the limits of the State.

" By your noble heroism and determined courage you have most effectually defeated the plans of the enemy for regaining possession of the States of Kentucky and Tennessee. You have secured positions from which no rebellious power can drive or dislodge you. For all this the general commanding thanks you collectively and individually. The loyal people of the United States thank and bless you. Their hopes and prayers against this unholy rebellion are with you daily. Their faith in you will not be in vain. Their hopes will not be blasted. Their prayers to Almighty God will be answered. You will yet go to other fields of strife; and, with the invincible bravery, and unflinching loyalty to justice and right, which have characterized you in the past, you will prove that no enemy can withstand you, and that no defences, however formidable, can check your onward march."

We seldom have a more striking exemplification of the power of the mind triumphing over the body, than General Grant presented during these hours of exhausting care and toil. He was then in feeble health, still suffering severely from his fall at New Orleans. He was so emaciated, and walked so feebly, that many feared he would never recover. Still, with all this bodily languor and suffering, his mind retained its accustomed energies, and he worked as indefatigably as if in the enjoyment of vigorous health.

There was an Indian chieftain of the Tonawanda Tribe, Colonel Ely S. Parker, who was on General Grant's staff. In a communication to "The Indianapolis Journal," he gives the following testimony to General Grant's personal bearing during these battles:—

" I need not describe to you the recent battle of Chattanooga. The papers have given every possible detail concerning it. I can only say I saw it all, and was in the five days' fight. It has been a matter of universal wonder in this army, that General Grant himself was not killed, and that no more accidents occurred to his staff; for the general was always in the front, and perfectly heedless of the storm of hissing bullets and screaming shells flying around him. IIis apparent want of sensibility does not arise from heedlessness, heartlessness, or vain military affectation, but from a sense of the responsibility resting upon him when in battle.

"When at Ringgold, we rode for half a mile in the face of the enemy, under an incessant fire of cannon and musketry, — nor did we ride fast, but upon an ordinary trot, — and not once, do I believe, did it enter the general's mind that he was in danger. I was by his side, and watched him closely. In riding that distance we were going to the front; and I could see that he was studying the positions of the two armies, and, of course, planning how to defeat the enemy, who were here making a most desperate stand, and were slaughtering our men fearfully. After defeating and driving the enemy here, we returned to Chattanooga.

"Another feature in General Grant's personal movements is, that he requires no escort beyond his staff, so regardless of danger is he. Roads are almost useless to him; for he takes short cuts through fields and woods, and will swim his horse through almost any stream which obstructs his way. Nor does it make any difference with him whether he has daylight for his movements; for he will ride from breakfast until two o'clock in the morning, and that, too, without eating. The next day he will repeat the dose, until he finishes his work. Now, such things come hard upon the staff; but they have learned how to bear it."

Immediately upon the meeting of Congress, soon after these events, both houses passed a resolution, "That the thanks of Congress be, and they hereby are, presented to Major-General Ulysses S. Grant, and through him to the officers and soldiers who have fought under his command during this rebellion, for their gallantry and good conduct in the battles in which they have been engaged ; and that the President of the United States be requested to cause a gold medal to be struck, with suitable emblems, devices, and inscriptions, to be presented to Major-General Grant."

This medal, the tribute of a nation's admiration, was designed by Leutze. On one side there was a profile likeness of General Grant, surrounded by a laurel wreath. His name, and the year of his victories, were inscribed upon it ; and the whole was surrounded by a galaxy of stars. On the opposite side was the figure of Fame, gracefully seated on the American Eagle, which, with outspread wings, seemed preparing for flight. In her right hand she held the symbolical trumpet. With her left hand she presented a scroll, on which were inscribed the names of, Corinth, Vicksburg, Mississippi River, and Chattanooga. On her head there was a helmet, ornamented in Indian fashion, with feathers radiating from it. In front of the eagle, its breast resting against it, was the emblematical shield of the United States ; beneath were sprigs of pine and palm twined together, indicative of the union of the North and South. Over all, in a curved line, were the words, " Proclaim liberty throughout all the land."

The States of New York and Ohio passed resolutions of thanks to General Grant and his army, and ordered the resolutions to be engrossed in their official records.

General Grant was not at all disposed to rest after the fatigue of the campaign of Chattanooga. He gathered up his strength to pursue the war with unabated vigor. He was still oppressed with innumerable cares. Inclement winter had come. The gathering of such large armies had exhausted the resources of the country. Our troops were very far from their base of supplies. The fall in the rivers had rendered them no longer navigable. The roads, encumbered with snow and ice, were almost impassable. And yet armies were to be fed and clothed. It is a great mistake to suppose that the skill of a general is confined to the ability with which he handles his troops upon the field of battle. The preliminary cares call for the highest exercise of earthly wisdom.

Many of General Grant's soldiers were without shoes; many had but a single blanket; the time of service of a large number of volunteer troops had expired. In the midst of these cares, which seem to have been enough to crush the strongest man, General Grant was planning a cavalry raid to sweep the State of Mississippi. On the 23d of December, he wrote to General Halleck, —

" I am now collecting as large a cavalry force as can be spared, at Savannah, Tenn., to cross the Tennessee River, and co-operate with the cavalry from Hurlbut's command, in clearing out entirely the forces now collecting in West Tennessee under Forrest. It is the design that the cavalry, after finishing the work they first start upon, shall push south through East Mississippi, and destroy the Mobile Road as far south as they can. Sherman goes to Memphis and Vicksburg in person, and will have Grenada visited, and such other points on the Mississippi Central Railroad as may require it. I want the State of Mississippi so visited that large armies cannot traverse there this winter."

About three weeks after this, he wrote, " Sherman has

gone down the Mississippi to collect at Vicksburg all the force that can be spared for a separate movement from the Mississippi. He will probably have ready, by the 24th of this month, a force of twenty thousand men. I shall direct Sherman, therefore, to move out to Meridian with his spare force, the cavalry going from Corinth, and destroy the roads east and south of there so effectually that the enemy will not attempt to rebuild them during the rebellion.

" He will then return, unless opportunity of going into Mobile with the force he has appears perfectly plain. Owing to a large number of veterans furloughed, I will not be able to do more at Chattanooga than to threaten an advance, and try to detain the force now in Thomas's front. Sherman will be instructed, whilst left with these large discretionary powers, to take no extra hazard of losing his army, or of getting it crippled too much for service in the spring.

" I look upon the next line for me to secure, to be that from Chattanooga to Mobile; Montgomery and Atlanta being the important intermediate points. To do this, large supplies must be secured on the Tennessee River, so as to be independent of the railroad from here (Nashville) to the Tennessee, for a considerable length of time. Mobile would be a second base. The destruction which Sherman will do the roads around Meridian will be of material importance to us in preventing the enemy from drawing supplies from Mississippi, and in clearing that section of all large bodies of rebel troops. I do not look upon any points, except Mobile in the south and the Tennessee River in the north, as presenting practicable starting-points from which to operate against Atlanta and Montgomery."

General Grant was now directing the complicated movements of three armies, extending over a region of more than a thousand miles. General Thomas was at Chattanooga, threatening Bragg. General Schofield was at Knoxville, keeping a close watch upon Longstreet. And General Sherman was preparing to advance into the interior of Mississippi. All looked to General Grant for instructions.

We have not space to describe these movements. Sherman's raid into Mississippi was a magnificent campaign. He drove the rebels out of the State, and destroyed the only remaining railroads. He supported his army upon the rebel stores which he captured, and brought back with his triumphant columns four hundred prisoners, five thousand negroes, a thousand white refugees, and three thousand animals. All this was accomplished in about four weeks, during which time he marched nearly four hundred miles. His losses were but twenty-one killed and a hundred and forty-nine wounded and missing.

About this time General Grant decided to make a tour through the outposts of his army. He visited Nashville, remaining only long enough to infuse new energy into the construction of railroad communications with Chattanooga. He then repaired to Knoxville. Being anxious to ascertain the condition of the roads between that place and Louisville, by the way of Cumberland Gap, he resolved to examine the route in person. It was midwinter, and it was bitterly cold among the mountains. Yet he traversed the long route on horseback, encountering the lowest temperature and the deepest snow which had been experienced there for many years.

It was indeed a journey of hardship and of peril. The officers who accompanied him were compelled often to wade through the drifted snow, driving their half-frozen horses before them. At Lexington, the now illustrious general was received with the most signal demonstrations of respect and admiration. Crowds from the surrounding country rushed to get sight of him. They thronged him, and clamored for a speech. One of his staff, General Leslie Coombs, mounted a chair and said, —

" General Grant has told me, in confidence, that he never made a speech, knows nothing about speech-making, and has no disposition to learn."

The latter part of January he visited St. Louis, to see one of his children, who was dangerously sick. Though he entered the city in the most unobtrusive way, the intelligence of his arrival spread rapidly, and crowds gathered around the hotel to see him. He was invited to a public dinner. His reply was characteristic : —

" Your highly complimentary invitation to meet old acquaintances, and make new ones, at a dinner to be given by citizens of St. Louis, is just received. I will state that I have only visited St. Louis on this occasion to see a sick child. Finding, however, that he has passed the crisis of his disease, and is pronounced out of danger by his physicians, I accept the invitation. My stay in this city will be short, — probably not beyond the first proximo. On to-morrow I shall be engaged. Any other day of my stay here, and any place selected by the citizens of St. Louis, it will be agreeable for me to meet them.

" I have the honor to be, very respectfully, your obedient servant,   " U. S. GRANT."

Over two hundred guests met in the spacious hall at the Lindell Hotel, to confer honor upon the distinguished visitor. The room was richly decorated, and General Grant was not a little embarrassed by the attentions which were lavished upon him. When the toast was given, " Our distinguished guest, Major-General Grant," the band struck up " Hail to the Chief." General Grant arose and said,—

" Gentlemen, in response it will be impossible for me to do more than to thank you."

In the evening he was serenaded; and an immense crowd surrounded the hotel, anxious to catch a sight of the hero, and clamorous for a speech. After some delay, General Grant stepped upon the balcony, and taking off his hat, in the midst of profoundest silence, said,—

" Gentlemen, I thank you for this honor. I cannot make a speech. It is something I have never done, and never intend to do ; and I beg you will excuse me."

" Speech, speech ! " shouted the multitude. Several gentlemen urged the general to say at least a few words. One earnest friend, placing his hand upon General Grant's shoulder, said, " Tell them you can fight for them, but cannot talk for them. Do tell them that." — " I must get some one else to say that for me," General Grant replied. Then, leaning over the railing, he said, slowly, deliberately, firmly,—

" Gentlemen, making speeches is not my business. I never did it in my life, and never will. I thank you, however, for your attendance here."

He then bowed and retired.

CHAPTER XVII.

Revival of the Grade of Lieutenant-General. — Speech of Hon. Mr. Farnsworth. — Of Hon. Mr. Washburne. — Action of Congress. — General Grant Nominated by the President. — His Letter to Sherman. — The Reply. — Public Enthusiasm. — Conferring the Commission. — New Plans for the Conduct of the War.

N the 4th of February, 1864, Congress passed a bill, which had been carefully matured by the military committee of the House, reviving in the army of the United States the grade of lieutenant-general, and authorizing the president to confer that rank on the major-general most distinguished for courage, skill, and ability. It was universally understood that the bill was designed to have the honor conferred upon General Grant. The Hon. Mr. Farnsworth, in an address to the House on the occasion, said, —

" We are now near the close of the third year of this war; and while it is true that many generals in the army may be up to-day and down to-morrow, and that their fortunes fluctuate, it is not true of the general to whom this legislation applies. His star has been steadily rising. He has been growing greater and greater day by day. By his masterly ability he now stands — without saying any thing to the disparagement of other generals — head and shoulders over every other general in the army of the United States. He has been tried long enough; and, if his star were to go down to-morrow, he has still done enough to entitle him to this prize."

Hon. Mr. Washburne, of Illinois, at the same time rendered the following tribute to the genius and merits of General Grant: —

" I am not here to speak for General Grant. No man, with his consent, has ever mentioned his name in connection with any position. I say what I know to be true, when I allege that every promotion he has received, since he first entered the service to put down this rebellion, was moved without his knowledge or consent. And in regard to this very matter of lieutenant-general, after the bill was introduced, and his name mentioned in connection therewith, he wrote me that he had been highly honored already by the Government, and did not ask or deserve any thing more in the shape of honors or promotion; and that success over the enemy was what he craved above every thing else; that he only desired to hold such an influence over those under his command as to use them to the best advantage to secure that end.

" Look at what this man has done for his country, for humanity and civilization, — this modest and unpretending general. He has fought more battles, and won more victories, than any man living. He has captured more prisoners, and taken more guns, than any general of modern times. When his blue legions crowned the crest of Vicksburg, and the hosts of Rebeldom laid their arms at the feet of this great conqueror, the rebel Confederacy was cut in twain, and the backbone of the Rebellion was broken.

" And that which must ever be regarded as the most

extraordinary feature of this campaign is the astounding fact, that, when General Grant landed in the State of Mississippi, and made his campaign in the enemy's country, he had a smaller force than the enemy. To his indomitable courage and energy, to his unparalleled celerity of movement, striking the enemy in detail and beating him on every field, is the country indebted for those wonderful successes of that campaign which have not only challenged the gratitude and admiration of our own countrymen, but the admiration of the best military men of all nations."

The bill reviving the grade of lieutenant-general passed both Houses almost unanimously. President Lincoln gave it his signature, and immediately nominated General Grant to that office. The Senate promptly confirmed the nomination.

" Grant himself used no influence," says General Badeau, " wrote no line, spoke no word, to bring about the result. I was with him while the bill was being debated, and spoke to him more than once upon the subject. He never manifested any anxiety, or even desire, for the success of the bill ; nor did he ever seem to shrink from the responsibilities it would impose upon him. If the country chose to call him to higher spheres and more important services, whatever ability or energy he possessed he was willing to devote to the task. If, on the contrary, he had been left at the post which he then held, he would not have felt a pang of disappointed pride." *

On the 3d of March, he was summoned to Washington by the secretary of war, to receive the credentials, and enter upon the duties, of his new office. As he left the

---

* Military History of Uylsses S. Grant, by Adam Badeau, vol. i., p. 570.

army with the intention of returning immediately to his command, he sent the following letter to his friend and efficient co-operator, General Sherman : —

"Dear Sherman, — The bill reviving the grade of lieutenant-general has become a law, and my name has been sent to the Senate for the place. I now receive orders to report to Washington immediately in person, which indicates a confirmation, or a likelihood of confirmation. I start in the morning to comply with the order.

" Whilst I have been eminently successful in this war, in at least gaining the confidence of the public, no one feels more than I how much of this success is due to the energy, skill, and the harmonious putting forth of that energy and skill, of those whom it has been my good fortune to have occupying subordinate positions under me.

" There are many officers to whom these remarks are applicable to a greater or less degree, proportionate to their ability as soldiers ; but what I want is to express my thanks to you and McPherson, as the men to whom, above all others, I feel indebted for whatever I have had of success.

" How far your advice and assistance have been of help to me, you know. How far your execution of whatever has been given you to do entitles you to the reward I am receiving, you cannot know as well as I.

" I feel all the gratitude this letter would express, giving it the most flattering construction. The word *you*, I use in the plural, intending it for McPherson also. I would write to him, and will some day ; but, starting in the morning, I do not know that I will find time just now.

" Your friend,

" U. S. Grant."

This letter was forwarded to General Sherman, at Memphis. His reply, on the 10th of March, is so noble, and so beautifully reflects the friendship existing between these illustrious men, that we cannot refrain from giving it entire : —

" DEAR GENERAL, — I have your more than kind and characteristic letter of the 4th instant. I will send a copy to General McPherson at once.

" You do yourself injustice, and us too much honor, in assigning to us too large a share of the merits which have led to your high advancement. I know you approve the friendship I have ever proffered to you, and will permit me to continue, as heretofore, to manifest it on all proper occasions.

" You are now Washington's legitimate successor, and occupy a position of almost dangerous elevation ; but if you can continue, as heretofore, to be yourself, — simple, honest, and unpretending, — you will enjoy through life the respect and love of friends, and the homage of millions of human beings who will award you a large share in securing to them and their descendants a government of law and stability.

" I repeat, you do General McPherson and myself too much honor. At Belmont, you manifested your traits, neither of us being near. At Donelson also, you illustrated your whole character. I was not near, and General McPherson was in too subordinate a capacity to influence you.

" Until you had won Donelson, I confess I was almost cowed by the terrible array of anarchical elements that presented themselves at every point ; but that admitted a ray of light I have followed since. I believe you are as brave, patriotic, and just as the great prototype, Washington ; as unselfish, kind-hearted, and honest as a man should be ; but the chief characteristic is the simple faith in success you have always manifested, which I can liken to nothing else than the faith a Christian has in the Saviour.

"This faith gave you the victory at Shiloh and at Vicksburg. Also, when you have completed your best preparations, you go into battle without hesitation, as at Chattanooga, — no doubts, no reserves ; and, I tell you, it was this which made us act with confidence.

"My only point of doubt was in your knowledge of grand strategy, and of books of science and of history ; but I confess your common-sense seems to have supplied all these.

"Now, as to the future. Don't stay in Washington. Come West : take to yourself the whole Mississippi Valley. Let us make it dead sure ; and, I tell you, the Atlantic slopes and Pacific shores will follow its destiny as surely as the limbs of a tree live or die with the main trunk. We have done much, but still much remains. Time, and time's influence, are with us. We could almost afford to sit still, and let these influences work.

"Here lies the seat of the coming empire ; and from the West, when our task is done, we will make short work of Charleston and Richmond and the impoverished coast of the Atlantic.   "Your sincere friend,

"W. T. Sherman."

In this whole transaction, there seems to have been a singular absence of all those petty jealousies and rivalries which so often dishonor human nature. On General Grant's journey to Washington, he received a despatch, very magnanimous in its tone, from General Halleck, whom he was to supersede. It was as follows : —

" The Secretary of War directs me to say that your commission as lieutenant-general is signed, and will be delivered to you on your arrival at the War Department. I sincerely congratulate you on this recognition of your distinguished and meritorious services."

General Grant's journey to Washington was made as rapidly as possible, in special trains. His fame now filled the land. At every depot, crowds were gathered to catch a glimpse of one whose achievements were so illustrious, and whose name was on all lips. Wherever he appeared, enthusiastic cheers greeted him. Upon his arrival in Washington, he quietly repaired to Willard's Hotel, and, unobserved, took a seat at a table in the dining-room, with his son by his side. A gentleman recognized him, and, rising, informed the guests that General Ulysses S. Grant sat at the table. Simultaneously, and as by an instinctive impulse, all rose; and cheer upon cheer rang through the hall. Many pressed around him to take him by the hand; and the crowd immediately became so great that it was with difficulty he could make his way to his private apartment.

In the evening he attended the president's levee at the White House. Here the enthusiasm which his presence created was very great. He engrossed the attention of the whole company. The crowd pressed him to an adjacent sofa, and lifted him from his feet, until he was compelled to stand where all could see him. Such a scene of enthusiasm was never before witnessed in the presidential mansion. President Lincoln, magnanimous, generous, unselfish, whose soul was never sullied with a jealous thought, stood by the side of Grant, and joined as heartily as any of the company with cheer after cheer in tribute to the merits of this great and good man.

But these ovations were only painful to General Grant. He had no taste for pageantry, and his modest nature shrank from these displays of admiration and homage. Though by no means insensible to manifestations of confidence and affection, he still wished to avoid them. Upon retiring that night from the levee, he said to a friend, —

"I hope to get away from Washington as soon as possible, for I am tired of the show-business already."

The next day, March the 9th, was the time appointed by President Lincoln for presenting him his commission as lieutenant-general. The impressive scene took place in the executive chamber, with true republican simplicity. All the cabinet were present, and also several other distinguished invited guests. President Lincoln rose from his chair, and thus addressed him : —

"General Grant, the nation's approbation of what you have already done, and its reliance on you for what remains to do in the existing great struggle, is now presented, with this commission constituting you *Lieutenant-General* of the Army of the United States. With this high honor devolves on you a corresponding responsibility. As the country here intrusts you, so under God it will sustain you. I scarcely need add, that with what I here speak for the nation goes my own hearty personal concurrence."

General Grant, taking the commission in his hand, replied, —

"Mr. President, I accept this commission with gratitude for the high honor conferred. With the aid of the noble armies who have fought on so many fields for our common country, it will be my earnest endeavor not to disappoint your expectations. I feel the full weight

of the responsibility now devolving upon me. I know
that, if it is properly met, it will be due to these armies,
and, above all, to the favor of that Providence which
leads both nations and men."

It is said that the ladies wished to have a ball in connection with the grand review of the Army of the Potomac, which was about to take place.

"Ladies," said the general, fixing his eyes sadly upon
them, and speaking in a very deliberate and serious tone
of voice, "this thing must be stopped. I am not a cynic,
and enjoy rational pleasures as well as any one else;
but I would ask you, in all candor and gentleness, if this
is a time for music and dancing and feasting among
officers in the army? Is our country in a condition to
call for such things at present? Do army balls inspire
our troops with courage in the field? Do they soothe
our sick and wounded in the hospitals?"   .

These ladies were truly patriotic; and it is but just to
them to record that they instantly recognized the propriety of General Grant's views, and gave to them their
cordial acquiescence.

All the energies of General Grant were now roused to
bring the war as speedily as possible to a triumphant
close. A council of war was held at the seat of government. Here General Grant was the first to propose that
it was essential to the defeat of the Rebellion that Richmond, its nominal capital, should be taken, that the
whole power of our scattered armies should be concentrated for the accomplishment of that decisive end. The
plan was his in its conception: the means for its attainment were all arranged by his mind. Orders were at
once despatched for the assembling of all the divisions of
the army, which could possibly be spared from other en-

gagements, to march upon Richmond. The continent seemed to shake beneath the tramp of these military hosts. Our steamers were loaded, our railroad trains were freighted, and all our great roads were thronged, with the gathering bands of war.

General Grant was so unassuming in his deportment, so simple and unostentatious in his movements, that he seldom excited an emotion of jealousy. Nearly all his subordinate officers had so much confidence in his justice, his disinterestedness, and his ability, that they co-operated harmoniously in carrying out his plans. One mind inspired the nation. Not often in the history of the world has any individual been invested with so much power. General Grant immediately took the field. He established his humble headquarters at Culpeper Courthouse, in the Old Dominion, not far from Washington; and his orders flew along the wires, all over our broad land, with lightning rapidity. Prodigious were the interests which he was compelled to grasp, and the combinations he was called upon to perform.

FREDERICSBURG
WILDERNESS
Howling Green
Shotsylvania C.H.
Rapidan R.
Pamunky
New Kent
Fair Oaks
RICHMOND
Orange C.H.
MANCHESTER
Coochland
James R.
Chesterfield
PETERSB9.
Palmyra
Charlottesville
Amelia C.H.
Cumberland C.H.
Maysville
Nottoway C.H.
Pr.Edward C.H.
Surrender of Genl. Lee
Annomattox C.H.
Annomattox
Marysville
Linchburg
Boyoton
CENTRAL
VIRGINIA

CHAPTER XVIII.

THE BATTLES OF THE WILDERNESS.

The Plan of the Campaigns. — Crossing the Rapidan. — The First Day's Battle. — Picturesque Spectacle. — The Second Day's Battle. — The Third Day's Battle. — Peculiarity of the Conflict. — Terrible Losses. — Battle of Spottsylvania Court-house. — Defeat of the Rebels. — Death of Wadsworth and Sedgwick. — Anecdotes of General Grant.

ENERAL Lee was at this time strongly intrenched, with a force of about a hundred thousand men, upon the south banks of the Rapidan River. He was there, with a well-disciplined army, protecting Richmond, and seriously threatening Washington and the neighboring northern cities of Philadelphia and Baltimore. The general plan of operations, as adopted by General Grant, consisted in reality of a series of campaigns, decisive and terrible, which were successfully carried out, and which terminated the war in an overwhelming and irreparable defeat to the rebels. Washington was to be covered, from any rebel raid through the Valley of the Shenandoah, by an adequate force under General Sigel, who had acquired a high reputation at Pea Ridge and in other battles in the West. Another large force, of both white and colored troops, under General Butler, after making a feint to attack Richmond by the way of the York River

and the Chickahominy, was suddenly to return in transports, descending the York River, rounding the point at Fortress Monroe, and ascending the James River, to land as near City Point as possible; thus menacing Richmond from the south and east.

This movement was sure to accomplish one of two results.   Should the rebels detach a large force from Richmond to re-enforce Lee upon the Rapidan, where General Grant was menacing him with the rapidly-increasing Army of the Potomac, then General Butler would move promptly upon the rebel capital.   On the other hand, should the rebels draw re-enforcements from Lee's army to concentrate an overwhelming force at Richmond to crush General Butler, then General Butler was to intrench himself in the best position he could select, and hold that army before him, so that Lee's army, upon the Rapidan, would be exposed to the force General Grant was gathering to overwhelm it.

In the mean time General Sherman, from Chattanooga, was to press with all vigor upon the rebel army which had fled into Georgia, so that no re-enforcements could be sent from there to the aid of Lee at Richmond.   Such was the origin of that magnificent campaign, so heroically achieved by General Sherman in his march from Chattanooga to Savannah.   Having cut the Rebellion in two, having destroyed its southern armies and its resources, General Sherman was to sweep northward with his triumphant host, capturing Charleston, Columbia, Wilmington, and all the other important rebel positions by the way, till his banners should again be united with those of General Grant around the walls of Richmond. Never was there a more bold and grand campaign conceived.   Never was there one more heroically executed.

General Meade was at this time in command of the Army of the Potomac. He was one of our most able and reliable generals, and had about a hundred thousand troops encamped and intrenched among the hills north of the Rapidan. The plan of the campaign was not made public, and was revealed only as developed by events. But it could not be concealed from the nation that a vast accumulation of troops was being made in the vicinity of the Rapidan, evidently for a march upon Richmond. General Burnside was accumulating a co-operating force at Annapolis, to advance by Acquia Creek, and unite with General Meade. General Grant established his headquarters with General Meade, that he might more efficiently aid in the one great object of crushing Lee's army.

The gathering storm was anxiously watched by the rebels, and every soldier whom they could spare from other posts was summoned to Virginia to meet it. Longstreet hurried up from his winter's encampment near Knoxville. Beauregard almost stripped the intrenchments of Charleston, and hastened with his troops to Richmond. Even from the remote banks of the Mississippi and the everglades of Florida, the hosts of Rebellion gathered for the battle.

On the 3d of May, General Meade's army, General Grant being present and in supreme command, silently approached the Rapidan, and at midnight, unseen and unopposed, crossed the stream, at fords and by pontoon bridges, a few miles below the intrenchments of the rebels. They then moved rapidly forward towards Chancellorsville, through a wild, rugged region of forest and underbrush, appropiately called the Wilderness. It was a brilliant day. The army was strong, well-fed, in its best attire, and in the best of spirits. All the day long the troops continued their unopposed march, — infantry, artillery, and cavalry, — by a flank movement threatening the rear of the foe. At night they encamped in a region of wonderfully picturesque beauty. Their camp-fires, blazing along the hill-sides and in the ravines, and illumining the forest, over a region eight miles in length, presented one of the most imposing scenes in the pageantry of war.

Early the next morning, Thursday the 5th, the march was resumed. The immense host, numbering nearly a hundred and fifty thousand men, advanced in three columns. General Warren was on the right, General Hancock occupied the centre, and General Sheridan, with his cavalry, covered the left. By this flank movement, General Grant compelled the rebels to abandon their strong intrenchments, upon which they had expended the labor of so many months, and either to attack him in the open field, or to fall back, towards Richmond, and occupy new lines of intrenchments.

The army had not moved far this day ere there were decisive indications that the enemy had moved from his works, and was advancing, with his whole force, from the west, with the evident design of cutting through our line of march. General Grant selected some ridges upon which he posted his troops, and, throwing up hurried earthworks, awaited the onset. The line of battle, thus formed in the heart of the Wilderness, extended about five miles over the hills, and through forests and ravines. The rebels, concealed in the forest, could mass their forces, and fall with concentrated strength upon any portion of our extended line which they might think the weakest. Thus they could easily, at the point of attack, outnumber us three or four to one.

At noon the battle commenced. General Lee was an able commander. His soldiers were desperately brave. With a strong column he plunged, like an ancient battering-ram, upon our line. The Union troops slowly yielded before the tremendous assault, and their line swayed back. But re-enforcements were speedily sent to the menaced spot; and the line was straightened, and the rebels were driven out of sight into the depths of the forest. The routed foe massed another column, and selected another point of attack. About three o'clock they charged with desperation, which could not be surpassed, upon our left centre. It was the surge dashing against the rock. A mass of twenty thousand rebels, with a determination of courage which elicited the admiration of their foes, hurled themselves upon a portion of the Union line not more than half a mile in length. The battle was terrific; and it raged long and bloodily, with re-enforcements rapidly gathered on each side. But again the rebels were completely foiled and driven back. The conflict was dreadful, brother against brother; and the field was covered with the wounded and the dead. Six thousand on the two sides were struck down by the missiles of war, — a number equal to the whole mature male population of a city of thirty thousand inhabitants.

The night was mild, but dark. The dead were buried. The wounded, torn and bleeding, were borne to the temporary hospitals in the rear. All the night long the surgeons were busy with knife and saw. The exhausted soldiers indulged in a few hours of sleep, dreaming of distant homes which many of them were never again to see, while the generals were preparing to renew the strife upon the morrow.

But how different the cause which animated the hostile armies!   General Lee wished to destroy the government of the United States, and upon its ruins to construct another government, which, trampling upon all the principles of democratic justice, should make the poor the slaves of the rich.   General Grant wished to defend those republican institutions transmitted to us by our fathers, and to save the national flag from degradation and our country from ruin.   There can be no question, in such a cause as this, upon which side the sympathies of Heaven were enlisted.

Another beautiful May morning dawned upon this sad world, which might be so happy, but which man's inhumanity to man has converted into a field of blood.

Scarcely had the sun arisen above the unclouded horizon ere a hundred thousand rebels were again on the move.   Instantly the roar of battle ran along the lines.   Assault after assault was made by the rebels, now upon this point and now upon that; but each was unavailing.   Though the Union line at times bent before the storm and swayed to and fro, and the ravines and hill-sides were crimsoned with blood and strewed with the dead, the stars and stripes gradually advanced upon the infuriated foe.   General Hancock drove a portion of the rebels more than two miles before him.   On this day the noble General Wadsworth fell, and the whole nation mourned his loss.   A bullet struck him on the head, and he dropped senseless, mortally wounded. There are few names which can stand so high upon the American roll of honor as that of James S. Wadsworth. Accursed be that Rebellion which has thus robbed our nation of so many of the noblest of her sons!

It was a day of terror and of blood.   The rebels were

perfectly familiar with the country, and in the dense forest they could mass their troops unseen to strike our line at any point they chose. The broken nature of the country was such that it was scarcely possible to bring artillery into action. Thus eight or ten thousand of the rebel infantry could easily emerge from the forest, rushing upon two or three thousand of the Union troops. All the day long the battle raged until darkness came. Our loss in killed, wounded, and missing was estimated at over ten thousand men. The rebel loss probably was not less. What imagination can gauge the dimensions of such a woe! The wail of agony or the cry of death which rose from that bloody field was re-echoed and intensified in twenty thousand distant homes.

The battle closed on a disputed field. The equally unyielding antagonists threw themselves down at night, almost side by side, each on the ground upon which he had fought during the day. Still the victory was decidedly with the Union troops. The rebels had endeavored to pierce our lines, and had signally failed. We had endeavored to resist their attempts, and had signally triumphed. Anticipating a renewal of the attack in the morning, our lines were strengthened during the night, and batteries were planted to protect important points. The gullies, ravines, and tangled underbrush of the forest, rendered it easy for either army to conceal its movements from the other.

It was not until nearly noon of the next day that it was ascertained that General Lee was on the full retreat, with his whole army, in the direction of Spottsylvania Court-house. He had left a strong line of skirmishers to conceal this movement. A vigorous pursuit was immediately commenced. As the two armies were pressing along in nearly parallel lines, the march became really a race, each eager first to reach the goal, which was a position of much strategic importance. The rebels, having the start by several hours, gained the point. But, during the day, divisions of the two antagonistic hosts, crowding along all the roads which could be found, were occasionally brought into contact, and fierce battles ensued. It was late in the hours of Saturday night when the two armies found repose in the spots which they had severally selected.

The three days' battle of the Wilderness, as it has been called, was now closed. It was one of the strangest battles which ever occurred. Hostile forces, amounting in the aggregate to nearly three hundred thousand men, fought almost incessantly for three days; and yet, buried in the glooms of the forest, they were scarcely visible to each other. Each army had about two hundred and fifty pieces of artillery, but the nature of the ground was such that they could scarcely be brought into action at all. Never before was there a battle of such magnitude fought in the midst of the ravines, gullies, and underbrush of an almost impenetrable forest.

General Grant had accomplished his purpose in outflanking the enemy, in compelling him to withdraw from his strong intrenchments, and to retreat, from his menace of Washington and the North, to the protection of Richmond. 'General Lee had utterly failed in his attempts to arrest our march, or to break our lines. He had, however, caused more than twenty thousand men, on the two sides, to fall, either dead or wounded, upon those hard-fought fields.

By the dawn of Sunday morning, our troops were drawn up in battle array about two miles north of Spottsylvania Court-house. They had marched fifteen miles since Saturday noon. The rebels had taken possession of intrenchments previously prepared, and were every moment adding to ·the strength of these earthworks. General Grant commenced a furious onset upon them, that they might have no time to add to their defences, and to recover from the confusion of their retreat.

All the day long the roar of battle continued, until darkness enveloped the scene. Both parties fought with equal desperation. The Union soldiers, however, though with very severe loss, drove the rebels out of their first line of intrenchments, and took twenty-five hundred prisoners.

Another night came; and again these panting, bleeding armies threw themselves upon the ground, for such repose as could be found amidst the dying and the dead. Both parties were in the ·extreme of exhaustion. For five days and nights they had been almost incessantly engaged in fighting or marching. But General Grant, the tireless leader of the patriot host, allowed his guilty foe no repose.

With the early light he opened upon the rebels a harassing fire from his batteries, while his skirmishers and sharpshooters annoyed them at every available point. But another victim who had attained to national fame died the death of a martyr in a holy cause on that sad day. General John Sedgwick was instantly killed, — the bullet of a sharpshooter passing directly through his brain. The loss of this distinguished man, whose noble characteristics won all hearts, was regarded as a national calamity.

Another night came; and for a few hours the storm of battle ceased, and the weary combatants slept. Tuesday morning, the 10th of May, dawned, ushering in such a scene of blood and woe as even this war-scathed, sin-blighted world has seldom seen. The rebels were still in their strong intrenchments at Spottsylvania. The patriot line bent around them in a circuit of about six miles in extent. There were here clearings of the forest and cultivated fields, affording ample range for artillery. Early in the morning, on both sides, the cannonade commenced, and the ear was deafened with the roar of five hundred guns. Hour after hour the battle waxed hotter. There were charges and counter-charges, the onward rush of the victors, the wild flight of the routed; and the vast field was swept again and again with the surging billows of war.

As the day was drawing towards its close, General Grant prepared for a simultaneous assault upon the rebel works by nearly his entire line. Calm, firm, determined, the patriot leader stood upon an eminence from which he could witness nearly the whole of the terrific strife. Twelve guns, fired in signal, put the mass in motion. They advanced with such cheers as patriots give. Instantly there came back a corresponding, defiant yell from the rebel lines. We say a *yell;* for it was ever remarked that the battle-cry of the rebel was like the yell of the Indian, and not like the cheer of the civilized man.

The rebels were driven from their position; and our advancing columns swept resistlessly on, taking possession of their first line of intrenchments, and capturing two thousand prisoners. But the twilight was now fading into darkness; and, under cover of that darkness, the rebels sought shelter in another line of intrenchments in their rear. Ten thousand killed and wounded, on each side, were the victims of this day of blood.

In one of the lulls of the battle during the day, a

general order was read to the army, announcing the magnificent successes which General Sherman was achieving in his campaign in Georgia, and also the successful landing of General Butler's troops far up the James River, in the vicinity of Richmond. These tidings, so inspiriting, roused the army to the wildest excitement and enthusiasm, and gave a resistless impulse to their charge.

There were few who had confidence in the plan of General Grant's campaign of Vicksburg, until success had demonstrated its wisdom. So, in this march upon Richmond, there were many obvious perils which military critics pointed out, but which General Grant had maturely considered ; and the result proved that he did not err in the decision to which his sagacity led him. It is said that a gentleman called upon him one morning, and found him in his tent talking to one of his staff-officers. "General," said the stranger, "if you flank Lee, and get between him and Richmond, will you not uncover Washington, and leave it exposed to the enemy?"—"Yes: I reckon so," was General Grant's taciturn and quiet reply. "Do you not think, general," the stranger continued, "that Lee can detach sufficient force to re-enforce Beauregard at Richmond, and overwhelm Butler?"—"I have not a doubt of it," Grant replied. "And is there not danger," the stranger added, "that Johnston may come up, and re-enforce Lee ; so that the latter will swing round, and cut off your communications, and seize your supplies?"—"Very likely," was the unconcerned response. General Grant had weighed all these possibilities, and his sagacity had taught him that the enemy would not venture to attempt any one of them. He had also decided just what to do, in case either of these movements should be attempted by the foe.

Indeed, the general seems to have conceived the plan of this campaign while in front of Vicksburg. While conversing with several officers on the subject of the capture of Richmond, the question was asked, " Can it be taken ? " — " With ease," General Grant replied. " By the Peninsula ? " the inquirer asked. " No," said the general. " If I had charge of the matter, I should want two large armies, — one to move directly on Lee ; and the other to land at City Point, and cut communications to the southward. Lee would be then compelled to fall back ; and the army from the north could press, and, if possible, defeat him.

" If he would open up communications again with the Cotton States, he must fight the army south of the James ; and, to do this, he must cross his whole force, — otherwise he would be defeated in detail. If he did so cross, the northern army could take Richmond. If he did not, that from the south could move up to the heights south of the James, and shell and destroy the city."

CHAPTER XIX.

THE MARCH FROM SPOTTSYLVANIA TO THE PAMUNKEY.

Scenes on the Battle-field. — General Hancock's Midnight Charge. — The Battle of Spottsylvania. — The Retreat of the Foe. — Grant's Congratulatory Order. — The Mud Blockade. — Advance to Guinea's Station. — The Race for Richmond. — The Pageantry of War. — Magnitude of the Army. — Advance to the North Anna. — Positions of the Two Armies. — Secret March to the Pamunkey. — New Base of Supplies.

HROUGH all the long hours of the night which succeeded this day of blood, groans of anguish, and occasionally shrill cries of torture, could be heard from the field where, during the battle, twenty thousand men had been struck down, wounded or dead. The next day there was active skirmishing, but no general engagement. The rebels, now acting only on the defensive, were busy in throwing up intrenchments to protect themselves from our impetuous charges. To prevent this operation, General Grant kept up a continual shelling of their lines. The unburied dead, and the sufferings of the wounded, made so strong an appeal to every heart, that neither army felt disposed to neglect that appeal for the renewal of the battle.

No one can imagine, without having witnessed the spectacle, what it is to see twenty thousand men struck down by the missiles of war in every conceivable form of mutilation. The temporary hospitals were all crowded. Thousands were waiting — their life-blood oozing away — for their turn to come to be placed beneath the knife of the surgeons. Prayers, sighs, groans, resounded on all sides. Piles of amputated limbs rose by the side of the surgeons' tents. In the terrible excitement of battle, one is unmindful of the carnage. But, after the battle, every-one is appalled by the contemplation of that unmitigated misery, for which there can be no earthly recompense. Thus passed this dreadful day. While the surgeons were plying the knife and the saw, and the burying parties were heaping the turf over the dead, shells were scream-ing through the air, and the thunders of hostile batteries shook the hills.

At night a tempest of thunder, lightning, and drench-ing rain swept the camp. In the midst of the darkness and the storm, General Hancock made an impetuous assault upon one division of the foe, took them completely by surprise, and, wresting from them seven thousand prisoners and thirty-two guns, drove the remnant wildly before him. His movement was like the sudden burst-ing of the tornado at midnight. As the victors rushed over the first line of rifle-pits, and upon the second, the rebels rallied with re-enforcements, and charged furi-ously. Again and again the foe dashed forward, only to be hurled back with prodigious slaughter. Gradually the whole force of both armies was brought into the conflict.

The sun rose, — noon came, — evening came; and still there was no intermission of the fight. Bayonets were interlocked: rebel and patriot grappled in death throes. There were actual heaps of the dead, friend and foe, rider and horse, "in one red burial blent." After fourteen hours of a struggle, perhaps as desperate as earth has ever witnessed, night mercifully came to separate the exhausted combatants. Again the appalling number of ten thousand men on each side had fallen, in killed and wounded, — twenty thousand in all. Both armies, at this rate, would soon have been consumed, were it not that each was constantly receiving strong re-enforcements. Thus the ranks were still kept full, notwithstanding the awful slaughter.

But in this day's terrible conflict, as in every other battle of this wonderful campaign, the Union army was slowly yet surely gaining its end. General Grant's right was pushed forward a full mile over the left centre of the foe. General Burnside had also, upon our left, driven the enemy before him. And General Hancock had gained an angle of the enemy's works which he held, notwithstanding the most desperate endeavors of the foe to dislodge him. General Lee was greatly chagrined at this discomfiture. He made five desperate but unavailing charges to drive the patriots back. Two or three times also, through the ensuing night, he renewed the struggle to save some guns, from which our troops had driven the gunners, but which we had not been able to draw from the field, in consequence of the fire of the rebel sharpshooters.

With the earliest dawn of Friday morning our skirmishers were pushed forward ; and behold ! the foe again had fled. Their dead — ghastly monuments of their defeat — were left unburied. It was a gloomy morning of clouds and rain. A wailing gale swept the tree-tops, — nature's sympathetic moan with human woe. The rebels had retreated to occupy a new line of defence several miles in their rear. Our troops took possession of the abandoned field.   Some were employed in burying the dead, others in searching for the wounded.   Reconnoitring parties were sent out to ascertain the route of the enemy, and the new position which he had taken.   Several sharp skirmishes took place between these parties and the rear-guard of the foe.   A few of the wearied soldiers had an opportunity to take a little of that repose which they all so greatly needed.   In the afternoon of this day General Meade issued the following congratulatory order to the army : —

" For eight days and nights, almost without intermission, in rain and sunshine, you have been gallantly fighting a desperate foe, in positions naturally strong, and rendered doubly so by intrenchments.   You have compelled him to abandon his fortifications on the Rapidan, to retire, and attempt to stop your onward progress; and now he has abandoned the last intrenched position, so tenaciously held, suffering in all a loss of eighteen guns, twenty-two colors, and eight thousand prisoners, including two general officers."

Another night came, dark and stormy.   The roads, saturated with water, and ploughed with the artillery and baggage-wagons of the retreating foe, had become quagmires.   All the night long, through darkness, mud, and drenching rain, the right wing of the Union army pressed forward secretly to gain new vantage-ground.   The troops reached the position they sought with the early dawn.   Their lines were strongly posted upon a series of ridges, running north-west and south-east, but about two miles beyond Spottsylvania Court-house.

The rebels were before them, protected by intrenchments, which, months before, they had prepared as a place of retreat.   The Union soldiers — iron men as they were in nerve and will — were so exhausted by their midnight march that they could not then move upon the enemy's works. It was Sunday, — the twelfth day of the campaign. Neither party was in a condition to renew the battle. Both parties vigorously plied the spade ; and there was an occasional skirmish, as the troops on either side were concentrated, and took positions in preparation for the conflict which it was inevitable must soon again ensue.

Monday and Tuesday came and went. General Grant sent a despatch to Washington, stating that the condition of the roads rendered any immediate movement of the troops impracticable, but that his army was in the best of spirits, and sanguine of success. A bright warm sun and a strong breeze rapidly improved the roads. Reconnoitring parties were sent to ascertain the position of the enemy. The army had now been refreshed by two days of comparative rest, and new supplies had been brought up of food and military stores.

General Grant ever sought to avoid a direct attack upon the breastworks of the rebels, and endeavored, by flank movements, to compel the enemy to evacuate his intrenchments. Thus far he had been eminently successful in this. Every flank movement had as yet been made upon the left of our line of march. He now decided to surprise the foe by a sudden and vigorous attach upon his left, which General Lee had gradually weakened.

Under cover of the night of Tuesday, General Grant prepared his columns for this movement. With the first dawn of Wednesday morning the cannonade commenced, and soon the roar of another pitched battle echoed over the hills. The Union troops, in their charge, pressed resistlessly on till they came to a long line of rifle-pits filled with sharpshooters, and protected by an almost impenetrable abatis.   In the rear of these rifle-pits, upon a gentle eminence, there was a formidable array of batteries.   It was evident that any farther advance would result in fearful carnage.   The troops therefore were withdrawn.   By eleven o'clock the battle was terminated.   In that short, fierce storm of war our loss, in killed and wounded, amounted to twelve hundred. As the rebels did not venture from behind their intrench-ments, their loss was probably much less.

For the remainder of the day the two armies vigilantly watched each other.   As soon as night came, General Grant sent a cavalry force, under General Torbert, to Guinea's Station, on the Richmond and Fredericksburg Railroad, a distance of about ten miles in a south-east direction.   He thus seized a considerable amount of rebel property on the road, and gained a position in their rear.   In the morning the remainder of the army was on the vigorous move for that point.   Thoughtful men, who watched these movements, were very anxious for our army, lest the foe should make a sudden sweep upon our rear, and cut off our supply trains.   But General Grant had provided for every emergence.   He had made ar-rangements for a continual change of his base of supplies as he advanced; and, until that change was effected, his line was carefully guarded.

The rebels were now nearly ten miles in our rear. They were hungry and destitute, and made a desperate attack upon our long line of supply-wagons advancing from Fredericksburg.   But they met with an unexpected reception, which speedily drove them back to the forest from which they had stealthily emerged.   Still the brief battle was so hotly contested that, on the two sides, twenty-four hundred men were either killed or wounded.   General Lee, finding that we were gaining positions in his rear which not only threatened his line of communications, but even his escape to the intrenchments of Richmond, thus rendering the capture of the city certain, hastily abandoned the strong works he was then occupying, and fled to seek another line of defence on the North Anna River.

As Lee attempted this movement, the ever-watchful eye of Grant was upon him; and a division was sent out, through the concealment of the forest, which suddenly plunged upon the rear of the enemy's retreating column, and captured four hundred prisoners. The rebels, as ever, fought desperately. They were, however, driven two miles across the Ny, leaving the path, over which they sullenly retired, strewn with their dead and wounded.

The next day was Friday. The country was rough, hilly, and heavily wooded. It was difficult for either army to ascertain the movements of the other. It was easy to conceal operations in the midst of forests and ravines, while clouds of skirmishers were pushed out to prevent observation. Still the one great fact was ever obvious, that it was Grant's object to get to Richmond as soon as possible, and that it was Lee's all-engrossing endeavour to arrest his march. They were both able generals. It was therefore not very difficult for each to decide, though in the dark, pretty nearly what the other would do.

On Friday the 20th, the armies scarcely caught sight of each other; yet both were actively on the march. General Grant was pushing rapidly on directly south, towards Richmond. Lee was a few miles west of him, on the race to get to some river's bank, or some line of natural or artificial intrenchments, where another stand of resistance could be made. It was not a little amusing to read in the rebel journals these operations described as " Lee chasing Grant." During Friday night, General Torbert, with his division of cavalry, reached Bowling Green, fifteen miles south-east of Spottsylvania Court-house. He encountered several divisions of the enemy, but dispersed them without difficulty. The main body of the army reached the same point on Saturday evening, having marched that day thirty-two miles. Even war has its days of pageantry and mirth, as well as its scenes of exhaustion, blood, and woe.

The march of the army on Saturday was picturesque and beautiful. It was one of the loveliest days of spring, with a cloudless sky, a bright sun, and an invigorating breeze. The roads were dry and in perfect condition. The scenery was enchanting, with its clear streams, its green meadows, its hills, its groves, its luxuriance, and bloom. The air was filled with bird-songs, and fragrance floated upon the breeze. An army of a hundred and fifty thousand men, with their banners, their gleaming weapons, their plumed horsemen, their artillery, their wagons, crowded the roads winding over the hills and through the valleys.

But few persons are aware of the magnitude of such an army. General Grant's vast host — infantry, artillery, cavalry, and baggage-train — would fill, in a continuous line of march, any one road to its utmost capacity for a distance of nearly a hundred miles. In this march the immense army crowded the whole region over a breadth of from ten to fifteen miles. · All the public roads and cross-roads and wood-paths were traversed. One mind presided supreme over these operations, as day after day and night after night, through darkness, through forests, through morasses, over streams and rivers, storming intrenchments, and fighting their way against a determined foe of a hundred thousand men, the Union troops pressed resistlessly on.

The next day was Sunday, and the march was continued. It was deemed quite important to cross the Mattapony River before the rebels should plant their batteries upon its southern banks. General Lee was continually watching his opportunity to strike General Grant by a flank attack on his long line of march. But the foresight of General Grant, and the heroism of his officers and soldiers, averted every danger. The foe made several attacks during the day, but in all he was repulsed.

Our troops were now within forty miles of Richmond. In the race for the rebel metropolis, there was no time to be lost. With the early dawn of Monday morning the 21st, General Grant's troops were again upon the march. By night they reached the North Anna River. Here the rebels had gathered in strength to dispute the passage. They were strongly intrenched upon some commanding positions north of the stream. General Hancock led the advance. He opened upon the foe with a furious cannonade, and followed it up by a charge. The rebels were driven from their intrenchments and across the stream, and were closely followed by our troops. The remainder of our army soon came up, and encamped that night on both sides of the river.

Tuesday morning, the whole army crossed at several points, sweeping away all resistance. The North Anna was a rapid stream, its southern banks being precipitous, and fringed with forest and underbrush. Our troops were in the heart of Virginia, but little more than a day's march from the capital.

The rebels could send forces from all points to oppose our progress. The passage of the North Anna cost General Grant the loss of a thousand men in killed and wounded.

On Wednesday the 25th, our whole army was in a strong position on the south side of the river. General Grant had also changed his base of supplies to Port Royal, on the Rappahannock, about thirty miles below Fredericksburg. This point could be reached by transports. Here our line had a front about four miles in extent, facing west. General Lee was but a few miles from us, and nearly opposite, on a parallel line facing east. A reconnoissance sent out by General Grant showed that Lee was so strongly intrenched that his works could not be carried without much carnage. He therefore, under cover of a strong demonstration against the foe, rapidly recrossed the river, and marched down its north-eastern banks to the Pamunkey,— which is formed by the junction of the North and South Anna.

A large body of skirmishers kept the enemy busy, so as to prevent him from obtaining any possible knowledge of this movement. General Hancock protected our rear. All the night of Thursday the march was continued; and at nine o'clock Friday morning General Grant took possession of Hanover Ferry, on the Pamunkey River, within sixteen miles of Richmond. Again he changed his base of supplies, and the transports brought an abundance of all things needed up the Pamunkey to the White House. He thus had a short line for his baggage-trains of only a few miles, perfectly protected.

The military ability displayed in this march from the Rapidan was of the highest order. All the efforts of an army of a hundred thousand men under General Lee, and of nearly an equal number in Richmond, to oppose his advance, were baffled. By a series of flank movements, the elaborate intrenchments of the foe were rendered of no avail. The successive changes in General Grant's base of supplies rendered his lines of communication so secure, that, notwithstanding the almost frantic endeavors of General Lee, Grant scarcely lost a wagon. So admirably was every arrangement made, and all possible emergencies provided for, that scarcely had our troops taken position at Hanover ere supplies were arriving at the White House.

During all this time, General Grant had no fault to find, no complaints to make, no quarrels with either superiors or subordinates. His words were few ; but every word, like his shot and shell, was to the point. His orders were never misunderstood. The officers who led his divisions were men of genius, of devotion to the cause, of self-denying patriotism. It may be doubted whether there was ever before a more united and harmonious army.

Upon reaching the Pamunkey, there was no delay, save an occasional halt of the advance to secure more perfect concentration. The march was cautiously continued all day of Friday, for the rebel forces were now thick around us. As we read the record of these movements, it seems impossible that men could have endured such fatigue. General Grant's rule seemed to be to march all night, and fight all day. On Saturday the foe was again encountered by a portion of our troops ; and, after a short but fiery conflict, the rebels were driven out of sight, leaving many of their dead and wounded in our hands.

On Sunday the 29th, the army crossed the Pamunkey, with all its baggage-train, in safety. It pressed forward rapidly through the day, prepared at all points for battle, and anticipating every hour that Lee would burst upon them with his whole force. Still there was no general attack during the day, though the troops were annoyed by an incessant series of skirmishes. The foe took advantage of every commanding position to open upon us the fire of his batteries; and at times a fierce battle raged for an hour, with charges and repulses. But in every instance the foe was eventually driven from his position, and the Union army pressed resistless onwards.

CHAPTER XX.

THE MARCH FROM THE CHICKAHOMINY TO PETERSBURG.

The Union Lines on the Chickahominy. — The Opposing Rebel Lines. — The Desperate Battle. — Days of Intrenching and of Battle. — Preparations for another Flank Movement. — The Wonderful March to Petersburg. — Surprise and Alarm of the Enemy. — Change of Base of Supplies. — Conflicts around Petersburg. — The Siege Commenced.

N Wednesday morning, the 1st of June, our troops had reached Cold Harbor. General Sheridan was placed in command there, with orders to hold the post at all hazards. He was fiercely assailed. But his cavalry, dismounting, and attacking the foe with carbines, drove them back. All the day long there was marching and fighting. We were now within a few miles of Richmond, and holding a very important position. The rebels, foiled in their attack by day, renewed it in the night. But again they met with a bloody repulse. The struggle cost us two thousand men.

General Grant posted his troops in a line, about eight miles in length, extending north-east and south-west, from Bethesda Church to Cold Harbor. The church was a sort of dilapidated barn. The town of Cold Harbor consisted of a rude country-tavern at the junction of two roads. The enemy was continually making assaults upon different parts of the line, though at no point meeting with any success. One thousand men on each side, of killed and wounded, were the victims of this day. General Grant maintained his position, which was important, as commanding these divergent roads.

The rebel line of intrenchments, for the protection of Richmond from an attack on the side of the north, was now directly before us. It was very formidable, having been reared by men who, beneath the stars and stripes, had been thoroughly educated, at West Point, in the art of war. Lee's army had now reached these forts, ramparts, and bastions. The garrison of Richmond had joined him. The works were manned with the heaviest guns, and crowded with desperate defenders. Without an hour's delay, General Grant prepared to test the strength of these works. All the night of Wednesday the rain fell in floods. All the night, in the dark and the rain, General Grant was preparing for an assault with his whole force in the morning. The result was very uncertain. If successful, General Grant would have an unobstructed march into Richmond. If unsuccessful, he had another plan to which he would immediately resort. During Thursday, several minor battles were fought, as troops were moved to be massed in positions in readiness for the decisive attack.

On Friday morning, our right wing rested on the Chickahominy; our left was protected by the Tolapotomoy Creek. All things were now ready for the grand movement. With the early dawn, at four o'clock, the skirmishers were sent forward; and, almost simultaneously, the roar of battle rose along both of the hostile lines. To distract the foe, impetuous charges were made at several points. All the energies of both armies were called into requisition; and there ensued a dreadful day of blood and misery, the horrors of which no pen can describe, and no mind can adequately conceive. The heroism displayed by the Union troops was beyond all praise. The rebels were sheltered behind their earthworks. Their intrenched batteries frowned from the eminences. The Union troops marched to the muzzles of these guns, which were belching forth canister and grape with murderous effect.

It would require a volume faithfully to describe the varied events of this one battle, or rather this series of battles, in which three hundred thousand men, along a line several miles in extent, struggled in the deadly conflict, all day long, with almost superhuman energies. Clouds of cavalry swept over the plain. Batteries were lost, and batteries were won. There were successful charges, and the cheer of victory rose above the thunderings of war's tempest. And there was the repulse, when the shout of the victors faded away into the wail of death. Night came, and the battle ceased. The carnage on both sides had been severe. In counting up our losses, it appeared that seven thousand were numbered among the killed, the wounded, and the missing. Though we gained several important positions, and made a decided advance, it was evident that the rebels were so firmly intrenched that they could not be driven from their works, except at too great a sacrifice of the lives of our brave soldiers.

With the light of Saturday morning, the two hostile lines were so near each other that at several points they were separated by a distance of only a few yards. While a brisk fire was kept up during the day from the batteries and sharpshooters, all who could be spared were busy with the spade in throwing up intrenchments, or in strengthening those already formed. About nine o'clock at night, the rebels attempted a surprise, by massing a strong force, and throwing it with immense impetus upon our extreme left. But Hancock's watchful eye was there. He received them without recoil, and threw them back, routed and bleeding. The rebel loss was very severe.

All day Sunday both armies worked diligently in the trenches. Sharpshooters on both sides were vigilant, and not a head or a hand could be exposed for a moment without being the target for many unerring bullets. Through all the hours of the day, there was almost an incessant fire of musketry and artillery, as the working parties, by tens of thousands, were burrowing in trenches, and throwing up ramparts. The region, miles in extent, became honeycombed with all the varied forms of military earthworks.

The night which ensued was very dark. A dense fog, chill and damp, settled down over both hosts. The troops slept upon their arms, each ready for an attempt at surprise. Just before midnight a very heavy column stealthily emerged from the rebel lines, and plunged with deafening yells upon a selected portion of our works. At the same moment a terrible, concentrated fire from the rebel artillery and mortars was opened upon that point. In an instant our vigilant troops were in line of battle. A deadly storm of musketry, grape, and canister, was poured directly into the bosoms of the advancing foe. The column was staggered, recoiled, fled; and the midnight tempest was over. It had burst, like a thunderbolt from the sky, and as suddenly had disappeared. No eye could penetrate the darkness and the fog. But groans of anguish and cries for help were heard emerging from the gloom. More than one thousand rebels, in those few moments, and on that narrow space, had been struck down dead or wounded. Their companions were compelled to abandon them, for flesh and blood could not stand against the storm of lead and iron which swept the field.

Tuesday was like Monday, — a day of incessant cannonading, of constant practice of sharpshooters, of frequent skirmishes; while the spade was vigorously plied. So many busy hands could in a short time dig rifle-pits, and throw up breastworks, which would effectually protect from the bullet, and conceal many movements. In fact, both armies were burrowing under ground, almost invisible to each other. Again, at midnight of Tuesday, the rebels made a desperate assault upon General Burnside's corps. That gallant officer was not found sleeping, and the foe was again repulsed bloodily. It is surprising that the rebels were not more successful in these attacks. General Grant's lines extended for several miles. It was easy for the rebels, in the darkness, and concealed by their works, to mass such a force as to be able to fall with ten men against one upon any portion of our line.

Wednesday was like Monday and Tuesday. The hills echoed with the roar of batteries. The rattle of musketry never ceased. There were frequent skirmishes; and ramparts and bastions were rising, as by magic, upon all sides. There were points in which the invisible foes were within a few yards of each other. They could hear the noise of each other's pickaxes, and could exchange jokes and taunts. Thus nearly a week passed away.

General Grant was all this time preparing for one of the most extraordinary movements of this or of any other campaign. It was not merely his object to capture Richmond; but he desired, still more strongly, to secure the utter destruction of Lee's army. There was danger, should General Grant prosecute the siege of Richmond from the north, that General Lee, abandoning his intrenchments, might retreat into the Carolinas and Georgia, and still continue the conflict. General Grant was therefore making preparations for another flank movement, by which, descending the north bank of the Chickahominy River, he might cross it some miles below the enemy's lines, and then, by a rapid march to and across the James, take a position in the rear of Lee's army, south of Richmond.

In preparation for this movement the base of supplies was changed, on Saturday, from the Chickahominy to the James River. On Sunday morning, June the 12th, the army, veiled from observation by its earthworks and by clouds of skirmishers, quietly commenced its march from its intrenchments. For miles these intrenchments were within reach of the enemy's guns. Unseen and unsuspected in the movement, this majestic host of a hundred and fifty thousand men, — infantry, artillery, and cavalry, — with their almost interminable line of wagons, pressed on towards their goal. All day long of Sunday and of Monday, and until Tuesday afternoon, with scarcely any rest, even at night, these iron men tramped on in silence, till the extraordinary feat was accomplished. They crossed the Chickahominy and the James, accomplishing a march of fifty-five miles without the loss of a wagon or a gun. This extraordinary movement was effected in the presence of an enemy a hundred thousand strong, desperate in courage, ably officered, and whose ramparts were in many places within fifty yards of the intrenchments from which General Grant marched his troops. Every possible path was crowded with the immense host. Through swamps and dust, and the blaze of noonday and the gloom of midnight, the army, guide by the energies

and protected by the sagacity of one mind, pressed forward till the marvellous feat was accomplished.

It will be remembered that General Butler had ascended the James River with a division of the army, to menace Richmond from the south, and thus to prevent re-enforcements from being sent to General Lee. This measure accomplished one of its expected results. General Beauregard in Richmond, leaving Lee to struggle unaided with Grant, hurried south with an overwhelming force to crush General Butler. It was impossible for General Butler to meet such an army in the open field. He accordingly threw up earthworks, and held his position. The enemy reared strong intrenchments in front of his lines, and held him where he was. Though transports, with any amount of supplies, could reach him by the James River, protected by the gunboats, he could make no advance.

On Wednesday morning the 15th, the Eighteenth Army Corps, which was in the advance, crossed the James River, and reached General Butler's encampment at Bermuda Hundred. Immediately crossing the Appomattox, these troops marched rapidly down the southern banks of the stream for an attack upon Petersburg. The rebels now were thoroughly alarmed. General Lee, to his amazement, found Grant's army nearly fifty miles south of him. The rebels in front of General Butler, in their eagerness to save Petersburg, abandoned their works, and advanced, with a rush, for the protection of that city. Lee's army, impetuously, and almost upon the run, crowded through the streets of Richmond, and hurried by turnpike and railroad to man the ramparts of Petersburg.

General Terry, who subsequently obtained such renown in the capture of Fort Fisher, pushed out from General

17

Butler's intrenchments, seized the vacated works of the enemy, and, advancing two or three miles, commenced destroying the railroad between Petersburg and Richmond.

Could one have looked down from a balloon upon the scene presented, a very extraordinary spectacle would have met the eye. Three hundred thousand men, in organized masses, were spread over a space about fifteen miles in breadth and nearly forty in length. They were marching in all directions, in apparently inexplicable confusion. The heads of antagonistic columns were continually meeting in deadly fight. Batteries were thundering from hill-tops. Squadrons of cavalry were sweeping the plains. Shot and shell shrieked through the air. Long lines of infantry rushed, like ocean surges, in the impetuous charge. Clouds of smoke were rising in all directions. Piercing the tumult of musketry and artillery, wild battle-cries blended with shrieks of agony and death-groans. Such a scene cannot be described. No mortal mind can conceive it.

In all the conflicts of the day, the Union troops were steadily gaining. The colored regiments fought with great gallantry, storming the enemy's works, seizing their rifle-pits, climbing their ramparts, and capturing their guns. In the march of this day, which was an incessant battle, the Union troops were greatly in the majority. But the enemy was very strongly intrenched, and General Lee with his whole army was but a few hours distant, and on the rush to re-enforce them. It was a matter of great moment to capture the enemy's works, if possible, before the arrival of Lee. The Union troops were consequently pushed forward, almost upon the full run. They succeeded in taking possession of the outer line of the rebel defences, with sixteen guns and three hundred prisoners, and had gained a position within two miles of Petersburg. But the city was found to be surrounded with a very formidable triple line of intrenchments. Into this second line the rebel army crowded rapidly and in great numbers, where they fought with even more than their customary desperation. Could they hold out but a few hours, an army of more than a hundred thousand men would join them.

Again and again our troops, as they arrived upon the extended field, rushed to the assault. But the works were strong, the foe determined. The fire of musketry, grape, and canister was deadly; and again and again the Union troops were repulsed with heavy loss.

Night came,—a troubled night of anxiety, and of preparation for the renewal of the stern conflict on the morrow. During the night, two thousand Union soldiers, struck by the missiles of war during the day, were to be borne to the hospitals, or consigned to their burial. It was so important to attack the rebel works before the arrival of General Lee that the next morning, notwithstanding the exhaustion of the preceding days, General Grant ordered another assault, at four o'clock. General Griffin's brigade was selected for this attempt. The morning had scarcely dawned ere this gallant band moved forward to capture an important post occupied by the foe. The charge was brilliantly successful, and the cheers of the soldiers announced far and wide their victory. General Griffin had driven the enemy from his position, captured a stand of colors, six pieces of artillery, and four hundred men.

During this whole day of Friday, the battle raged over a field many miles in extent. There were occasional lulls, and again the storm of war would burst forth with renewed uproar. The enemy contested every foot of our progress; yet, step by step, General Grant gained ground, moving slowly, yet with the resistlessness of fate. At night General Burnside had attained a position within a mile and a half of the city. He threw a few shells into the streets, which Lee's army was already entering. As these shells came shrieking and exploding in the midst of the dwellings of Petersburg, they must have created terrible forebodings of the still more dreadful storm which was now sure to come.

General Lee felt the importance of driving General Burnside, at every hazard, from the commanding post he held. He massed an overwhelming force, and, on Friday night, hurled these columns upon Burnside with all the energies of despair. The battle was short, but terrible and deadly. The combatants fought across the breast-works, often hand to hand. General Burnside was over-powered, and driven from his position, with about equal loss upon both sides.

As soon as the morning of Saturday dawned, the battle was renewed everywhere. Cannon replied to cannon, charge to charge; and these two armies, alike desperate, alike determined to conquer or to die, grappled each other as armies have seldom grappled before. Alas, that men can fight so bravely, as did the rebels, in the most infamous cause for which men ever drew the sword, — to overthrow the Constitution of the United States, and to rear upon the wreck of our free institutions, of our noble democratic principle of 'equal rights for all men, a government whose corner-stone should be *the enslavement of our brother-man !*

The onset of our troops was so terrible, and the ene-my's position in his second line so extended, that General

Lee judged it expedient to abandon that second line, that he might concentrate his force within a more limited inner line of works. This was mainly accomplished Friday night, and during the day of Saturday. When Saturday night came, our troops could look back upon three days of almost incessant fighting. Never in the history of the world had more resolution, fearlessness, and skill been displayed upon the field of battle. And yet it was found impossible to penetrate the strong ramparts of the foe. In these three days, the Union army had lost not less than ten thousand men in killed, wounded, and missing. As the rebels fought under the protection of their works, their loss was probably much less. It had now become evident that the intrenchments of the foe were too strong to be carried by direct assault. General Grant consequently commenced the regular siege of Petersburg and Richmond, but without the slightest misgiving as to the result. Re-enforcements were continually sent to him, to replenish his diminished ranks; and he quietly remarked to a friend, " I shall take Richmond, and General Lee knows it."

CHAPTER XXI.

THE SIEGE OF PETERSBURG.

Investing Petersburg. — The Railroads. — General Birney's Raid. — The Cavalry Raid of Generals Wilson and Kautz. — General Grant's Despatch. — Feelings of the Soldiers. — The Bombardment of the City. — Sympathy between President Lincoln and General Grant. — Ewell's Raid.

HE city of Petersburg, containing a population of about fifteen thousand, is situated on the south banks of the Appomattox River, twelve miles above City Point, where the Appomattox enters the James. It is about twenty-five miles south of Richmond. The patriot community was much disappointed, and so doubtless was General Grant, to find that the city was so strongly fortified that it could not be taken by assault.

It was General Grant's plan gradually to extend his lines around the city, so as completely to invest it on the south and the west, and to cut its railroads, by which alone it could now receive supplies. The first railroad which the Union troops came to, south of the city, and which was easily seized, was the one which ran from Petersburg to Norfolk, in a south-easterly direction. The next one, about ten or twelve miles west of this, ran due south to Weldon, Goldsborough, and Wilmington, in North Carolina, thence branching off into the heart of the Southern States. This road was one of great importance to the rebels, opening to them all the resources of the South. There was still another road, called the Petersburg and Lynchburg Road, running nearly west, which was also almost essential to the existence of an army in Petersburg.

General Lee was well aware that General Grant understood the value of these roads, and that it would be his first endeavor to take them. He therefore gave the most assiduous attention to their protection. On the night of the 20th of June, General Grant sent out the Second Corps, under General Birney, to advance towards the Weldon Road. In the darkness they moved from their intrenchments, and commenced a rapid and noiseless march, aiming to strike the rails several miles south of Petersburg. The route was long; and the hot sun of a summer's day soon blazed down upon the troops, while clouds of dust smothered them, from the tramp of ten thousand men and horses. It is not pleasant, in a dusty day, to ride behind a single stage-coach. No one, who has not been blinded and smothered on the march, can imagine what it is to be in the midst of a column, miles in length, of horsemen, footmen, and wagons, trampling through dust which seems to be, not merely ankle deep, but at times actually over one's head, filling eyes, mouth, and nostrils.

About noon, the troops reached what is called the Jerusalem Plank-road, which ran from Petersburg to Jerusalem, about half-way between the Norfolk and Weldon Railroads. Here the enemy was found in strength. As from a gentle eminence General Birney looked down upon the frowning batteries, and the long lines of ramparts and rifle-pits, crowded with soldiers before him, it was clear that he could go no farther without hard fighting. The rebels had the great advantage of occupying the inner lines, so that they could with great rapidity push re-enforcements to any menaced point. The Union soldiers, exhausted with the march and parched with thirst, were not prepared for an immediate charge. They took their positions, cooked their suppers, and bivouacked for the night,—in preparation for the battle of the morrow.

Our army now occupied a circuitous line around Petersburg, on its southern and eastern side, about thirty miles in length. General Foster's division of the Tenth Corps was north of the James River, at Deep Bottom. South of the river, a few miles from him, General Butler was stationed with his force, at Bermuda Hundred. Still farther south, at a distance of some eight or ten miles, the main body of the army was gathered, in a long, strong line some miles in extent, directly fronting Petersburg. With their hundred-pounders, a round-shot or shell was occasionally thrown into the city.

The Eighteenth Corps held the right of this beleaguering host, the Ninth Corps held the centre, and most of the Fifth Corps the extreme left. These troops were in direct communication, so as to afford each other immediate support. A few miles south and west of the extreme left of our line, General Birney was now encamped with the Second and a portion of the Sixth Corps, on his march for the Weldon Railroad, and facing the foe.

Such was the position of our army on the night of the 21st of June. The rebels were concentrated at Petersburg, protected by the strongest intrenchments which could be reared. It is manifest that Lee could mass vast forces at his leisure, and burst forth upon any one portion of our line for its destruction. Such was his constant aim. It was the very difficult task of General Grant to protect his whole line against such a calamity.

General Lee found one corps of our army at the Jerusalem Road, separated by miles from the rest, on the march, and unintrenched. There was already a strong force of his own army in well-constructed ramparts directly before them. Troops were hurried forward to crowd those ramparts in defence, and then to emerge from them, and overwhelm the assailants.

While General Birney's troops were making their march, on Tuesday the 21st of June, President Lincoln visited the army at Petersburg, and held a long interview with Generals Grant and Butler. Early on Wednesday morning, General Birney moved forward to test the strength of the foe. He sent first the cavalry, under Wilson and Kautz, to make a rapid circuit south, and strike the railroad about ten miles below Petersburg. They were to burn bridges and depots, tear up and bend the rails, and inflict all the other injury which was possible. The remainder of the troops moved in two columns directly against the enemy.

By some mishap, these columns, diverging in their march through a dense forest, were not within supporting distance of each other. There was a gap between them. The eagle-eyed foe detected the error. A strong division of the enemy swept through the vacant space, and, turning, fell impetuously upon the flank of the second division, led by General Barlow. The Union troops, thus assailed at great disadvantage and by superior numbers, fought heroically. But the assault was so resistless that their line was doubled up, many prisoners were taken, and awful carnage ensued. The rebels captured all the guns of Knight's battery; took several whole regiments as prisoners; and were triumphantly advancing, spreading havoc around, when the Twentieth Massachusetts, under Captain Patten, from a good position, with well-aimed muskets, poured so deadly a volley into the bosoms of the foe as to check and stagger them in their march.

Volley after volley followed in swift succession. This respite of a few moments allowed the broken corps to rally. The fight continued, desperately, bloodily, all the day, — in the forest, — on the hill-sides, — through the ravines. But the disaster of the morning was irreparable. When night came to terminate the conflict, our troops had made scarcely any advance, and had lost five hundred in killed and wounded, and over two thousand prisoners. In regard to the results of this expedition, General Grant says in his despatch, —

"Sixty miles of railroad were thoroughly destroyed. The Danville Road, General Wilson reports, could not be repaired in less than forty days, even if all the materials were at hand. He has destroyed all the blacksmith-shops where the rails might be straightened, and all the mills where the scantlings for sleepers could be sawed. Thirty miles of the South-side Road were destroyed. Wilson brought in about four hundred negroes, and many of the vast number of horses and mules gathered by his force. He reports that the rebels slaughtered without mercy the negroes they retook. Wilson's loss of property is a small wagon-train used to carry ammunition, his ambulance-train, and twelve cannon. The horses of our artillery and wagons were generally brought off. Of the cannon, two were removed from their carriages, the wheels of which were broken and thrown into the water; and one other gun had been disabled by a rebel shot breaking its trunnions, before it was abandoned. He estimates his total loss at from seven hundred and fifty to a thousand men."

The next day the heat was terrible. Neither army seemed disposed to attempt to strike any very vigorous blow. General Birney sent out reconnoissances; and there were several pretty sharp skirmishes during the day. The next morning, Thursday, 23d, a cautious movement was made in advance.

Wilson and Kautz succeeded in reaching the Weldon Railroad, tore up its rails for a considerable distance, and swept across still farther west to cut the Lynchburg, or Danville Road, as it was also called. In this raid, upon which about eight thousand men were sent, with twenty-eight pieces of artillery, every man had his particular duty assigned him; and the operations were conducted as regularly as the evolutions on a parade-ground.

General Grant planned and gave minute directions for all these movements. The soldiers had now learned to place implicit confidence in his judgment. "It is wonderful," writes the army-correspondent of "Harper's Weekly," "how entirely the army confides in General Grant. Every soldier's tongue is full of his praises. No matter how severely wounded, no matter how intensely suffering, if there is strength enough in him to speak, every man in all the hospital wards will tell you, if you ask his opinion, —

" ' He is one of us, — this unconditional-surrender general; and he will bring us through, God willing, just as surely as the sun shines.'

" Then they will tell you stories of his watchfulness and care, the fearlessness and intrepidity of this man whose plume they delight to follow; how he is everywhere, by night and by day, looking after the comfort of his men, and quietly prosecuting the strategic work of the campaign; how he rides unexpectedly to the remote outposts, speaking a pleasant word to the pickets if faithfully on duty, and administering reprimands if not vigilant and watchful; how he shuns fuss and show, going about often with only an orderly; how his staff — plain, earnest men, like himself — get down at times from their horses, that sick and wounded men, struggling hospitalward, may rest their weariness by riding to their destination; how, in a word, he is a thoughtful, resolute, kind man, sympathizing with the humblest soldier in his ranks, penetrated with a solemn appreciation of the work given him to do, and determined, by Heaven's help, to *do* it, right on the line he has occupied. And, when they tell you this, these maimed heroes lying in the hospitals add always with a magnificent *élan*, — an energy which has a grand touch of pride in it, —

" 'And we'll help him do this work: we will stand by him, come what may; we will perish, every man of us, rather than have him fail, and the Cause dishonored: we will be proud of every scar won in fighting where he leads.' "

Ten days now passed, during which but little was apparently done. Still our troops were busy every hour in preparing for the blows, terrible and decisive, with which they soon were to strike the rebel army. They were daily taking new positions, throwing up new intrenchments, concentrating and consolidating their lines. Every day there was more or less of fighting, and often a very fierce interchange of shots between the hostile batteries. The rebels in their desperation sought in vain a weak spot in our lines. On the 25th, General Sheridan, with a train of baggage-wagons six miles long, crossed in safety the James, near Fort Powhattan, protected by the gunboats. The rebels attacked him ferociously, but were constantly thwarted and repelled. He fought his way against the thronging foe, from the Pamunkey to the James, saving every wagon, cannon, and musket. In the incessant battle, he lost of his division — consisting of about six thousand men — about five hundred in killed and wounded.

The bombardment of a city is one of the most terrible things in the world. To the inmates of the city it must be awful beyond description. From General Smith's front, a thirty-pound Parrott shell was thrown every five minutes, day after day, into the city. Long practice enabled the gunners to throw these terrible missiles with great accuracy. At length General Grant got several heavy siege-guns in a position which commanded the city, and at once commenced throwing a shell every fifteen minutes during the night.

These shells were dropped in all parts of the city, through all the hours of the night. They exploded with thunder roar, scattering ruin and death around. No one could tell where they would fall. All were alike exposed. If one fell upon the roof of any building, it sank with a crash to the cellar, and, there bursting, blew up the whole edifice, and buried all the inmates in a common grave.

On Thursday night the 30th, several large fires were kindled by the shells. Hour after hour the miserable city burned. While the flames were raging, the shells were still falling. The glare of the fire, the dense volumes of billowy smoke which rose, and the mournful ringing of the alarm bells, presented a scene which saddened the hearts even of those who were inflicting this terrible chastisement upon the foe. They felt that the war, with all its horrors, must be prosecuted until the rebels would abandon their endeavor to overthrow those free institutions of our land in which the hopes of humanity for all coming time are enshrined. There were probably but few in the city at this time but the rebel soldiers. The door was wide open for the escape of all who wished to leave.

Very cordial sympathy existed between General Grant and President Lincoln during all these operations. It was very fortunate for the country, that, in these great emergencies, two men so honest, sincere, unaffected, unselfish, were at the head of our civil and military administration. Secretary Stanton co-operated with both with harmony never disturbed by a ripple even of ill feeling or of jealousy. As General Grant entered upon this campaign, President Lincoln wrote to him the following letter. It was dated, Executive Mansion, Washington, April 30, 1864 : —

" LIEUTENANT-GENERAL GRANT, — Not expecting to see you before the spring campaign opens, I wish to express, in this, my entire satisfaction with what you have done up to this time, so far as I understand it. The particulars of your plans I neither know nor seek to know. You are vigilant and self-reliant ; and, pleased with this, I wish not to obtrude any restraints or constraints upon you. While I am very anxious that any great disaster, or capture of our men in great numbers, shall be avoided, I know that these points are less likely to escape your attention than they would be mine. If there be any thing wanting which it is within my power to give, do not fail to let me know it.

"And now, with a brave army and a just cause, may God sustain you!

"Yours very truly,

"A. LINCOLN."

To this General Grant gave the following reply, dated Headquarters Armies of the United States, Culpepper Court-house, May 1, 1864: —

"THE PRESIDENT, — Your very kind letter of yesterday is just received. The confidence you express for the future, and satisfaction for the past, in my military administration, is acknowledged with pride. It shall be my earnest endeavor that you and the country shall not be disappointed. From my first entrance into the volunteer service of the country to the present day, I have never had cause of complaint, have never expressed or implied complaint against the administration, or the Secretary of War, for throwing any embarrassment in the way of my vigorously prosecuting what appeared to be my duty.

"Indeed, since the promotion which placed me in command of all the armies, and in view of the great responsibility and importance of success, I have been astonished at the readiness with which every thing asked for has been yielded, without even an explanation being asked. Should my success be less than I desire and expect, the least I can say is, the fault is not with you.

"Very truly your obedient servant,

"U. S. GRANT."

General Lee endeavored to distract the attention of General Grant, and to draw off his troops from the siege of Richmond, by sending, under General Ewell, a carefully-selected army of twenty-five thousand men, who could move with much celerity, to menace Washington. General Hunter had been left to guard the valley of the Shenandoah from such a raid. The Union force in the valley was not, however, sufficiently strong to resist such an army as Ewell commanded. As these solid battalions swept like a flood down the valley, our scattered troops in haste evacuated their positions, losing many valuable stores.

The rebels crossed the Potomac at several points, and sent strong bodies of their fleet cavalry in various directions, plundering and destroying. The panic all through that region was terrible. Hagerstown, in Maryland, was seized by the rebels, plundered, and twenty thousand dollars extorted from the inhabitants to save their four hundred buildings from the flames. Mosby's cavalry came clattering into the streets of Frederick City. Here, again, they robbed the stores ; and as it was rather a wealthy town, of about six thousand inhabitants, they extorted from them a ransom of two hundred thousand dollars.

Conscious that their time was short, they tarried scarcely an hour at any one place. Onwards these marauding bands swept. They struck the Baltimore and Ohio Railroad, and destroyed it for several miles. Troops were rapidly gathering from the North to chastise these bold raiders. General Wallace had rendezvoused about ten thousand men at Monocacy Junction. Ewell fell upon him with twenty thousand. There was a desperate battle, in which the Union troops were driven back with severe loss. Washington and Baltimore were in terror. Detachments of the foe were reported within sixteen miles of Baltimore, loading their wagons with plunder, driving off herds, levying contributions, tearing up rails, cutting telegraph wires, and burning bridges. All the alarm bells of the city were rung, summoning the whole male population for the defence of the place.

At Washington, the enemy was reported at Rockville, but thirteen miles from the city, and, soon again, as within five miles of the metropolis, where they applied the torch to the mansion of Governor Bradford, and laid it in ashes. General Augur — in military command at Washington — summoned the marines, the home guards, and even the employees in the Government Departments, to aid in defence of the capitol.

Detachments of cavalry swept rapidly around to the north of Baltimore, and destroyed portions of the Northern Central Railroad. Another band, on fleet horses, ventured even to the Philadelphia, Baltimore, and Wilmington Road, destroying the track, and firing several trains. But now the troops were so rapidly gathering from the North that these bold raiders, acting upon the principle, that the " better part of courage is discretion," commenced their retreat. They had inflicted an immense amount of mischief, and had filled their wagons with supplies. But they had not induced General Grant to relinquish, in the slightest degree, his grasp upon the foe at Petersburg.

General Grant was well aware that the raid could be only very transient, that the North would speedily send down a sufficient military force to put the invaders to flight. Instead, therefore, of abandoning his works to rush to the defence of the Northern cities, he merely sent a few troops in transports to render Washington secure, and pushed his siege with renewed vigor. As the raiders retreated, they were pursued by the volunteer force, though not with much vigor. A few prisoners were taken, a few hundred were killed, and some of their well-filled wagons were captured. The raiders had gained provisions and other stores sufficient to supply their army for a few additional days, but they had accomplished nothing in the way of raising the siege of Richmond.

CHAPTER XXII.

PROGRESS OF THE SIEGE.

Labors of a Beleaguering Army. — Attack upon Richmond from the North. — The Mine: Its Construction, Explosion, Results. — Gregg's Raid to the Weldon Road. — Its Seizure. — Desperate but Unsuccessful Struggles of the Rebels. — Treachery of the Rebels. — Military Railroad. — Tidings of the Capture of Atlanta. — Obduracy of Jeff. Davis. — Immensity of General Grant's Cares.

HERE is no rest in the trenches of a besieging army. Every day is a battle. Sharpshooters are constantly on the watch for an exposed head or hand. Batteries open their concentrated fire upon the rising ramparts. Shells mount shrieking through the air, and drop in the midst of the workmen who are burrowing in the parallels. There is incessant toil with the spade, now under a blazing sun, and again in drenching storms. Often new positions are to be gained at the expense of a terrible conflict. The besieged are ever making desperate sorties, by night as well as by day, plunging, with overwhelming force, upon some point of the investing line where they hope to destroy both the works and the workmen.

In such labors as these the month of July passed away. General Grant was daily advancing, step by step, nearer to the foe. His lines of circumvallation, ever changing, were about twenty miles long. He was about to make another attempt to seize and hold the Weldon Railroad. The plan he adopted for the accomplishment of this end was to send secretly a strong force, under the impetuous Sheridan, to attack Richmond upon the north. Should Lee send a large force from Petersburg to protect Richmond, General Grant could then strike heavily upon the weakened rebel lines. Should General Lee fear to withdraw troops from Petersburg, and thus send no reenforcements to the ramparts above Richmond, Sheridan would be able to seize very important positions there.

On the 26th of July, the Second Army Corps secretly commenced its march from our extreme right, and, followed by Sheridan's cavalry, crossed the Appomattox at Point of Rocks. Pushing rapidly forward, by midnight of the same day they reached the James River, and crossed it at Jones Neck. The secret passage was effected by means of a pontoon bridge muffled with hay. With rapid strides the troops continued their march until they reached Deep Bottom, within twelve miles of Richmond. Here they found an encampment of the rebels, whom they easily scattered, capturing their intrenchments and a battery. The tidings were flashed from Richmond along the wires to Lee at Petersburg. Much alarmed, he immediately despatched twenty thousand men with twenty pieces of artillery to aid in repelling the assailants.

General Grant, having thus gained his object, opened a vigorous cannonade upon the enemy's works, in preparation for a general charge. The bombardment was continued by night. The flash of the guns, the meteoric shells circling through the air, the flames of wide and wasting conflagrations bursting out in various parts of the city, and the incessant roar of the explosions, presented one of the sublimest scenes in war's dreadful drama.

For a month, Lieutenant-Colonel Pleasants had been diligently and sagaciously at work, with the Forty-eighth Pennsylvania, in digging a mine to blow up one of the most formidable of the forts of the enemy. It was his plan, immediately after the explosion, to have several thousand troops rush through the chasm, and seize upon a very important eminence beyond. The mine was started from a ravine opposite to General Burnside's corps. Unfortunately, some of the officers looked contemptuously upon the scheme, and did not co-operate with that energy which was essential to its success. Had General Burnside's plans been cordially adopted, there can be no doubt that the result would have been highly advantageous.

A gallery was dug four and a half feet high, and of the same width, for a distance of five hundred feet into the hill. The earth brought out was covered with bushes to conceal it from the view of the rebels. The miners burrowed their way along until they were directly under the rebel fort. Here they dug two lateral galleries, one thirty-seven and the other thirty-eight feet in length. In these galleries eight magazines for the powder were constructed. These magazines were charged with four tons of powder strongly tamped.

Directly over this sleeping volcano stood the rebel fort, garrisoned by two hundred men, with six guns and all the necessary camp-equipage. The men were singing, dancing, and playing cards, but little conscious of the awful doom which was awaiting them. At the moment of the explosion, a terrible cannonade was to be opened upon all the rebel works in the vicinity. Under cover of this bombardment, the storming party, rushing through the gap cut by the mine, were to seize the crest of Cemetery Hill beyond, which so effectually commanded Petersburg that the city would be in our power.

Just after midnight of Friday, July 29, all the arrangements were completed: the fuse was laid through the long, dark, damp gallery, and the mine was ready to be sprung. The cannoneers stood at the siege-guns ready to open their fire. The field artillery was harnessed for the rush. Sheridan's cavalry were astride their horses to make a charge upon another portion of the enemy's works. The Union troops were cautiously drawn back, that they might not be injured by the eruption which would throw rocks, guns, and the bodies of men, far and wide.

It was a beautiful morning, clear and serene, the moon shining brightly. At half-past three o'clock the fuse was lighted. The morning was beginning to dawn; and the rebels could be seen sitting about, and strolling upon and in front of their parapets, enjoying the refreshing coolness, entirely unsuspicious of danger. Our army was awake, and every point of favorable observation was crowded with men, waiting with interest the expected upheaval.

Minutes seemed hours; and yet a whole hour passed, and there was no explosion. It was probable that, in the dripping passage, the fuse at some point had become injured and had gone out. Lieutenant Douty and Sergeant Reese boldly entered the gallery to ascertain the difficulty. They found the fuse extinguished about a hundred feet from the entrance. Relighting it, they crept back. It was then nearly five o'clock. The troops were beginning to pronounce the whole affair a failure. There came a trembling of the earth, — a smothered roar, — and then a volcanic burst of flame and smoke. Rocks, timbers, earth, guns, and men were thrown, in a vast spreading column, a hundred and fifty feet into the air. These were all enveloped in heavy folds of billowy smoke, which wrapped in its funereal pall, blended with the *débris*, the mangled forms of two hundred men.

For a moment there was a pause, as all eyes regarded the gigantic apparition. The next moment a hundred guns opened their roar, and in rapid fire hurled round-shot and shell in and upon the rebel works. For miles upon miles the resounding thunder rolled. As the vast column thrown into the air fell in wide-spread and indescribable ruin, an immense chasm appeared, several hundred feet long, fifty feet wide, and twenty feet deep.

-Thus far the mine had been a triumphant success. For some cause, not easily explained, the charging column, after a delay of ten minutes, — when seconds were of priceless value, — rushed into the gap, and there halted, and commenced throwing up intrenchments. The important point to be gained was the crest of Cemetery Hill, four hundred yards beyond.

" Ledlie still halted in the excavation. Wilcox and Potter soon followed him, and the three divisions became intermixed, and general confusion prevailed. An hour of precious time was lost. Ledlie made no attempt to move in or out, and Potter and Wilcox could not go forward while he blocked the way." *

This delay was fatal. The rebels recovered from their stupor. They opened fire upon the crater from all the guns which could be brought to bear upon it, and planted

* Charles Carleton Coffin.

new batteries upon the eminences to enfilade the troops crowded together in that narrow spot. Still it was more than an hour before a single shot was fired by the rebels. It is mortifying to think that a victory, so easily within our grasp, should have been thus lost. Potter at last succeeded in extricating his troops from the confusion, and pushed on towards the crest. But being unsupported, and the rebels being then prepared to meet him, he was driven back by the storm of grape and canister which was hurled into his ranks.

The rebels concentrated their fire into the crowded crater, where our brigades had thrown up some slight intrenchments. The day was lost. Nothing remained but to escape as rapidly as possible from the gorge, which the soldiers truly designated as a slaughter-pen. It was certain death to remain. It was almost equally certain death to attempt a retreat, as the rebel batteries swept the only possible line of escape. On this bloody day, in which we might so easily have gained a signal victory, we lost, in killed, wounded, and prisoners, four thousand men. The enemy lost but a thousand.

The plan did not originate with General Grant. He saw, however, that it was a wise undertaking, and gave to it his consent. All engrossed as he was with the immense cares of the campaign, he very properly left the details of this local enterprise to those who had conceived the design. In the subsequent examination of this affair by the Committee on the Conduct of the War, General Grant said, —

"General Burnside wanted to put his colored division in front; and I believe, that, if he had done so, it would have been a success. Still I agreed with General Meade in his objection to the plan. General Meade said, that if we put colored troops in front, and it should prove a failure, it would then be said, probably, that we were shoving those people ahead to get killed, because we did not care any thing about them. But that could not be said, if we put white troops in front."

This Committee on the Conduct of the War assign the following as reasons why the attack should have been successful: —

1. The evident surprise of the enemy at the time of the explosion of the mine and for some time after.

2. The comparatively small force in the enemy's works.

3. The ineffective fire of the enemy's artillery and musketry; there being scarcely any for about thirty minutes after the explosion, and our artillery being just the reverse as to time and power.

4. The fact that our troops were able to get two hundred yards before the crater, towards the west, but could not remain there, or proceed farther, for want of supports.

This repulse was a great disappointment, but it did not occasion the slighest shade of despondency in the army or throughout the country. Still the weary days glided along. There was incessant digging, marching, fighting. There were bombardments and skirmishes and charges and bold raids, day after day. No pen can ever describe them all. The rebel intrenchments were very strong, — so strong that there could easily be spared from their impregnable ramparts a force sufficiently numerous to enable them to command the valley of the Shenandoah.

About the middle of August, a series of movements was commenced on the north bank of the James. The rebels fought bravely from behind their intrenchments. Still our troops, with amazing recklessness of courage, stormed the ramparts, and obtained positions within six miles of Richmond. This attack upon Richmond from the north was intended as a feint, to draw off the troops of Lee in that direction.

In co-operation with this movement, Gregg's cavalry division was sent, on the morning of the 18th, with four days' rations, to make another attempt to gain possession of the Weldon Railroad. They left their encampment at four o'clock, and at eight o'clock struck the road at a station six miles south of Richmond. One portion of the command immediately commenced tearing up and destroying the track. Another strong, well-armed detachment advanced two or three miles towards the city, and intrenched themselves in a position to repel the foe. The tidings soon reached the ears of Lee. He hurried forward two brigades for the rescue of the road. There was a sanguinary battle, which continued until night. The rebels were driven back with the loss of about a thousand men. As it was certain that General Lee would make the most desperate endeavors to regain the road, our troops toiled through the night in enlarging and strengthening their defences.

The next day the rebels came down from Petersburg in overwhelming force. With the utmost fury they commenced the battle. The result was long doubtful. They were just upon the point of a very decisive and bloody victory, when the Ninth Army Corps opportunely arrived to the support of their exhausted comrades of the Fifth; and the exultant rebels were decisively repulsed. Their exhaustion was so great, and their loss so heavy, that they did not venture the next day — Saturday — to renew the attack. The precious hours, the Union troops employed in strengthening their works.

Sunday morning the rebels, having recruited their strength and received large re-enforcements from the city, moved forward with much energy, for another struggle to regain the road. They were repulsed with great slaughter. Monday, they renewed the attack; and again their charging lines melted away before the awful storm of grape and canister belched from our ramparts. Tuesday, these desperate men, with renovated numbers, marched forth again to the assault; and again, torn and broken, they retreated, leaving the ground covered with their slain. We had gained the Weldon Road, two and a half miles from Petersburg, and all the powers of Rebeldom could not force General Grant to relinquish his hold. The loss of the road was a terrible calamity to General Lee. It cut off so important a line for supplies and recruits as to forebode the destruction of his army. Lee therefore resolved to make another attempt, with all his available strength, to regain the road. He concentrated an immense force, gathered from every point of his encampment from which troops could be spared, and massed them in heavy columns concealed in the forest.

At a given signal they all rushed upon our lines, leaped over our breastworks, and engaged in a hand-to-hand fight. The struggle on both sides was marked with desperation which had not been surpassed during the war.

The carnage was dreadful. Our troops fought desperately against these overpowering numbers. Though they lost two thousand prisoners, and a thousand in killed and wounded, they still held their position during the day. When night came, they fell back a few miles along the railroad, to a still stronger position, where they could defy all the efforts of the enemy to dislodge them.

General Grant did not allow General Lee an hour of

repose. From the rebel forts and bastions north of Richmond to their ramparts south of Petersburg, there was a distance of about thirty miles. General Grant, by making demonstrations, now at this point and now at that, kept the rebel troops in a state of constant harassment, compelling them incessantly to traverse this distance, to and fro, of thirty miles, to protect menaced points.

Occasionally a day would be appointed for shelling the city. All the day long, the roar of the bombardment shook the hills, as shot and shell fell like hail into the streets and upon the dwellings of Petersburg. There was but little sense of honor with these bold, bad men who were fighting for the destruction of free institutions. They often bayoneted our wounded; shot in cold blood our colored soldiers, refusing them any quarter; and literally starved to death the prisoners they took.

The great issues of the war did not depend at all upon the death, here and there, of individual soldiers. There was consequently often a tacit truce between the pickets, when the men on both sides would walk unmolested in front of their works, and there was a friendly interchange of newspapers, tobacco, and coffee, while the Union and Confederate soldiers would good-humoredly talk and joke together. It was deemed a point of honor that the signal should be given, on such occasions, before hostilities were resumed. One day while our men were out as usual, exposed on the plain before their works, the rebels opened fire upon them without any warning. The Richmond editors rubbed their hands with glee over this achievement, which they pronounced to be a " delicious piece of retaliation " for the bombardment of Petersburg. Two hundred Union soldiers were thus murdered; for this was deliberate murder, not honorable warfare.

On the 4th of September, tidings reached General Grant's army, that General Sherman had taken Atlanta. The joyful event was celebrated by the salute of a hundred shotted guns discharged upon the doomed city, and by the cheers of a hundred thousand men. The rebels, in defiant reply, opened fire from every gun. This brought into action all the batteries along our lines, and, for an hour, war's tempest raged in its most sublime uproar. Scarcely any thing human can be conceived more impressive than this response to General Sherman's telegram announcing his great victory.

Thus the weeks of battle and of blood rolled on. Not for an hour was there any cessation. The Weldon Road was now our own, and the rebels found ever increasing difficulty to obtain supplies. Early in September we had a well-constructed railroad, passing through the heart of our camps, a distance of nearly thirty miles, from City Point — our base of supplies — to the position at our extreme left on the Weldon Road. An effort was now made by some distinguished and benevolent men in the North, with the consent of the Government, to stay the further effusion of blood by peace. But Jefferson Davis, the rebel chieftain, would listen to no terms which did not destroy the Government of the United States. " The North," said he, " was mad and blind. It would not let us govern ourselves. So the war came. Now it must go on till the last man falls in his tracks, and his children seize his musket and fight his battles. We will govern ourselves. We will do it, if we have to see every Southern plantation sacked, and every Southern city in flames."

CHAPTER XXIII.

General Grant's Report. — General Butler's Movement upon Richmond. — March to the South-side Railroad. — Midnight Bombardment. — Renewed attempt upon the South-side Railroad. — President Lincoln's Second Inaugural. — Sherman's Wonderful March. — Ravages of the March. — Capture of Savannah.

HERE were two approaches by which General Grant was now crowding upon Richmond. One was from the north, by the roads which led from Malvern Hill and Deep Bottom. The other was from the south, leading either through or around Petersburg. From both these directions General Grant was waging an incessant battle. In his official report, he had said to the Government, —

" From an early period in the Rebellion, I had been impressed with the idea that active and continuous operations of all the troops that could be brought into the field, regardless of season and weather, were necessary to a speedy termination of the war. From the first, I was firm in the conviction that no peace could be had, that would be stable and conducive to the happiness of the people, both North and South, until the military power of the Rebellion was entirely broken. I therefore determined first, to use the greatest number of troops practicable against the armed force of the enemy, preventing him from using the same force, at different seasons, against first one and then another of our armies, and from the possibility of repose for refitting, and producing necessary supplies for carrying on resistance ; second, to hammer continuously against the armed force of the enemy and his resources until, by mere attrition if in no other way, there should be nothing left to him but an equal submission, with the loyal section of our common country, to the Constitution and laws of the land."

General Grant, being now firmly in possession of the Weldon Road, made preparations for another advance in his investing circle towards the west, to seize the South-side Railroad, which ran from Petersburg directly west to Burkville and Lynchburg. The loss of this important line of communication would be irreparable to the rebels To cover the movement, another very vigorous attack was to be made upon Richmond from the north.

In the night of Wednesday, Sept. 28, the Eighteenth and Tenth Corps, in light marching order, moved from Bermuda Hundred up to Jones Neck, where they crossed the James on muffled pontoons, and marched to the vicinity of Deep Bottom. General Grant, with General Butler, who was in command at Bermuda Hundred, accompanied the expedition. The troops pressed along as rapidly as possible, and before daylight encountered the enemy's pickets, and drove them in. Fighting their way onward, through many brisk skirmishes, after a march of three miles, they came to a road running from the one they were upon to the James River, near Fort Darling, but a few miles below Richmond.

Here they found a long line of intrenchments, very strong in their construction, heavily armed, and crowded with troops. The line was strengthened by connecting forts. The adjacent eminences, lining the left banks of the river, frowned with batteries. Drury's Bluff, crowned by Fort Darling, was upon the opposite side of the river. Our troops found themselves in the midst of a labyrinth of fortifications, which the rebels had been constructing for three years. For miles there was an interminable series of forts, ramparts, bastions, rifle-pits, and connecting passages. Defeated at any one point, the rebels had but to retreat a few yards in the rear to another equally strong.

General Grant, as we have said, accompanied this expedition. Quiet and undemonstrative as he was, his presence inspired the troops with tenfold ardor. A broad, open plain skirted the approach to the frowning ramparts. The country around was a wilderness region, sparsely inhabited, filled with forests. Our troops formed in the dense woods, dashed out over the plain, and, in the face of an appalling fire, which struck down eight hundred of their number, clambered over the first line of intrenchments, and carried them with loud cheers. We thus captured one of the forts, which was called Fort Morris. Sixteen pieces of artillery — several of them heavy siege-guns — were the trophies of the gallant achievement.

Scarcely a bullet struck the rebels, as they fled to other protected points in the rear, and immediately opened upon the victors, from every gun which could be brought to bear upon them, a deadly fire. The position could not be held.

In the mean time, General Birney, in command of the Tenth Corps, with Paine's colored division of the Eighteenth Corps, had marched from the New Market Road, down the Kingsland Road, towards the river. Here, on a

commanding eminence called New Market Heights, they
found the foe, as ever, strongly intrenched, and surrounded by all the means of defence which modern military
art could supply. The colored troops led the charge
with great gallantry. Though in the impetuous rush
nearly six hundred men dropped by the way, struck down
by the deadly fire of the foe, the rebels were driven pell-
mell from their works before this long line of eager, black
faces. White troops never fought better. General Grant
was delighted with their heroism, and they were re-
warded with a special letter of congratulation. General
Birney pushed on with his exultant troops along the New
Market Road, until he came within six miles of Richmond.

General Kautz, with his cavalry, was sent out to recon-
noitre. The horsemen passed rapidly along the Central
Road until they reached a spot within a few miles of
Richmond, where several batteries opened fire upon them.
General Terry also crossed from the New Market to the
Central Road, and followed the path the cavalry had traversed. These movements alarmed General Lee. He
had no means of knowing how large was the force assailing him from the north. There was danger that Richmond might be penetrated through some weak point, and
captured.

On Friday morning, both of the Union corps were concentrated before Harrison Battery, within three miles of
the city. They had cut through the most advanced
works of the enemy, and were now prepared to deal
ponderous blows upon the inner line. The thunder of
their guns shook the dwellings of the rebel metropolis.
Richmond was thrown into consternation. Every available man was brought into requisition. General Lee,

with his re-enforcements, pushed forward with the utmost precipitancy to meet the emergence.

In the mean time, General Grant, leaving General Butler to conduct the movement before Richmond, had hurried back a distance of over thirty miles to superintend his grand movement upon the South-side Road, for which this attack upon Richmond was merely preparatory. The column of advance was composed of two divisions of the Ninth Corps, and most of the Fifth. General Warren was in command. The weather was fine, the roads in admirable condition. The troops, in the best of spirits, commenced their march as if setting out on an excursion of pleasure. They left Four Mile Station on the Weldon Road, and, by a circuitous route of about twenty miles, approached the Lynchburg Road at a point called Poplar Grove.

General Lee had availed himself of all his resources to prevent the possibility of the capture of this railway, which was so essential to the sustenance of his army. On the march our troops encountered a series of forts, intrenchments, and rifle-pits, which involved them in several very bloody battles. Exhausted, bleeding, with thinned ranks, these determined men toiled on. Rain came, and, with the rain, the mud. Along the flooded roads, and beneath the blackened sky, the tempest of battle flashed and roared. We gained victory after victory, but always at a heavy price. The enemy, when unable longer to resist the impetuous charges, fled to other works in the rear. Thus the Union troops fought their way along, mile after mile. Though the enemy was found in such strength that we were not able to get possession of the South-side Railroad, our troops gained a position but a few miles from it, at Poplar Grove Church, from which no efforts of the rebels could drive us. Thus, step by step, General Grant was advancing in his great achievement.

General Butler's movement on the north was eminently successful. He gained and held positions which annoyed Lee exceedingly. Though the rebel general exerted his utmost strength, sacrificing thousands of men in the struggle to drive General Butler back, all his efforts were unavailing. At every point the Union army was steadily making progress, and seldom did General Grant lose any position which his troops had won.

The latter part of October, there was another movement organized against the South-side Road. The column selected for this important enterprise upon the railway consisted of Hancock's Second Corps, Weitzel's Eighteenth Infantry, and the Cavalry Corps of Kautz and Gregg. The march was to be conducted with the greatest secrecy, by remote and obscure roads. No bugle-calls were to be sounded, no camp-fires were to be built. Generals Grant and Meade accompanied the expedition.

But in some way, — no one knows how, — the rebels had gained information of the movement, and had secretly gathered a large force to repel it. The troops started just before daylight. After a short march, as they were fording a small stream, they found themselves almost ambushed in the midst of the foe. Batteries frowned all around them. Felled trees encumbered the roads. From every point they were assailed, by both infantry and artillery. They fought desperately and, as usual, victoriously, slowly forcing their way along. Their ammunition was nearly exhausted, and with the night a heavy rain set in. As it was evident that the rebels were gathered at that point in great force, and that their series of intrenchments could only be carried at the expense of a fearful slaughter of the Union troops, it was deemed best to abandon the expedition. All the night long, through the darkness and the rain, the troops, exhausted as they were, marched back to the camps which they had left so hopefully in the morning. But no one was disheartened. General Grant had his hand upon the throat of the Rebellion; and, notwithstanding its writhings, he would not relinquish his grasp until the monster was strangled.

Thus days and weeks of incessant warfare passed without any very decisive results, though, daily, Lee was losing and Grant was gaining.

It is important that there should be some reference to General Sherman's wonderful march from Chattanooga to Savannah; for this was a very essential part of Grant's campaign against Richmond. In a speech which General Sherman made in Louisville from the balcony of the Burnett House, after the close of the war, he said, —

" While we are here together to-night, let me tell you, as a point of historical interest, that here, upon this spot, in this very hotel, and, I think, almost in the room through which I reached this balcony, General Grant and I laid down our maps, and studied the campaign which ended the war. I had been away down in Mississippi, finishing up an unfinished job I had down there, when General Grant called for me, by telegraph, to meet him in Nashville. But we were bothered so much there that we came up here, and in this hotel sat down with our maps, and talked over the lines and the operations by means of which we were to reach the heart of our enemy. He went to Richmond, and I to Atlanta. The result was just as we laid it out in this hotel, in March, 1864."

In President Lincoln's second inaugural address, he said, standing upon the steps of the Capitol, in words which were echoed throughout all Christendom, —

"The Almighty has his own purposes. ' Woe unto the world because of offences ! for it must needs be that offences come ; but woe to that man by whom the offence cometh !' If we shall suppose that American slavery is one of those offences which in the providence of God must needs come, but which, having continued through his appointed time, he now wills to remove, and that he gives to both North and South this war as the woe due to those by whom the offence came, shall we discern therein any departure from those divine attributes which the believers in a living God always ascribe to him ? Fondly do we hope, fervently do we pray, that the mighty scourge of war may speedily pass away. Yet if God wills that it continue until all the wealth piled by the bondman's two hundred and fifty years of unrequited toil shall be sunk, and until every drop of blood drawn with the lash shall be paid by another drawn by the sword, as was said three thousand years ago, so still it must be said, 'The judgments of the Lord are true and righteous altogether.' "

On the 25th of December, 1864, General Sherman had achieved his sublime march from Atlanta to Savannah. With his majestic host he had swept across the whole State of Georgia, in a path sixty miles in width and over three hundred in length, destroying every thing which could assist the rebels to carry on the war. About sixty thousand troops were gathered under his banners. Three thousand five hundred wagons were in his train, requiring the services of thirty-five thousand horses in addition to the cavalry.

The destruction was awful. The army marched the whole distance in twenty-four days. In the entire command, but five hundred and sixty-seven men of all ranks were either killed or wounded. Ten thousand negroes, liberating themselves, entered Savannah in the train of the army. Thirteen hundred and thirty-eight of the Confederate army were made prisoners. Twenty thousand bales of cotton were burned, besides twenty-five thousand captured at Savannah. Thirteen thousand head of beef-cattle, nine million five hundred thousand pounds of corn, and ten million five hundred thousand pounds of fodder were taken from the country. Foragers were every day sent out, along the whole line of route, to gather all the sheep, hogs, turkeys, geese, chickens, sweet potatoes, and rice from the plantations. Five thousand horses and four thousand mules were impressed for the cavalry and trains. Three hundred and twenty miles of railway were destroyed, by burning every tie, twisting every rail while heated red hot over the flaming piles of the ties, and laying in ruins every depot, engine-house, repair-tank, water-tank, and turn-table. Thus the communication between the Confederate armies in Virginia and in the West was effectually severed. General Sherman estimated the damage done to the State of Georgia at a hundred million dollars. Of this, twenty million dollars inured to our advantage. The remainder was simple waste and destruction.

Such is war. These dreadful blows were necessary to bring the wicked rebellion to an end. The discipline of the army was well maintained. After the capture of Atlanta, General Sherman considered it a military necessity to dismantle and destroy the city, before he cut loose from his base of supplies, and commenced his perilous

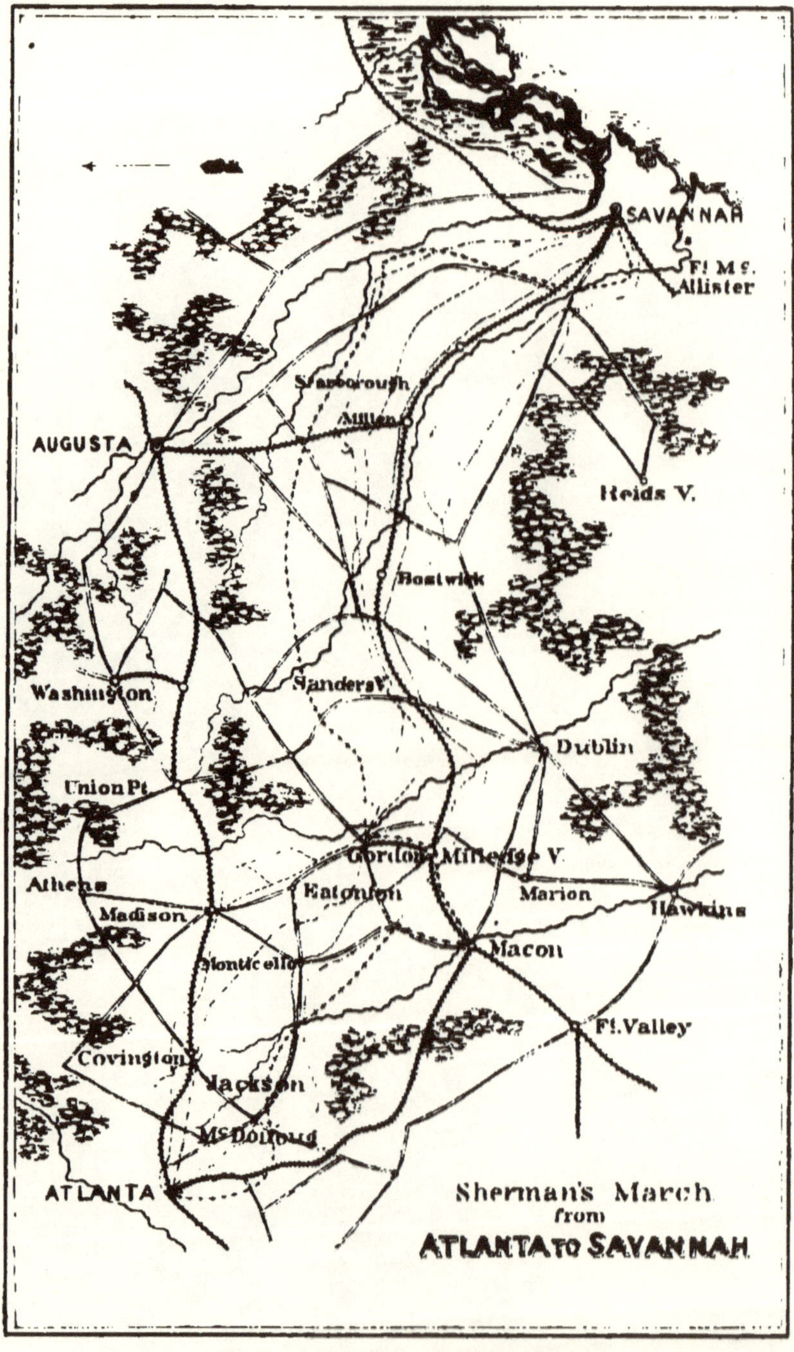

SAVANNAH
Ft. Mc.
Allister
Scarborough
Millen
Reids V.
AUGUSTA
Bostwick
Sanders V.
Washington
Dublin
Union Pt.
Gordon Milledge V.
Athens
Eatonton
Marion
Hawkins
Madison
Monticello
Macon
Ft. Valley
Covington
Jackson
McDonoug
ATLANTA
Sherman's March
from
ATLANTA TO SAVANNAH

march where for. nearly a month his army would be lost from all communication with the North.

The wonderful march from Atlanta to Savannah was accomplished in four columns, each masked in all directions by clouds of skirmishers. From the time the army left Atlanta until its arrival before Savannah, — about twenty-four days, — not a word of intelligence respecting it was received by the Government, or by the people of the North, except through Confederate newspapers. So many points were threatened by General Sherman, and each with such force, that it was impossible for the enemy to decide whether Augusta, Macon, or Savannah were his immediate objective.

The march was magnificently accomplished. We have not space here for its thrilling details. On the 25th of December, President Lincoln received the following telegram from General Sherman : —

"I beg to present you, as a Christmas gift, the city of Savannah, with a hundred and fifty heavy guns and plenty of ammunition, and also about twenty-five thousand bales of cotton."

To this President Lincoln immediately replied, —

"MY DEAR GENERAL SHERMAN, — Many, many thanks for your Christmas gift, — the capture of Savannah. When you were about to leave Atlanta for the Atlantic, I was *anxious*, if not fearful ; but feeling that you were the better judge, and remembering that 'nothing risked, nothing gained,' I did not interfere. Now, this undertaking being a success, the honor is all yours ; for I believe that none of us went further than to acquiesce. And taking the work of General Thomas into the count, as it should be taken, it is indeed a great success.

"Not only does it afford the obvious and immediate

military advantages, but in showing to the world that your army could be divided, putting the stronger part to an important new service, and yet leaving enough to vanquish the old opposing forces of the whole, — Hood's army, — it brings those who sat in darkness to see a great light.

" But what next ? I suppose it will be safe, if I leave General Grant and yourself to decide. Please make my grateful acknowledgments to your whole army, — officers and men.

" Yours very truly,

" A. LINCOLN."

Thus closed the year 1864. Everywhere the armies of the Union were triumphant: everywhere the Rebellion was reeling and staggering beneath the blows which were dealt upon it.

CHAPTER XXIV.

THE FINAL VICTORY.

Pride of the Rebels. — Anxiety of the North for Peace. — Sherman's March through the Carolinas. — The Ravages of War. — Grant's Comprehensive Plans. — Continued Battles. — Lee's Plan of Escape. — The Last Struggle. — Lee's Utter Discomfiture. — His Flight. — The Surrender. — Overthrow of the Rebellion. — Grant's Farewell Address.

S we entered upon the fourth year of the war, it was evident to every intelligent observer that the affairs of the Rebellion were hopeless. General Lee was unquestionably as fully aware of this as was any one else. The prolongation of the conflict could only prolong the reign of misery and death. Still pride impelled the rebel leaders, notwithstanding the fearful woes they were bringing upon their own section of the country, to persist to the last extremity. It was not a heroic, but a cruel and a wicked resolve. It accomplished no good, and only entailed untold misery upon tens of thousands of helpless families.

The North was anxious for peace, and was willing to offer almost any terms consistent with national honor and territorial integrity. President Lincoln had visited the army at Petersburg, and, for the first time, witnessed war in all its horrors. His kind heart was harrowed by the revolting spectacle.

" He walked over ground covered with bodies of the slain, more numerous than he could count or cared to count. He saw living men with broken heads and mangled forms, and heard the hopeless groans and piteous wails of the dying whom no human hand could save. He witnessed the bloody work of the surgeons, — those carpenters and joiners of human frames, — and saw amputated legs and arms piled up in heaps, to be carted away like the offal of a slaughter-house; and he turned from the horrid sight, exclaiming, ' This is war, horrid war, —the trade of barbarians.'. Appealing to his principal officers, he inquired, ' Gentlemen, is there no way by which we can put a stop to this fighting ? ' "*

But Jefferson Davis and his confederates had madly resolved to overthrow our free institutions, and they would listen to no terms whatever which did not destroy the life of the nation. Nothing was left for General Grant but to strike, with all his strength, the final blows. Sherman swept like a tornado through South and North Carolina. All opposition melted away before him. Charleston, humiliated, scathed, utterly ruined, fell 'into his hands. His conquering legions went wherever they would, capturing whatever they wished to capture, destroying whatever they wished to destroy. The destruction of Lee's army was mathematically certain, so soon as Sherman should cross the Roanoke, and, in immediate co-operation with General Grant, should complete the investment of Richmond. The magnificent combinations of General Grant were now coming to a triumphant conclusion.

General Sherman commenced his march from Savan-

* Sherman and his Campaigns, p. 394.

nah, with an army full sixty thousand strong. He marched along roads several miles apart, but nearly parallel, in columns of about fifteen thousand men. Each column, with its baggage train, filled to its utmost capacity about ten miles of road. The troops were mainly subsisted upon the country through which they passed. All public property which could aid the Rebellion was destroyed. Depots, car-shops, manufactories, were burned. The path of desolation which the army left behind it, nearly sixty miles in breadth, was dreadful.

South Carolina had rendered herself peculiarly obnoxious to the nation. Her representatives in Congress had long been insolent in tone to the highest degree, avowedly seeking to provoke a quarrel. South Carolina had first seceded, and had bombarded Sumter, seeking thus to " fire the Southern heart," and to constrain the other slave States to unite with her in dissolving the Union. She had thus sown the wind. And now, when the whirlwind came, with its sweep of desolation and woe, few pitied her, as she sat sullen and unrepentant in the midst of her ruins.

The triumphant Union columns pressed along, sweeping all opposition before them. As our troops advanced, the rebels retreated precipitately from Charleston. There the Rebellion commenced, and, in the providence of God, upon that city fell the most direful punishment. For fourteen months it had been in a state of siege. During that time, thirteen thousand shells had been thrown into the town. These terrible missiles, rising high into the air, plunged upon the roofs of churches, hotels, dwellings, stores, and, passing to the basement, exploded with force which left the whole edifice but a pile of ruins. A sad scene of desolation was presented to our troops as they entered the war-scathed city. The whole of the lower part of the town presented but a blackened area of roofless houses, crumbling walls, upheaved pavements, grass-grown streets, with here and there a few men and women wandering listless and woe-stricken.

It was now certain that General Sherman would soon be able to unite his army with that of General Grant, and then a few remaining blows would put an end to the Rebellion. The campaign in Georgia and the Carolinas, destroying the railroads and all the resources of war there, was essential to prevent Lee from retreating to those regions, and there prolonging the conflict for years. The mind of General Grant ranged the whole vast field of the struggle, and planned all the details of the movements which were to combine in effecting the final result. On the 20th of February, he wrote as follows to his energetic cavalry-leader, General Sheridan : —

"As soon as it is possible to travel, I think you will have no difficulty about visiting Lynchburg, with a cavalry force alone. From thence you could destroy the railroad and canal in every direction, so as to be of no further use to the Rebellion. Sufficient cavalry should be left behind to look after Moseby's gang. From Lynchburg, if information you might get there would justify it, you could strike south, heading the streams in Virginia, to the westward of Danville, and push on, and join Sherman.

"This additional raid, with one now starting from East Tennessee under Stoneman, numbering four or five thousand cavalry; one from Eastport, Mississippi, numbering ten thousand cavalry; Canby, from Mobile Bay, numbering thirty-eight thousand mixed troops, — these three latter pushing for Tuscaloosa, Selma, and Montgomery ; and Sherman, with a large army eating out the vitals of

RALEIGH
Pittsboro
GOLDSBORO
Salisbury
Newton
Lincolnton
Charlotte
FAYETTEVILLE
Sneedsboro
Lumberton
Cheraw
WILMINGTON
Camden
Florence
COLUMBIA
Cades
George T.
Orangeburg
Black
CHARLESTOWN
Robert V.
SAVANNAH
Sherman's March
from
SAVANNAH TO GOLDSBORO

South Carolina, — is all that will be wanted to leave nothing for the Rebellion to stand upon. I would advise you to overcome great obstacles to accomplish this. Charleston was evacuated on Tuesday last."

At daylight on the morning of the 25th of March, Lee made his last offensive movement. He massed an immense force, and endeavored to break Grant's line at Fort Steadman, — a square redoubt, covering about one acre, and defended by nine guns. The rush was so sudden and impetuous that in about a minute the fort, which was about five hundred feet from the enemy's lines, was captured by the foe. But scarcely had the rebels' first yell of victory died away ere Colonel Tidball's artillery opened upon them; and the rebels, at the same time attacked in the rear, were forced out, pell-mell, with the loss of eighteen hundred prisoners, and a total loss of three thousand men.

President Lincoln witnessed this battle from an elevation in the vicinity. A general attack was ordered ; and our troops, in retaliation, took the intrenched picket-line of the enemy, and held it, notwithstanding all Lee's efforts to get it back. General Grant was well satisfied with the results of the day. He said, in the evening, —

"It will tell upon the next great battle. Lee has made a desperate attempt, and failed."

The rebels were gathering in great strength, under General Joe Johnston, in the vicinity of Goldsborough and Raleigh, hoping there to overwhelm General Sherman. General Grant sent General Sheridan, with his cavalry, to the assistance of Sherman, and also sent General Schofield, with two divisions, to advance to his aid by the way of Newberne. A junction was soon effected between these forces, the rebels being bloodily repulsed in all their endeavors to prevent it. Triumphantly General Schofield's troops and General Sherman's, advancing from different directions, entered Goldsborough together, and grasped hands in excess of joy. It was the union of the two armies. They were now in a position to co-operate, and to strike the few remaining blows before which the Confederacy was doomed to fall.

General Sherman hastened to the headquarters of General Grant, where he arrived on the evening of March 29th. An eye-witness has thus described this interview : —

" I was sitting in the office of General Grant's adjutant-general, on the morning of the 28th of March, and saw President Lincoln, with Generals Grant, Sherman, Meade, and Sheridan, coming up the walk. Look at the men whose names are to have a conspicuous place in the annals of America : Lincoln, — tall, round-shouldered, loose-jointed, large-featured, deep-eyed, with a smile upon his face ; he is dressed in black, and wears a fashionable silk hat. Grant is at Lincoln's right, shorter, stouter, more compact; wears a military hat, with a stiff, broad brim ; has his hands in his pantaloons pocket, and is puffing away at a cigar, while listening to Sherman. Sherman, — tall, with high, commanding forehead ; is almost as loosely built as Lincoln ; has sandy whiskers, closely cropped, and sharp, twinkling eyes, long arms and legs, shabby coat, slouch hat, his pants tucked into his boots. He is talking hurriedly, gesticulating now to Lincoln, now to Grant, his eyes wandering everywhere. Meade, — also tall, with thin, sharp features, a gray beard, and spectacles ; is a little stooping in his gait. Sheridan, — the shortest of all, quick and energetic in all his movements, with a face bronzed by sun and wind ; courteous, affable, a thorough soldier. The plan of the lieutenant-general was then made known to his subordinates, and each departed, during the day, to carry into execution the respective parts assigned them." *

General Grant's line was now about forty miles in length, extending from the north side of the James to Hatchie's Run. General Weitzel was in command of the position on the north side of the James River. The crisis was approaching, and Grant watched every movement of Lee with a sleepless eye. His great apprehension was that Lee would attempt to escape, and effect a junction with General Johnston, who had an army near Raleigh, estimated by General Sherman at between thirty and forty thousand infantry, and ten thousand cavalry. The united armies of Lee and Johnston, falling suddenly upon Sherman, might crush him.

It was Grant's intention, the moment Lee commenced this movement, to fall furiously, with his whole force, upon the evacuating columns. On Friday, the last day of March, the Fifth Corps was moved south and west to take an important position near the bridge over Gravelly Run. The enemy was strongly intrenched here. The Second and Third Divisions attacked them, and were driven back in confusion. General Griffin rode up to General J. Lawrence Chamberlain, and said, —

" General, the Fifth Corps is disgraced. I have told General Warren that you can retake that field. Will you save the honor of the corps ? "

It was an appalling undertaking. With one brigade, already exhausted by hard fighting, and weakened by severe loss, General Chamberlain was to attack the foe

* Four Years of Fighting. By Charles Carleton Coffin, p. 488.

flushed with victory. He formed his lines, dashed through the stream, and drove the enemy back, for more than a mile, to the edge of a hill. Here, as the enemy appeared in greater force, he was ordered to halt, that the strength and position of the foe might be ascertained. But he begged permission to press on, asking only for several regiments to support his flanks *en échelon.* He then, upon the double-quick, swept the field, and gained a lodgement on the White Oak Road, which enabled the Fifth Corps to render essential service in cutting off the retreat of Lee.

On this day, Grant saw indications that Lee was about to move. He hurled his whole army against the rebel lines. For three days, the battle raged with as much determination and carnage as had been at any time witnessed during the war. On the 3d of April, Lee's line was crushed at all points, and the next morning both Petersburg and Richmond were evacuated. Lee, with his shattered army, was in full flight. The glad tidings that morning ran along the wires, creating indescribable joy : —

"Richmond and Petersburg are ours. A third part of Lee's army is destroyed. For the remainder, there is no escape."

The rebels retreated mainly by two roads, — one across the Appomattox towards Amelia Court-house, and the other bending to the left towards Lynchburg. They were hotly pursued. Their path was strewed with the *débris* of a routed army, and many prisoners were picked up. The flight and the pursuit were continued on the 3d and on the 4th. The Fifth Corps had gained a commanding position, half-way between Amelia Court-house and Burksville, effectually cutting off the further retreat in that direction. The rebel army was now at our mercy.

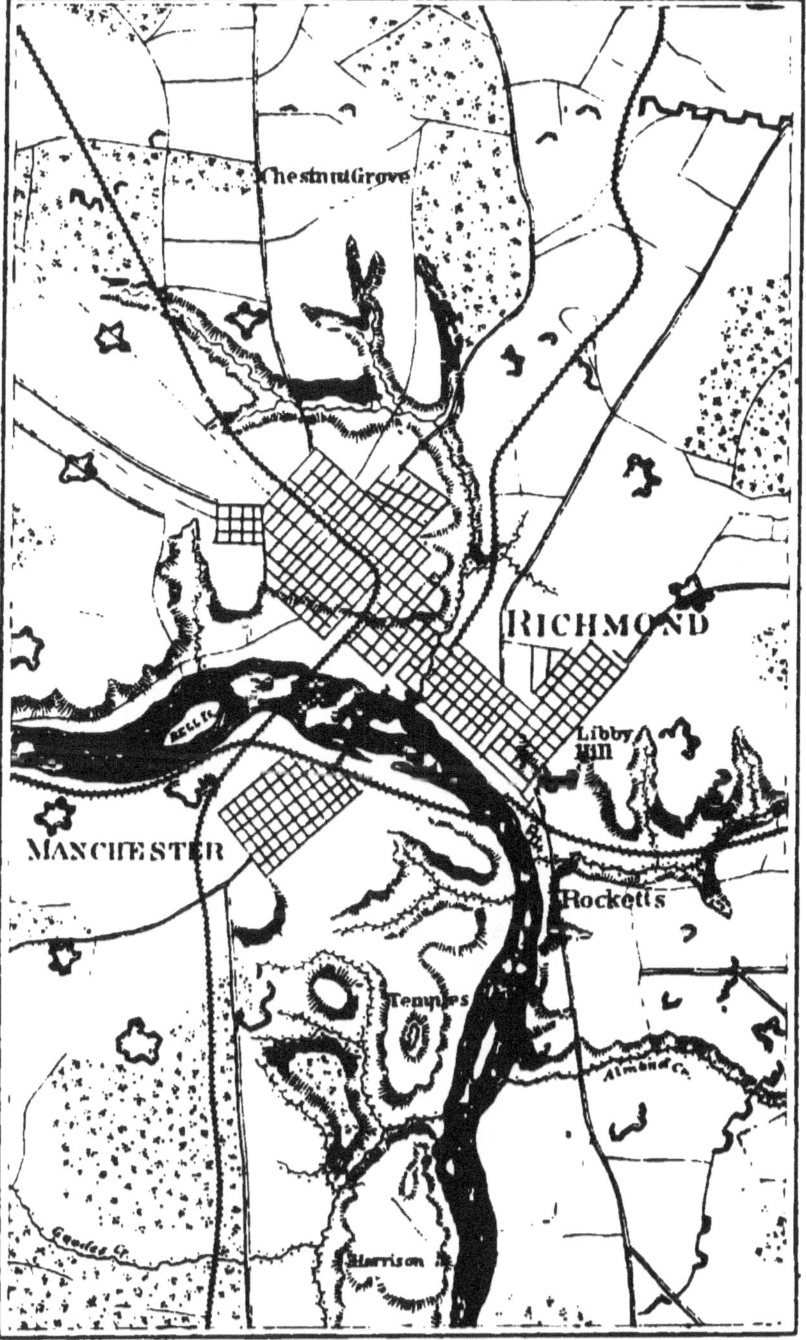

Chestnut Grove
RICHMOND
Libby Hill
BELL Id.
MANCHESTER
Rockett's
Tennis
Almond Cr.
Goodes Cr.
Harrison

· It could not escape. There was nothing before it but
surrender or destruction. General Grant, anxious to
avoid the further effusion of blood, condescended (and
under the circumstances it was a great condescension) to
make the first advances, and to urge General Lee to
surrender. On the 7th, he sent the following despatch
to Lee:—

" The result of the last week must convince you of the
hopelessness of further resistance, on the part of the
Army of Northern Virginia, in this struggle. I feel that
it is so, and regard it as my duty to shift from myself
the responsibility of any further effusion of blood, by
asking of you the surrender of that portion of the Con-
federate-States Army known as the Army of Northern
Virginia."

General Lee, while affecting to doubt whether his condition were entirely hopeless, still asked for the conditions on which the surrender would be received. General Grant replied,—

" Peace being my first desire, there is but one condition
I insist upon ; namely, that the men surrendered shall be
disqualified for taking up arms against the Government
of the United States, until properly exchanged."

General Lee's response to this was evasive, assuming
that he did not think that the emergency called for a
surrender, but that he would meet General Grant to talk
over the " restoration of peace." General Grant replied ;
and his reply shows the clearness of his intellectual
vision:—

" As I have no authority to treat on the subject of
peace, the meeting proposed could lead to no good. I
will state, however, general, that I am equally anxious
for peace with yourself, and the whole North entertains

the same feeling. The terms upon which peace may be had are well understood. By the South laying down their arms, they will hasten that most desirable event, save thousands of human lives, and hundreds of millions of property not yet destroyed. Sincerely hoping that all our difficulties may be settled without the loss of another life, I subscribe myself,

"Very respectfully, your obedient servant,

"U. S. GRANT."

General Lee must have seen that it was in vain to attempt to parley, or to prevaricate, with so clear-sighted and straight-forward a man. He returned a despatch consenting to the interview. But General Grant was then miles away, pushing the pursuit with all vigor. He received Lee's despatch at half-past eleven of the 9th. He hurried to the front, and held an interview with Lee. The terms were very simple. All the officers and men were to give their parole not to serve against the United States until exchanged. All the arms, artillery, and public property were to be packed and stacked, and turned over to the officers appointed by Grant to receive them. The officers were permitted to retain their side-arms and their private horses or baggage.

There was nothing for Lee to say but yes or no. He said yes. At half-past three, P.M., the terms were signed. Our troops had overtaken — as we have mentioned — the main body of Lee's army, upon a plain surrounded by hills, from which there was no possible escape. They were just ready to open fire, when they were astounded by the outbursts of cheer upon cheer from the exhausted, bleeding, despairing rebel troops. They had first received the tidings of the capitulation, and their joyful shouts conveyed the glad news to our army. The cheer was echoed back, and the voices of friend and foe blended in that joyful cry. The Union troops, who were pressing along in the rear, caught the shout, learned its significance, and passed it along their ranks in thunder roar. For miles, the hills and the forests rang with the acclaim of that grand, patriot army, rejoicing that the spirit of rebellion was now trampled down forever.

Johnston's condition was hopeless. He could be instantly crushed beneath the armies of Grant and Sherman. Johnston promptly surrendered. General Sherman consented to terms which were certainly inconsiderate, but the reasons for which were not then fully understood; and he was censured with very undue severity. The terms he proposed were not ratified by the Government; and General Sherman, co-operating with General Grant, received the surrender of Johnston's army upon the same terms with those accepted by General Lee. The scattered rebel bands, upon receiving these tidings, either surrendered, or dispersed to their homes. The number surrendered amounted to 174,223. The number of rebel prisoners then on hand was 98,802. The whole Union military force, on the 1st of May, amounted to 1,000,516. Jefferson Davis, with several members of his cabinet, accompanied by a small body of cavalry, endeavored to escape, hoping to reach some Southern seaport, and take ship for foreign lands. He was hotly pursued, and was caught at Irwinsville, in Georgia, on the morning of the 10th of May. He exposed himself to much derision, by being captured disguised in the garb of a woman.

The war was ended. The nation was saved. General Grant was pronounced, by the unanimous voice of his countrymen, the Washington of the conflict. In the following address, issued on the 2d of June, 1865, General Grant took leave of all the armies which had been so long guided by his genius in their arduous campaigns : —

"SOLDIERS OF THE ARMIES OF THE UNITED STATES, — By your patriotic devotion to your country in the hour of danger and alarm, your magnificent fighting, bravery, and endurance, you have maintained the supremacy of the Union and the Constitution ; overthrown all armed opposition to the enforcement of the laws, and of the proclamations forever abolishing slavery, — the cause and pretext of the Rebellion ; and opened the way to the rightful authorities to restore order and inaugurate peace, on a permanent and enduring basis, on every foot of American soil.

"Your marches, sieges, and battles, in distance, duration, resolution, and brilliancy of results, dim the lustre of the world's past military achievements, and will be the patriot's precedent in defence of liberty and 'right in all time to come. In obedience to your country's call, you left your homes and families, and volunteered in its defence. Victory has crowned your valor, and secured the purpose of your patriotic hearts. And with the gratitude of your countrymen, and the highest honors a great and free nation can accord, you will soon be permitted to return to your homes and your families, conscious of having discharged the highest duty of American citizens.

"To achieve these glorious triumphs, and secure to yourselves, your fellow-countrymen, and posterity the blessings of free institutions, tens of thousands of your gallant comrades have fallen, and sealed the priceless legacy with their lives. The graves of these a grateful nation bedews with tears, honors their memories, and will ever cherish and support their stricken families."

We must here close our sketch of the life of General Grant. It is more than probable that he has but just entered upon that career of usefulness in which he is destined to serve his country. Since the close of the war, his measures of firmness and of. conciliation have been such as increasingly to endear him to his countrymen. He has ascended another step in the line of military promotion, in receiving the appointment of GENERAL of the Armies of the United States. There is but one more exalted honor which can be attained. The nation seems to be waiting the appointed time when it can honor itself by conferring its highest gift upon Ulysses S. Grant.

Stereotyped and Printed by Geo. C. Rand & Avery.

4191

L